I0776454

"...This fantasy had me hooked by the second chapter and it became harder to put the book down…[Rita] contains good language content and is an excellent read for junior and high school students. As a parent I found this story enjoyable and a well-written book that kept you in suspense wondering what would happen next."

Deloris Johnson

Reader Review on Reader's Favorite

"[Takano Rynn] An easy read for the young adult in your family. It was enjoyable to read more about these two characters and was easily caught up in the surprise plot twists along the way."

Riley

Amazon Five Star Review

"Once again author Bianca Rowena captures our hearts and imagination with her thrilling sequel to [Rita]. Her writing is fast paced and clear . . . you slip into Rita and Takano's world right from page one. Everything about this book sparkles! I absolutely loved it. If I could give it 10 STARS I would! Anxiously awaiting the next book in this wonderful, imaginative series!"

Kindle 5 Star Customer Review

RITa

Book One of the Rita Series

Bianca Rowena

Bianca Watson Publishing

Rowena, Bianca
Rita (formerly titled, The Gift Stone) / Bianca Rowena.–2nd ed.

Summary: When her village is threatened by the evil Takano Rynn,
leader of the Ruling Order, Rita defeats him in battle and
believes him to be dead. She leaves her Temple life to hide
in the masses of Central City where she befriends
members of the Opposition Parrin, Star and the little robot
Beeps. But is Takano Rynn really dead?
Or will he come back for his revenge?

ISBN 978-1-9992041-1-2 (Softcover : alk, paper) / 978-1-9992041-2-9 (e-book)
[1. Young Adult Fiction—Fantasy. 2. Romance.] I. Title.

Designed by Uzichu | Printed in Canada | Second Edition 10 9 8 7 6 5 4 3 2

First published as *The Gift Stone* in Canada in July 2017 by Bianca Watson Publishing
The Gift Stone / ISBN 978-1-9992041-1-2 (Softcover) / 978-1-9992041-2-9 (e-book)

*To all the hardcore Reylo fans on Wattpad,
thank you for all the support and the One Million
views!And to my smart, talented daughter, Jessica,
who was the first person to love this story.*

CHAPTER 1

F ALLEN LEAVES CUSHION MY steps as I run up Green Hill. The morning air is filled with the scent of oncoming rain and a frosty chill.

It's colder than I had expected. I'll have to cut my run short today. It's not worth getting sick over, even if my running days are fast coming to an end, as the Snow Days draw near.

I stop at the top of the hill to wipe the sweat off my brow. Out on the horizon the bright reds and golds of the sunrise lie trapped beneath a ceiling of dark clouds.

The sun rises first on Central, as the saying goes.

I look out into the distance, toward Central City.

Temple Mother's words come to mind. "Hurry up girls," she'd say. "It's already tomorrow in Central."

I smile, imagining the hustle and bustle of the city where it's always tomorrow. If I lived in Central, would I be free to run to my heart's content?

Fog hovers low to the ground. I squint, trying to see into the mist.

It's moving.

Hooded figures emerge from the fog, advancing with military-like precision. I recognize their cloaks.

It's the dark army of Takano Rynn. They're marching towards Green Hill. Towards me.

I glance back at the Temple, half in ruins, but still my home. It sits silent in a cloak of darkness beneath the storm clouds. The Sisters will still be sleeping and the Commoners too, in the small village beyond. They're all observing the Rest Day, all but me.

I turn back to the moving fog. Soldiers appear from the mist, dressed all in black, the color of Dark Leader Takano Rynn and his followers. Their faces are hidden beneath their hoods, like their leader. He is at the head of the group and his dark form takes shape as he emerges from the fog, taller than the rest. He moves with purpose, eyes glowing beneath his hood.

I shrink back into the shadows of a nearby tree.

What could the most feared leader in the Galaxy possibly want with our forgotten little village, here on the outskirts of all wars, trade, or anything of importance?

The leader's gift of influence is so strong that it reaches to me through the darkness, drawing me forward, urging me to surrender myself to him, like all who have ever been unfortunate enough to end up in his presence.

"I am a Temple Girl," I whisper. "My mind is not easily overthrown."

Takano's unseen grip wavers just long enough for me to free myself from his hypnotic influence. I have to warn the Sisters. They won't stand a chance against Takano Rynn's evil.

I turn back the way I came, and run.

CHAPTER 2

C OLD WIND WHIPS AT my face as I run into the Temple courtyard. I don't turn to see if the soldiers are in pursuit. I have to warn the sisters.

When I reach the fountain, I slow to a jog. Water used to flow from its center, before the frosts came, and now patches of ice glisten on the cobblestone floor.

I make my way carefully around the ice and stop at the front gates to catch my breath.

There's no time to go around to the back. I look up at the tall metal bars of the gate, which I know is locked.

I run towards it and jump, grabbing onto the cold metal bars. The hinges creak and the gate rattles as I climb. My hands stick to the frozen metal, pinching my skin each time I pull away to grab another bar.

I ignore the pain and climb upward.

The gate wobbles as I lift my leg over the pointed spikes at the top. I balance carefully on one foot, then lift the other over.

My foot slips suddenly and I stifle a scream.

"Stars above!" I hiss. My hands lose their grip and I fall towards the pavement. I ready myself for the landing, putting my hands out in front of me.

My fall is slowed down by a heat coming from my palms, pushing back at me from the ground. Or maybe I'm imagining it.

I land safely on my feet, in a crouching position. Not bad, for a Temple Girl.

I smile. Maybe all the hours of physical training I did in secret are actually paying off. But the other girls...what are they going to do when Takano Rynn's army arrives?

None of them have any real training to defend themselves. But they wouldn't fight, even if they could. Violence goes against our Vows.

I run to the Temple doors and throw them open. They slam against the inside wall, the sound echoing through the sanctuary. The Temple birds scurry off in a flutter of wings, startled by the sudden noise. Inside, the heat is unbearable. Silence fills the sanctuary again.

I hurry down the center aisle, careful not to run.

Running in the sanctuary is forbidden.

A light flickers from Temple Mother's study.

I stumble up the balcony stairs, my heart pounding harder and harder. When I reach the study I'm out of breath.

"Rita?" Temple Mother stands at the window overlooking the back gardens. She seems surprised to see me. I try to speak but am too out of breath. She frowns, then turns her attention to the window again. "The gardens are all settled for the season, are they not?"

"Yes, Mother," I say. "But I wasn't in the gardens this morning."

Mother frowns. "You've been running again, haven't you?"

I shake my head. "There are soldiers. Takano Rynn. The army. They're coming."

"What are you saying?" Mother leans forward suddenly, grasping the side of her desk with one hand for support.

"They're coming, *here*," I say. "I saw The Dark leader and his army."

Tears rush to my eyes. We are no match for Takano Rynn. He will slaughter us all, as he did to all the Temple Boys years before.

"Did you have a bad dream, child?" Mother asks.

"No..." I blink, suddenly confused. Was it just a vision? But I saw the moving fog and the army. I saw Takano Rynn's glowing eyes.

"Perhaps you should go take more rest," Temple Mother continues. "You look fevered."

Suddenly she lets out a small gasp and I tense.

She senses it too, now. He's coming.

Her eyes go wide. "Run, child"

"But, the others—"

"Don't let him find you, Rita!"

I scramble to my feet and hurry out of the room to the stairs.

Should I warn all the girls first? Or run ahead to the village to wake the people? They won't have time to flee, with their children and babies.

I stop at the bottom of the stairs. The front doors are still closed. I can't let the Dark Army come in here.

I won't run. I have to confront Takano Rynn. He may have strange powers, but he is still just a human, like me. I have strengths too. How many times did I fight beasts out in the forest beyond the Green Hills, ones more powerful than ten men?

Every one of the beasts had a weakness. Takano Rynn must have a weakness, too.

I glance around the room for a weapon. The brass fireplace poker has a handle and a sharp, pointed end. It isn't a sword, but it will have to do. If Takano Rynn is bringing his army to the Temple, then he'll have to go through me first.

"Rita?" Brianne's timid voice brings me from my thoughts. She stands at the entranceway leading to the bed chambers, still in her sleeping robes.

"Are you okay?" she asks, her eyes wide.

"Go hide," I tell her. "Hide well."

I hurry to the fireplace and grab the metal poker.

"I'm going to fight. And if I don't return, you must feed the Temple birds for me. Understand?"

"But—"

"Tell the others to hide, too."

I don't wait for her reply but run down the middle aisle of the sanctuary and out the front doors.

CHAPTER 3

TAKANO RYNN STOPS. HE knows I'm near, but he can't see me in the tree above him.

I hold the brass poker tight in my hand, ready to lunge it into his heart. The soldiers wait for their leader to move forward. But he stands still, his cloak flapping in the cold wind. I wait too, silent in the branches.

Could they just be passing through? Perhaps they have no interest in our Temple or the village beyond.

I raise my metal rod. I can't take that chance. If I strike the leader, the rest will scurry, like the mindless drones they are.

Takano Rynn's hooded head turns left, then right, his hidden eyes searching the trees. The wind picks up again. Now's my chance to throw the metal poker. The rustling of the trees will mask the sounds of my movements.

Takano Rynn's head turns in my direction and I freeze.

My mind is not easily overthrown.

I pull my arm back, using my other hand to hold onto a sturdy branch, then launch the heavy rod into the air. It zips through the darkness towards its target.

Takano Rynn jumps back, anticipating the unseen object before it makes impact. But he's not quick enough. The rod misses its target, his heart, and pierces his side instead. He cries out, doubling over in pain.

I hit him!

I hit the feared leader of the Ruling Order.

Soldiers begin to shout, pointing in my direction. I know they can't see me yet, but they will soon enough. I start to climb. The closer I remain to the soldiers, the less likely they are to find me. They'll be expecting me to flee. With any luck they'll run ahead in pursuit and pass by beneath me.

The shouts grow closer and I climb higher. The branches scratch my palms, drawing blood.

I haven't stopped the soldiers at all, but only made them angrier. They run past, below me, their heavy boots trampling the grass in soft thuds that seem to shake the ground itself.

The tree branches sway in a gust of wind and I shut my eyes against the cold, hugging the tree trunk tight.

The storm will be here soon. At least the army is no longer headed for the Temple or the Village. Maybe I have stopped them after all.

Wet dew lands on my face and I open my eyes. Large snowflakes float all around, so light they can't seem to decide which way is up or down.

The sun is obstructed from view and the hills lie in darkness. I can't see the soldiers but their shouts move farther away, in the opposite direction of the Temple.

I look back towards the village.

Did Temple Mother rouse the sisters?

Did Brianne tell the others to hide?

Snowflakes swirl in front of my face, making it hard to see. I blink, searching the small clearing where I hit Takano Rynn. Has anyone remained behind with him?

Then I spot him, standing in the same place he was when I threw the metal poker, his face turned up to me, eyes hidden beneath his hood. My stomach tightens and I grasp the branch in front of me tighter.

Can he see me?

The snow gathered around his feet is stained red with the blood dripping from his side. He pulls out a sword. The metal gleams in the dim light of the early morning.

He lifts his free hand towards me and I'm suddenly pulled forward by some unseen power. It rips me from the tree and I lose grip of the branch.

The snowy ground rushes towards me fast. I throw out my hands in front of me.

"Stop!" I yell.

The wind stops and everything becomes silent. I'm suspended for a moment, no longer falling. Even the snowflakes have paused in mid-flight. I look over at Takano Rynn. He's completely still as well.

I set one foot gently onto the ground, then the other.

What happened?

Did Takano Rynn make everything stop?

Suddenly the deafening sound of rushing wind returns and everything gets thrown back into motion. Gravity pulls me to my knees and I land hard.

Takano Rynn comes to life, swinging his sword down at me as though nothing happened.

I roll away just in time and his sword pierces the ground, inches from my side. My shoulder hits something hard and I cry out.

It's my metal poker. I grab it and jump up into standing position. Takano Rynn's sword comes down at me again and I swing the rod to block the attack.

Sparks fly, lighting up Takano's eyes. I see the anger and hate in them. I push back against his sword with all my might and he pushes down.

"Coward!" I yell. "Show your face if you will fight me."

Takano releases me and lowers his sword. Snowflakes float frantically around his black form.

I grip my metal rod tight, ready for an unexpected attack, or some kind of trick. My chest heaves with labored breaths as I wait. The cold, wet ground seeps through the fabric of my gardening trousers.

I get up, clutching the metal rod tight and keeping my eyes on Takano. He lifts his hand to his hood and pulls it back to reveal his face.

CHAPTER 4

ALL THE ANGER AND fear inside of me disappear when I see Takano Rynn's face.

What had I expected to see? A monster with gnarled features? Surely not an appealing man with dark wavy hair, blue eyes and pale skin. I'd seen other men before, of course, in the village. But none like this, clean and unblemished, like a stone statue; like someone who has never known a day of hard work out in the field.

His jaw clenches and he frowns, as though displeased with my silent reaction.

I lower my fireplace poker and we stand facing one another, the snowflakes drifting between us. They settle onto Takano Rynn's dark hair. He raises his free hand towards me and an invisible hold seizes me. My throat tightens.

What kind of man relies on magic to fight a weaker opponent? I want to tell him he's a coward again, but I can't speak. The metal rod slips from my fingers and lands with a thud onto the grass.

Takano Rynn's expression changes as his eyes search mine. I'm drawn into their cold, blue pools. I fight against the pull of his influence.

"You know where it is," he says, his voice emotionless. I clench my hands into fists, but can do nothing else.

He moves closer until his breath brushes against my neck.

"You're different," he says.

My heart races. I don't want to look at him, but now I can't look away. I shudder and he pulls back, walking around me slowly.

Sure, he can be calm, having an unfair advantage. I'd have killed him by now if he didn't have his powers.

He takes slow steps, his hands clasped behind his back. Then he stops suddenly, gripping his side and fighting back a cough. His hold on me wavers.

Blood drips onto the snow. Blood, just like mine or the sisters', or anyone else who is human. So then why am I surprised to see it? He is still a man.

"You caught me off guard," he says, straightening to his full height again. "There aren't many who would walk into death, rather than flee from it. I didn't expect an attack from a Temple Girl."

"Let me go," I say between clenched teeth.

"Tell me where Gift Stone is." He moves close again, locking his gaze on me. I feel the pull of his influence trying to take control of my thoughts.

The Gift Stone? The old legend which only little Temple Girls believe? That's why he's been attacking the defenseless Temples all across the galaxy?

"You have a strong mind," he says.

"Stop!"

He doesn't stop but freely searches my thoughts, like a physician's fingers examining a body.

"How sweet," he says. "You are worried about your sisters." He pauses. "Oh, I see. They're not your real sisters, are they? You're all alone in this world."

I don't respond.

"Where is the Gift Stone?" he asks again, his voice calm but carrying a hint of impatience now.

He brings his sword up to my throat. "Is it hidden in this Temple?"

"There is no Gift Stone," I whisper.

"Of course there is. Tell me where they're hiding it or I will kill every last one of the Temple Girls until I find it." He pushes the sword against my throat. "You told the young one, Brianne was it? To go hide it."

"No," I swallow hard. "I didn't tell her to hide anything. I told *her* to go hide."

A humorless smile crosses Takano Rynn's face.

"She can try to hide. But I will find her."

"You will not harm her," I hiss at him, my anger giving me strength. A heat rushes through me, starting at the roots of my hair and pooling in my fingertips. I let go and allow Takano's invasion of my thoughts, which gives me a way into his.

Our minds connect and I feel his surprise as he tries to resist. But it is too late. I can see his thoughts. He truly is looking for the Gift Stone, which he's been told is hidden in one of the Temples. He believes that if it's found by someone else, it can be used against him and he may be defeated by its power.

The pain from his wound seeps into me as well, along with his anger, determination and hate. Behind these surface emotions is a childlike curiosity about me and my ability to resist him. It confuses him. He thinks I've been in contact with the Gift Stone and that is what is made me strong.

"It does not exist," I say. "It's only a myth, a hope of those desperate to see your evil reign come to an end."

I break free of our connection, but not before sensing an unexpected vulnerability. He's afraid I might have harnessed the power of the Gift Stone and can defeat him right here and now. It's just enough doubt for me to have an advantage over him.

I grab his sword out of his hand in one swift movement.

"Rita!" he cries out. "Stop!"

The surprise of hearing Takano Rynn call out my name catches me off guard and I hesitate. He reaches for his sword and I snap back to attention, swinging at him with all my strength. A clash of metal hitting metal rings through the air. He's wearing some kind of armor. His chest must be covered, beneath his cloak.

I step back. I'll never defeat him if he's covered in metal. Anger rises inside of me.

"You're nothing but a coward!" I yell, swinging the sword again. "A coward who killed all the Temple Boys because you were afraid." I swing again, no longer in control of my anger. "Afraid one of them would rise up against you." I stop to look him in the eyes. "You're even afraid of *me*."

Takano's gaze grows dark. He lunges at me with a loud cry. I duck and roll away, losing my hold on the sword. Suddenly he's towering over me, gripping my wrists and pinning me down to the ground.

"You're strong," he says, breathing heavily. I struggle to break free but he's stronger, even with his wound. "You're like me," he says, his eyes searching mine.

"I will *never* be like you." I snarl.

"Join me."

His eyes draw me in again and his thoughts enter mine once more.

We can be powerful together.

"Never!" I roll him off of me and reach for the sword again, but I'm not fast enough. He grabs it first and swings it down at me.

I roll out of the way but the sword clips my shoulder. I cry out and kick upwards into Takano's side, where his wound is still oozing blood. He grunts and falls to the ground, dropping the sword. I snatch it up and jump onto my feet.

Takano coughs, crouched down before me, gasping for breath. I lift the sword high, my heart racing. He stops struggling for air and collapses to the ground, becoming completely still. My arms tremble as I hold the sword tight, ready to strike.

I can kill him. Now's my chance.

I look down at his unmoving body. Takano Rynn, the mighty and powerful leader, now vulnerable and helpless before me. Will he die of the wound I gave him? Is he already dead?

I lower the sword. It wasn't just anger I saw inside of him when our thoughts merged, there was curiosity and a desire, not just for the Gift Stone, but for companionship. He wants to find someone with powers like him. But that person isn't me.

I sigh. *I am not like you, Takano Rynn.*

The shouts of the soldiers in the distance echo through the trees. I look up but the fog is too thick to see anything. They're looking for their leader. I won't be able to fight them all.

I take one final glance down at Takano's body. Then I drop the sword, and run.

CHAPTER 5

THE GEARS OF THE Above Train grate loudly as it speeds down the old metal track. I look out the dirty windows at the buildings below. Some reach up as high as the tracks, which weave between the city skyscrapers.

The people far below look like tiny, colorful bugs, moving about. I smile at the thought of being lost in the masses down there. This will be my home now, since I can no longer live in the Temple. Murderers aren't allowed to step foot on Temple grounds. But out here, I can fade into obscurity, like a drop in the ocean. Nobody knows where Takano Rynn has disappeared to, nor that it was me who opened his side and left him to die that snowy morning.

How could they know? We were alone during that battle. Such a strange twist of fate. After living a quiet life as an orphan at the Temple, I am now on the run for killing the leader of the Ruling Order.

I thought I may get kicked out of the Temple one day, for my love of running, but not for killing a man.

Takano Rynn's lifeless body lying in the snow flashes through my mind. I grip the bar in front of me tighter and take in a shaky breath of the stuffy, recycled air.

Maybe there will be peace now that the leader of the Ruling Order is gone. Maybe what I did wasn't all bad.

Join me...

I shake my head to dispel the image of his eyes from my mind.

Even if I had the Gift Stone and the power to lead the people in peace, would I have the courage to do it? The way Takano Rynn's brother Lord Morlin once did? Well, he tried to, until Takano killed him too.

I glance around at the locals on the train with me. They look bored, resigned to their fate of riding this old metal beast off to wherever they are going.

No one smiles. They are all listening to their devices with their earphones in. I have no destination, but they know exactly what they are doing, getting on and off, switching trains at the right stops, at the right times. No one flinches when the brakes squeal or the wheels crunch and bump over the tracks. I flinch every time.

On and off they go, swallowed up into the city and replaced again by new passengers with new frowns on their faces.

Brianne's smile comes to mind and I blink back tears. I'll never see her again. I didn't even say goodbye or give anyone an explanation before I took off in the night.

A blur of leaves outside the train windows replaces the metal buildings as we soar above trees now. They remind me of home, except that here a large electric fence encircles them and no one can touch them.

Once we pass the trees, we climb up again, nearing the heart of Central City. The apartments and houses are crammed together in skinny tall blocks. There are no large family homes here with yards and fences, like back at the village.

The train's gears complain loudly as it comes to an abrupt stop. People barely have enough time to get off before the train starts up again, rushing to make the next station.

A guy about my age crams in with the newcomers and stands next to me. He reaches over my shoulder to grab onto the metal bar that I'm holding onto.

I turn slightly to look at him, trying not to be obvious. He has dark skin and a pleasant face. He smiles briefly at me then looks out the windows. His well-worn brown jacket smells like the outdoors.

His arm touches my shoulder and I flinch, but he doesn't seem to notice. At the Temple and in the Village we never had a reason to get this close to each other. Such nearness was reserved for young children and their mothers, or for newlyweds. Not for Temple Girls.

But I wasn't always a Temple Girl. I had a mother and a father once.

I blink back tears. My parents are out there somewhere. Maybe even here in Central. I used to pretend they lived here, when I was little. Now I'm actually here.

A familiar hope stirs inside of me. I probably won't run into my parents at the train station, but one day I'll find them.

I grip the metal bar tighter and look out over the sea of people. They sway to and fro, left and right, then right and left. A few glance in my direction and I look away. Do they know Takano Rynn's is dead, yet? Or who killed him?

I pull the hood of my Temple cloak down farther over my face and tuck the loose strands of my blonde hair out of sight.

A girl with short, white-blonde hair and markings on her skin watches me with a smirk. Her markings are in the image of a sea creature that runs down her neck and onto her shoulder. It must have hurt to be marked so deep that the image never sheds from the skin.

"Where did you get your markings?" I ask, over the noise of the train. She doesn't respond.

The train breaks to another screeching halt and I fall against the boy with the brown jacket.

"Sorry," I say quickly but he doesn't seem to even notice.

The train speeds up again and the noise returns.

"I can't wait to get back to my little robot," she continues. "I hate vacations."

"What are vacations?" I ask.

She turns to me then, and looks down at my Temple clothes. "You've never been on vacation?"

I open my mouth to answer, then close it. I may very well have been on a vacation, or in one, and not know it, since I don't know what a vacation is.

If I can't answer truthfully then I shouldn't speak at all. That's the Temple teaching.

"Why are you in Central?" the markings girl asks.

"I'm going to live here."

She nods, like it's the logical answer.

"I've got nothing to return to at home," I add, "like you do." I stop. Why did I say that?

"You mean my robot?"

"I guess."

"You can get something in Central, something you can look forward to returning to at night."

"I need a place to return to first."

The dark-skinned boy speaks, startling me. He is standing so close that I'd forgotten he was still there.

"The things you want to get back home to, don't usually cost anything," he says, glancing at the white haired girl.

"I didn't steal her," she says to him. "She cost me a lot."

He gives her a disbelieving look but doesn't respond.

"Steal who?" I ask, only now realizing that these two know each other.

"Beeps, my robot," the girl says. "Parrin here doesn't think robots have real emotions."

Parrin shakes his head but doesn't say anything.

"What province are you from?" the markings girl asks me.

"I'm from the Northern Provinces."

I adjust my Temple clothes. The many layers are designed for the cold North not for Lower Central. Yet I didn't expect it to be this warm. I brought nothing else with me, not even a traveling case, just the clothes I had on when I left. Nothing I used at the Temple was mine to take.

"Central sucks the life out of you," the boy named Parrin says. "Too many people and not enough air."

I think back to the open spaces in the far away province where my village is. All that emptiness would sometimes feel suffocating too.

"I don't mind sharing air," I say.

Parrin smiles; a small grin that I would have missed if I wasn't paying attention. I feel a twinge of hope. The people here aren't monsters, like Temple Mother made us believe.

They're outcasts perhaps, on their own in a scary city. But they're still human.

I glance up at the information scrolling across the screen at the front of the train car.

The words *Downtown Central–Main Street* are displayed.

We're nearing the heart of Central. It's my stop.

Parrin's arm still rests on my shoulder and I don't want to move away. His nearness is comforting. Maybe I don't have to get off at Downtown Central; I could stop anywhere.

"We're getting off at the next stop," the markings girl says, as though reading my thoughts.

"I'll get off there too," I say, quickly.

Parrin and the white-haired girl exchange a glance and my cheeks heat up. Are they a couple and don't want me to tag along?

The train comes to a stop and Parrin grabs hold of my arm, pulling me quickly to the doors. My gasp of surprise goes unheard in the commotion of people trying to get off the train while others are getting on at the same time. We rush out the doors seconds before they close again.

I knew that things would be different in Central, but I'm not sure I'm ready for this.

People press in all around me. It's hard to breathe. There are too many people. I've only just arrived here and I've already made significant physical contact with another person. I pull my arm out of Parrin's grasp as soon as we're clear of the doors. It really shouldn't matter anyway. I'm not a Temple Girl anymore.

And yet, it still matters.

CHAPTER 6

T HE CROWD OF PEOPLE push against us and we're moved forward into tunnels that lead to different levels or out to the streets of Central. The citizens disperse, in a hurry to get to wherever they're going. We're left standing at the entrance of one of the tunnels. I wipe the sweat from my forehead.

"You should take off your layers of Temple clothes," Parrin says, "before we go out onto the streets. It's even warmer out there."

His friend crosses her arms. "I thought they were some kind of farmer clothes," she says. "My name's Star, by the way."

I smile. "I like your name," I say. "Mine's Rita."

"Cute," Star says.

"How do you know they're Temple robes?" I ask Parrin.

He shrugs. "I used to be a Temple Boy." He starts walking again.

"What?" I hurry to keep up with his long strides as he heads down a tunnel, it's walls lined with public service announcements about the Ruling Order.

How could Parrin have been a Temple Boy? There aren't any left. Takano killed every last one of them.

"But there are no Temple Boys anymore," I say.

Could he be Gifted? I would be able to tell though wouldn't I? The same way I could feel Takano's power even at a distance; his influence.

I stop walking and pull my hood off quickly before I can change my mind. Air washes over my head and neck, and I sigh in relief. Parrin's eyes go wide.

"What?" I say, immediately defensive. But I know what. It's my blonde hair. It always surprises people who haven't seen it before. Sometimes it's so blonde that it seems to glow, under certain lighting, or in moonlight. Or so I've been told. It's best to keep it covered.

"Wow," Star says. "You won't last in Lower Central with long hair like that. It's way too hot here." She looks at me for a moment, as though assessing me. "You could get a lot of money for that hair. The Upper Citizens pay a nice price for real hair, especially that color."

"She can't cut it," Parrin says. "It's holy."

I twist my braid into a knot behind my head. Star's right about the heat and Parrin's right about my hair, that a Temple Girl's hair is never cut.

"Aren't you going to become unclean by being here?" Parrin asks me.

I frown, wanting to ask him the same thing. But he said he used to be a Temple Boy, not that he is one anymore.

"I'm sure she's left all that Temple stuff behind and that's why she's here," Star says. "Let's go. Beeps must be worried about me by now."

"Where is everyone?" I ask, already missing the hustle and bustle of the train.

I glance around the abandoned train station. Everyone is gone. An eerie sound floats out from the tunnel, like the distant cry of haunting spirits. A wind perhaps or the lingering sounds of the rushing train that has left.

"No one can stay in the tunnels once they get off the train, not since the Ruling Order took over. If you hang around too long in here, they arrest you."

I look for Ruling Order guards but don't see any.

"But Takano Rynn is rumored to be dead now," Parrin adds. "He's disappeared. Maybe things will change, finally."

My stomach tightens at hearing Takano Rynn's name.

"I don't think he's really dead." Star plays with one of her piercings in her eyebrow. "If he was, then there would be chaos in the streets and rioting. But nothing seems to have changed."

"It's only been a few days," I say.

"You know about Takano Rynn's disappearance?" Parrin asks. "The news traveled all the way to the outer provinces? Not even Central citizens know about it yet."

I shrug and avoid looking at him.

"He's not dead," Star says. "I can sense it."

"Even if he was dead, Dukath would find some other evil lord to take Takano's place." Parrin crosses his arms and looks down the length of the tunnel.

"Dukath?" I ask.

"He's just a myth." Star waves her hand at Parrin.

"He's real." Parrin frowns. "He's the one that even Takano Rynn bows down to."

"Well, then the Opposition—"

Parrin bumps against Star's shoulder and she stops talking. I wait for her to continue but she doesn't.

"What about the Opposition?" I ask.

"Don't say that word too loudly here," she says, then turns to Parrin. "Are we ready to go? I need to get to the base."

Parrin nods. "But first we should help Rita be a little less conspicuous."

He takes hold of the top button on my robe then begins to unwind the string that's wrapped around seven times one way, then seven times the other way in a special ritualistic pattern. I expect him to keep going in the same direction and not realize that he's actually winding the string up again, after the seventh turn. It's a common mistake for even the Temple Girls when they lose count, but Parrin stops at seven and starts the other way.

"How do you know about the buttons?" I ask.

"What's with all the string wrapped around those buttons?" Star asks, watching us.

"It's a tradition," Parrin answers for me. "It carries meaning."

He starts on the next button and I push his hands away.

"I can do it myself."

I undo the rest of the buttons as fast as I can, then unwrap the thick cloth belt around my waist. Parrin starts helping again, holding the belt for me as I take off my outer robe. It falls to the ground and he snatches it up, frowning.

"Temple robes shouldn't be thrown onto the ground," he says, pushing the garment back into my arms.

"I've got a friend who'd be interested in buying that," Star adds.

"So do I." Parrin digs into his pocket and pulls out some exchange currency. I'm not too familiar with the currency but I can tell it's a large amount. He hands it to me.

"Here. For the robe and belt."

I take the delicate papers from him. They feel rough to touch, as though they've exchanged many hands before reaching mine. "Thank you."

Star watches Parrin with interest. "That's a lot of currency, just for a robe."

Parrin shrugs. "She needs a place to stay."

We start walking again and I feel too light without my robe on, even though I'm carrying it in my arms. As though reading my thoughts, Parrin takes the robe from me.

"I'll carry it, since I bought it," he says.

As we near the end of the station tunnel, the noise and heat return. It's even warmer than on the train. The simple servant's dress I'm now wearing is made of a light fabric but it still reaches down to my worn leather boots and up to the white decorative collar around my neck.

I take a deep breath, trying to get more air as I follow Parrin and Star out onto the street. The city smog burns my throat. I squint at the blaring lights and colors of the storefronts lining the street.

Everything is flashy, demanding attention. Fake trees made of metal and plastic light up one side of the street. The shops on that side are made to look like buildings that they are not; castles, farmhouses and one even built in the image of a Temple, but only on the outside. The sign above says *Dee's Discount Skin Markings.*

We move through the crowd and I lose sight of Parrin and Star. Then Star's colored white hair stands out in the crowd and I find them again. I could take Parrin's hand, or Star's, to keep us from getting separated, but the thought makes me too nervous.

We keep walking, in a hurry. Why am I following them?

Parrin glances back occasionally to see if I'm still with them. For a moment I think I see him take Star's hand. But I can't be sure.

We head down a darker alley, moving away from the bright lights and crowds. Small groups of people stand quietly in dark corners, watching us as we pass. Parrin ignores them. They look poor but their clothes are still flashy, only more worn out.

Star is ahead of us now. She stops at a hidden door beneath a flight of metal stairs and opens it. The sound of laughter and the smell of smoke waft out. I head for the door but Parrin puts his arm out in front of me to stop me.

"Let Star go alone. We'll wait here," he says.

I nod and look up at the side of the building. A maze of ladders and metal stairs zigzag between the apartment doors high above, going up and up as far as the eye can see.

I close my eyes to stop a sudden wave of dizziness. How could anyone use those stairs and ladders without getting nauseous from the height?

Parrin remains silent as we wait, as though lost in thought.

A loud bang echoes down the dimly lit alley and I jump, moving closer to Parrin.

"Just a ladder being let down," he explains.

"Oh." I cross my arms and step back, my cheeks heating up. Am I really going to be okay in Central, if I'm already jumping at every noise? Where will I even spend the night tonight?

The door Star disappeared through opens again and she steps out with a smile on her face. At her feet is a little robot, no taller than her knees.

The small, dust-covered robot wobbles on its wheels, moving fast like an excited toddler.

"You'd better keep her safe while I'm on this mission," Star says to Parrin.

The robot comes to a stop beside Star but doesn't stop fast enough and bumps into her legs. Then it tries to correct itself and rolls forward, bumping into Parrin's legs. He crouches down and pats her head.

"Okay Beeps, are you going to behave yourself?"

Beeps responds with an assortment of beeping sounds. I smile. It's obvious where she gets her name from.

"And you're going to make me breakfast every morning, right?" Parrin asks her.

Beeps' little noises sound like a *no* response, to me. Parrin laughs.

"Okay, I'm out," Star announces.

Parrin stands and gives her a friendly handshake. She grasps his hand tight and pulls him into a quick hug.

"Stay safe," Parrin says to her. "Don't fly that plane into a black hole."

"Can't make any promises," she says, letting go of his hand.

She gives me a salute, then walks away down the dimly lit alley.

Parrin and I watch her in silence until she disappears around the corner.

"Where's she going?" I ask, to break the silence.

Beeps responds but I don't understand her answer.

"Come on," Parrin says, heading down the alley in the opposite direction Star went. "It's not a good idea to stay here too long."

I have no reason to follow Parrin anymore. He gave me money and I can get food and a place to stay now.

Beeps stops to look back at me when I don't follow them. Then Parrin stops too.

"Are you coming?" he calls over his shoulder.

I hesitate for a moment, then hurry after them.

CHAPTER 7

"**S**O WHERE ARE WE going?" I ask Parrin.

A merchant cart almost runs into us as we round the corner. I grab Parrin's arm to hold him back before he gets hit.

"Thanks," he says.

Beeps squeals as the cart catches one of her wheels and flings her into a group of scantily clad girls. They giggle and keep walking.

"There's a hotel on the second level that should be safe for you to stay at, for a few days anyway, until you find something more permanent." Parrin looks up. "The Lower Citizens can't go on the second level, except for merchants with clearance."

"Then who uses the second level?"

"Upper Citizens, visiting here from Outer Central. The third and fourth levels are for higher citizens who work in the city but don't want to live in Lower Central."

We continue down the street and I fight the urge to stop and look at everything. The shops are full of flashy trinkets that catch the eye. I want to stop and see what they are. Toys? Devices? Decorations? I spot a shelf full of books with colorful covers made of embroidered cloth. Brianne would love one of these.

I look back at Parrin and see that he's gone.

"Parrin?" I yell.

A group of rough looking citizens gathered near a smoke shop, stop talking and look at me. One smiles, showing a row of stained teeth.

"Hey girl. Is that your real hair?" the tallest one asks. He starts to walk in my direction and the others follow.

"No," I call back in reply, then pick up the pace. Beeps speeds off suddenly and I run after her.

People step aside and make room as she zooms ahead. I keep running too, not wanting to lose sight of her.

We stop at the base of a flight of white stairs which lead up to a metal gate above. There's a guard stationed at the front of the gate and I spot Parrin's brown jacket. He's speaking with the guard in what seems to be a heated discussion.

Parrin glances down at me, as though sensing that I've arrived. I head up the stairs but he shakes his head, and I stop. Beeps bumps against my leg.

"Oh, you can't go up," I say, realizing her wheels would never make it up the stairs. I lean down to take her in my arms. Her body is heavier than I expect. "I think Parrin wants us to wait for him down here anyway," I say.

When I look up again I see that both Parrin and the guard are gone. "Great," I mumble, sitting down on a step.

Beeps says something that by now I can tell is a question of some sort, which I'm guessing is related to Parrin's sudden disappearance.

"I don't know Beeps, maybe Parrin just has to talk to someone to get me clearance for the second level or something."

I pull Beeps close to my legs, feeling protective of her now that we're on our own. The Lower Citizens stay clear of the stairs and I feel safer knowing that there are guards nearby watching the entrance to the second level.

"We'll just have to wait I guess." I pat Beep's head and give her a smile. "Maybe you can teach me a few words in robot."

Beeps doesn't respond and her hesitation makes me laugh.

"I'm smarter than I look," I tell her.

She starts beeping some words and I try to guess what they are, but between the two of us we're so hopeless at understanding each other that it makes me laugh so much I have to clutch my side. It feels good to laugh again. It's been a long time since I've laughed.

Beeps tries to project something onto the ground for me to look at but the lights near the stairs are too bright and I can't make out the words. I don't notice the time pass as we continue trying to understand each other, until suddenly the street becomes dark.

"What's going on?" I look down the road and see that the street lamps have turned off. Only a few store signs are lit up now, leaving shadows in every corner.

Beeps says something but I don't understand.

I look around. All the people are gone and we're alone. Is this some kind of nighttime curfew?

A nearby shadow turns into a man with broad shoulders, walking out from an alleyway. He heads towards me and I stand. Another man is behind him, his eyes also on me. They're wearing black and for a second I think they're part of Takano Rynn's army. But they don't have the army patch on the right arm.

Beeps starts to wheel around in circles and I glance back to the top of the stairs. The lights have been shut off at the gates as well, and I can't tell if anyone is up there.

Should I run up to find a guard?

I turn back to the approaching men. They're a lot closer now. If I go up the stairs I'll be trapped coming back down.

"Come on Beeps," I whisper.

I run and Beeps follows, her wheels squealing as she speeds past me. The men are running now, too. Their large build makes them slower runners and I have practice running.

The city smog burns my eyes and throat. The sound of music and voices comes into earshot, like a crowd is just around the next corner. I hear the footsteps of the men behind us but I don't look back, focusing on my running instead, the way I would if running in the forest back home.

We round the corner at the end of the long street and a bright light blinds me for a second.

I head for a busy club, not too far off. My eyes adjust to the brightness of the busy street, which is apparently not under curfew like the other area nearby.

The stores and buildings here are colorful, reminding me of Summer Festival. Two Ruling Order guards walk down the opposite side of the street, slowing their stride when they see me. They have large weapons made of a lightweight plastic. I look away, not wanting to show fear that they're watching me. I haven't done anything wrong.

The large men that were chasing us are gone, but I can't shake the uneasy feeling of being exposed and vulnerable.

My chest burns from my run and I try to calm my heart by controlling my breathing. I head towards the club where there's a line-up of loud people. As I get closer my heart rate slows and my shoulders relax.

At the end of the street the road opens up into a brightly lit shopping center area, with lots of activity. I hurry past the rowdy Lower Centrals, waiting outside the doors of the club, dressed in glittery clothes and painted elaborately, to enhance their facial features. Loud music booms from inside the building.

"Beeps?" I look around but don't see Star's robot.

Before I start to panic, I spot her, swerving between the legs of a group of people.

I sigh. I could have lost her. I need to pay closer attention. Parrin would never forgive me, and neither would Star. I wouldn't have forgiven myself if I lost Beeps! I can tell she's more than just a simple robot. But where did Parrin go? Why did he leave us on those steps for so long and then never return? Did something happen?

Beeps lets out a series of high-pitched sounds and I kneel down to pat her little head.

"Sorry for running off so fast," I tell her. "We'll be fine if we stick together. Okay?"

She responds with her robot *okay*, which I am now familiar with, and I get up to start walking again.

My braid weighs heavy down my back, making me sweaty. People stop talking and stare as we pass by. Star's words come to mind, *you won't last in Lower Central with long hair like that.*

I reach for my hood then remember that I sold my cloak to Parrin. My stomach grumbles.

I'm not at the Temple anymore, where the meals are prepared for me every day on time and where I have a safe place to sleep. I will need to find my own food and shelter.

I look down to make sure Beeps is still with me. She gives me a questioning beep.

"We'll be just fine," I say to her. "I'll take care of you."

CHAPTER 8

THE SMELL OF GRILLED meat draws me to a messy looking restaurant. Beeps rolls along silently beside me. I keep my eyes on her as we move closer to the doors. It would be so much easier if I had a rope tied around her to keep her from wandering off.

My stomach growls and I walk faster. The windows of the restaurant are covered with posters advertising local events.

I stop at the front doors and peer between two posters to look inside. All the tables are occupied and the sound of cheerful voices drifts out to the street. I step back from the window. I'm far too tired from all the traveling and running to eat at a busy place like this. But going in would get us off the streets.

Beeps makes a questioning noise, and looks up at me.

"Stay close," I say. "We're going in."

I open the doors and the loud conversation and delicious smells of grilled meat hit me all at once.

A short, rough-looking man stands at the front counter. He narrows his eyes at me.

"No Upper Levels here," he says.

"I'm not an Upper Level," I reply. "I just need to eat."

He doesn't respond but turns and walks away.

Beeps makes her questioning noises again and before I can answer, the man reappears at a low gate to the left of the counter. "Come with me," he says, waving a hand to us.

We follow him through the busy restaurant to the back. The noise is so different from mealtimes at the Temple. How can they even eat in so much disorder and confusion?

"You can sit on the floor there." The man we are following points to a row of cushions along the wall where no one else is sitting. I dig my hand into my pocket and pull out one of the bills that Parrin gave me.

The man's eyes go wide. "We have private rooms too," he says quickly, reaching for the bill.

"I'm also looking for a place to live." I hold the money away from him.

The man glances at Beeps and then at me.

"I won't ask where you got that money, but for a little more I can give you a good meal and a place for the night." He licks his lips, his eyes darting around the room then back at me. "We have nice rooms, for long term living, at the back of the restaurant, privileged renters only."

"How much?"

"Too much for you, girl." He smiles, showing missing teeth. "You won't get rent for less than a small fortune anywhere in the city. And you can't rent unless you're a Registered Citizen."

"I am," I lie.

"I doubt that." He laughs, then coughs, clearing his throat before speaking again. "There are a lot of night crawlers on the streets looking for their next victim to steal from once all the shops close. They'll cut your head off for that golden mane of yours." He looks me up and down and I shiver. "I'll tell you what," he continues. "For that bill I'll give you food and a stay for one night. And for the length of your hair, I'll give you the room to live in for four season's time."

Beeps makes a high-pitched noise but I ignore her.

"It's a deal," I say to the man. "I'll cut my hair tomorrow. Right now I need food and a place to sleep."

The man's smile widens and he turns to walk away, waving at us to follow him. We walk through a doorway that has beads hanging on strings as a barrier to the other side. They catch in my hair as I step through.

I guess I really will have to cut my hair then.

I wrap my arms around myself, getting a chill despite the heat in the place. I would've had to cut it eventually anyway.

We stop at a locked door and our host pulls out a wad of keys. He unlocks the door and walks in. We follow him down a long hallway that has doors on either side.

This must be the residence he was talking about.

The hall is dimly lit but the rooms seem safe here, protected by the locked door at the end of the hall and by the busy restaurant on the other side. It's a lot quieter here and my shoulders relax.

Beeps' wheels crunch over the dirt on the floor as we make our way to the other end of the hall. We stop at a door that has two thin bars of iron forged into a number '12' and hammered onto the front.

"Here we are," the man says. "You'll have to eat in the restaurant if you want a meal. No food allowed in the rooms."

I nod. "Thank you. I think we'll eat first then return to the room."

The man frowns but doesn't reply. I take out the bill again from my pocket and hand it to him. He snatches it out of my hand.

"I'll tell the waitress to bring you a meal at the back of the restaurant," he says, then hurries away before I can ask what kind of meal I'll be getting.

CHAPTER 9

BEEPS ROLLS INTO MY leg again as I try to unlock our apartment door. She's been beeping the same sounds over and over, trying to get my attention. I'm pretty sure I know what she's saying. She wants to help me with the lock, but I've been ignoring her.

I sigh, finally relenting, and step away from the door.

"Okay fine Beeps, but you don't even have hands." I offer her the key and she shakes her tiny head.

A little compartment on her body opens up and a small retractable arm, with a grip at the end, extends up towards the lock. The grip is replaced by a long, sharp object that she inserts it into the lock. The door opens.

"I don't think that's how we're supposed to be opening the door to our apartment, Beeps. But good job!"

She gives a reply that I assume is 'you're welcome.'

I pull the door open the rest of the way and step in. My knees hit the side of a bed before I can even go inside. I reach in and flip on the light switch.

A dim yellow glow floods the room, a room which is just one large bed.

"Oh..." I lean in to look around the corner. The edges of the bed touch all four walls. Up near the ceiling a long shelf runs along the length of the room. There is a phone on the wall beside another door, which I'm hoping leads to a washroom.

"Well Beeps, looks like our new home is a bit small." I reach down to pick her up. She lets out a tiny beep as I lift her. "What in the galaxies are you made out of?" I say, lifting her onto the bed with a loud grunt.

Beeps squeals, bouncing on the mattress and rolling onto her side, then onto her face. I laugh and she lets out a series of sounds that I'm quite certain are not-so-nice comments.

"Sorry Beeps, but you'd laugh too if you saw how funny you looked right now."

A loud bang from down the hall startles me, but I can't see to the end of the long corridor to make out what's caused the noise. I climb up onto the bed and quickly close the door behind me, then lock it.

I sigh at the comfort of the bed and roll onto my back.

Finally, I'm off my feet. I walked all the way to the train station from the Temple. I even stood while eating my meal at the restaurant, moments before, not wanting to sit onto the brown and yellow soiled cushions on the floor. The food was worth it, though.

My eyelids grow heavy and I almost fall asleep. I blink and turn my head to look at Beeps. She's wobbling in place, having trouble staying upright on the soft bed. I smile.

"You alright?"

There's a short beep in response.

"I don't know how much time we're going to be spending together, or how I'm going to find Parrin again," I say to Beeps.

Her head drops and she makes a soft sound. I sit up. "No, no, I don't mean he won't be back, or that Star won't see you again. Parrin is smart and he'll find us. I just mean that you and I, we're going to be a family for a little while."

Beeps lifts her head and lets out a high pitched, happy sounding sequence of sounds.

"And," I continue. "If we're going to be a team, I really am going to need to learn your language, okay?"

Beeps nods.

"Good, now let's start with some basics."

Beeps responds and I recognize the sound as a *yes*.

"I know that means yes."

She repeats the sound.

"Good." I smile. "And I'm pretty sure I know what your *no* sound is too." I lay back down and look up at the low ceiling. "What other words should we start with?"

Beeps rolls onto her back beside me and a compartment opens up in her body. A small flashlight appears. It lights up the room in a bright blue. I squint, waiting for my eyes to adjust to the brightness.

Beeps projects some commonly used words and phrases onto the ceiling tiles, then she lets out a sequence of beeps.

"Are those the sounds that go with that phrase?"

"Yes," Beeps says in her robot language.

I smile. "Okay. Can I ask you to give me the sounds for some words that I want to know?"

"Yes."

"Great!."

Beeps responds again and the words *you're welcome* light up above us on the ceiling.

"I knew that one," I say with a smile. "And I've only known you for like an hour. Are you proud of me?"

"Yes," Beeps says. "You're smarter than Parrin."

I read the words above and laugh.

"Well, I do have a gift for understanding people." My eyelids grow heavy again. "I'm glad you're here, Beeps."

"Thanks," she replies.

"I never had any friends back at the Temple," I say. "Not really. I mean, Brianne..."

A lump forms in my throat but I push through the pain and continue.

"She was nice to me. But even she was scared of me. All the girls were. I don't know why..."

I stop for a moment. Maybe I do know why. Maybe they saw that I was capable of murder, even back then they must have sensed that in me.

Beeps waits silently for me to continue.

"Whenever I felt lonely I would go into my garden and visit all my plants and vegetables. They didn't say much but they were still alive, you know?"

Beeps responds and I open my eyes to look up at the ceiling to see what she's said.

"You had plants that could talk?"

I smile. "No. But in a way they communicated with me. I knew when they were happy because they grew fast and healthy. And I knew when they were sad and had no ambition to grow." I roll onto my side and yawn. "Can we continue robot language class in the morning? I'm so tired."

"Yes," Beeps responds, and a second later, I fall to sleep.

CHAPTER 10

I RACE THROUGH THE back alley, running faster than I ever have. With no robes or heavy garments to drag me down I can run freely. My new clothes cover a lot less than my Temple undergarments did. Yet I don't feel exposed, just free.

The tiny silver top I bought for myself earlier is too small to cover my stomach. And the small, orange shorts are too tight, yet they make me feel protected, like I'm wearing close fitting armor.

The world seems bigger now that I no longer wear my head covering. The sky is open wide above me. I can see higher and farther than I ever have.

I run from the city streets all the way to the industrial area on the outskirts of Central. There are less people the farther away I get from the city, but more vehicle traffic.

I stop at an intersection where the streetlight turns red and I take a moment to stretch my legs.

Large carts carrying merchandise from the factories roll past on the road. My fanciful dreams of how I imagined Central to be, seem so far-fetched, now that I'm actually here. But it feels good to know I made it. My apartment is small and I've been eating unhealthy at the restaurant. But I did finally buy clothes to help me fit in with the Citizens. Beeps and I are finally settling into our new home and I'll need to find a way to make money soon if we want to remain here.

I look out over the soot covered factories in the distance.

I need to find work today. Parrin's money is starting to run out. The factories will hire anyone, even unregistered Citizens like me, or so I've been told. It's not a place I'd want to work a long time, but it's a start.

I see the peak of a temple in the middle of all the dirty rooftops, the normally gold steeple is gray with soot. But it can't be a real temple, not here in Central. It must be a replica, some sort of entertainment center for performers, or a restaurant with a temple theme. The thought is a bit appalling, but I have to go see.

The street signal changes and I head for the steeple.

The distance is longer than I expect, but the temple peak stands above every other building, guiding me until I reach its front doors.

The air out here is less polluted than in the city center, but the sun is unrelenting, with no barrier to damper it. I'm drenched in sweat from running. There is no courtyard and fence around the property, like there would be at a real temple.

The doors open up right onto the dust filled streets, with no gate to keep out the unworthy. I hurry inside without a second thought, desperate to get out of the burning heat. My skin is not used to being exposed like this, having always been covered under my temple robes all my life.

Inside, it is dark. I'm blinded from being out in the sun, but the scents are familiar. I half expect to see Temple Mother materialize in the aisle, ready to reprimand me for leaving all my chores and responsibilities to the other sisters. And yet, I've done so much worse now.

The hum of machines and bustle of the merchant vehicles is shut out by the thick walls. There is only silence and cool air. It reminds me of home. The only home I've ever known, at the Temple. My life with my parents is a faded memory I can no longer conjure up.

My eyes adjust to the dim light and I see that this temple is different than the one back home. The engravings on the walls are unfamiliar.

I look up to the ceiling. The top half of the temple is completely black, charred by fire. What kind of fire would consume the top half of the church in this way? Then I remember the rumors of Takano Rynn burning down all the temples for boys.

I gasp. Is this a temple for boys? If so, I'm definitely not supposed to be inside. The walls below the charred ceiling are lined in gold, with symbols and art etched into the fine metal. The gold is a deep yellow and, in some places, tinted red. I've never seen so much gold in my life.

I swallow hard, awed by this place, but also afraid.

I know nothing about the ancient sayings and stories. But this is not my world anymore.

There are no brothers minding the temple, which makes sense since Takano killed them all. But there are also no devout citizens sitting on the benches and asking for graces. It feels like I'm inside a large tomb.

I head cautiously down the middle aisle, half expecting to burst into flames as punishment for being where I should not be. Statues watch me from their alcoves on either side of the temple walls as I pass by. One in particular stares at me in accusation, with marble eyes. I can't seem to escape his glare, no matter which angle I look at him from.

There's something familiar about him.

I walk up to his alcove to get a closer look. Most of his face is hidden in shadow by the hood he wears, etched into stone over his head. Only his long beard and piercing, marble eyes are visible.

I look at the engravings at the bottom of the statue, but I can't read them. And yet, I know who this is.

Takano Rynn's grandfather.

This statue was made before he turned into the evil lord that he later became.

That will never be me.

I'm surprised at the thought. Of course this could never be my fate, I'm not a Gifted lord.

"I killed your grandson," I say to the lifeless statue. "But I'm not like you. I have no desire to kill again. I've saved lives by stopping Takano Rynn."

I'm not sure if I'm trying to convince the lifeless statue of my innocence, or myself. I'm not proud of what I've done. I don't want power or vengeance.

Join me...

I push down the guilt that rises up when I think of Takano asking me to join him. It's inconceivable, and yet to him it was a plea for companionship.

Now he is gone and I will never think of it again.

I turn to leave the accusing glare of Takano's grandfather, and head back down the center aisle to the front doors. The cold dampness on my clothes chill me to the bone as the air moves around me. It reminds me of winter nights at the Temple.

They all knew I wasn't good enough to be there. I was taken in as an orphan. I was never a real Temple Girl. I disobeyed the rules all the time. Yet I never saw myself capable of murder. How can I judge Takano Rynn or his grandfather for becoming who they became, with the responsibility of the power they wielded? How much more easily would I have killed for my own reasons, if I had such power?

I suddenly feel desperate for the burning heat of the city, a heat that lulls my body and mind into a sleepy reality in which I don't have the energy to feel anything but tiredness. I'd prefer that to the cold, harsh wakefulness of being inside this temple.

I push through the temple doors and am hit with sunlight, full in the face.

A vehicle honks its horn, startling me. The drivers of the merchandise carts curse as they swerve to avoid hitting me. I ignore their hollers and head back the way I came. My hair sticks to my face and I swipe at the flyaway strands. The factories will be too hot to work in, with long hair. I've been avoiding cutting it this whole time but there's no reason left to keep my Temple vows. My hair will get too much attention and possibly get me killed. I promised Mr. Jardan, our landlord, that I'd give it to him as payment for our living quarters.

The though of my new living quarters makes me think of Beeps back home all alone. I pick up the pace. I'll pay Mr. Jardan today and find work later.

Once I'm back in the city, I stop at the first general shop I see. The windows are covered in ash from the nearby factories, so I can't see much of what's inside.

A bell rings when I pull open the heavy door. The shop owner stops polishing a glass bowl in his hand and glances at me.

"I've already paid my taxes," he says, his expression turning angry.

I pause for a moment, confused. "I was hoping to buy scissors."

The shopkeeper's shoulders seem to relax.

"Scissors, I have."

He comes out from behind the counter and goes directly to a shelf of random items, easily locating a pair of scissors in all the disarray. He gives me a suspicious look. "What's someone like you doing in Lower Central?"

I push my long braid over my shoulder in an attempt to hide it behind me. "I used to be a Temple Girl, but I'm not anymore." The words sting and I want to take them back. But it's true.

"I can pay you for your hair," the shopkeeper says.

"No." I pull some coins out of my pocket. "I just want the scissors, thank you."

I grab the scissors from him and drop the coins on the counter.

"A Temple Girl can't cut her own hair," he says.

I frown. Does everyone know the legends?

"For a small fee," the Shopkeeper continues, "I will have my sister cut it for you. Come." He walks down the aisle, between shelves, towards the back of the shop.

I hesitate. The Temple rules no longer apply to me now that I've left. Do they? I'll just cut my hair myself.

But what if there is some truth to the legends?

There's no point in thinking about it now. I might as well get it over and done with.

I hurry after the shopkeeper, anxious to get back to the restaurant to check on Beeps. I've already been away too long.

I step into the back area of the shop. The rooms are more organized here than at the front of the store. The space looks like living quarters.

An earthy incense tickles my nose and I stop a sneeze before it comes out. I glance around the room. The furniture looks like those of the Upper Citizens, only more worn and old. The reflection off a shiny object catches my attention. I walk over to have a closer look.

Glass ornaments line the shelf. I pick up a tiny glass sea creature. There are other sky creatures made of glass, with tiny crowns, as well as various land creatures of old; ones that went extinct long ago.

"This way," the shopkeeper says.

I set the glass sea animal down carefully and follow him through another curtain to a lounge area with soft carpet.

The room is lit in many colors, coming from a lamp in the shape of another sea creature, with long tentacles reaching to the ground.

"Do you like octopi?"

The voice startles me and I jump. A lady with short blue-gray hair watches me from a seat in the far corner of the room.

"I don't know what they are," I say.

"They're sea creatures." She gets up and walks over to me. Her clothes are made of a light material that floats as she moves, skimming the ground. "You're a Temple Girl."

I bristle, as though I've been accused of some wrong-doing. How does she know? I glance at the shopkeeper, who has now withdrawn to a corner of the room, but is watching curiously.

"I was," I tell the woman.

"You still are."

"I left." I shift from one foot to the other, not wanting to talk about my upbringing, with a stranger. Maybe everyone will stop asking if I'm a Temple Girl once I cut my hair.

"You never truly leave," the older lady says. She steps closer to me and I resist the urge to back away. Her eyes are almost white as she studies me. "You've met Takano Rynn," she says.

My face flushes and I don't respond. How does she know?

My heart pounds but I hold my ground. Does she know I killed Takano Rynn?

"You have his power," she whispers.

The scissors slip from my grasp and drop silently onto the carpet.

I shake my head. "I don't have powers like that."

"You have the Gift," the lady continues. "I was given a dream, that you would come."

I clench my fists tight. She doesn't know what she's talking about.

I pick up the scissors and glance over at the shopkeeper again. His expression is unreadable.

"Only one person in the Galaxy has the Gift," I say.

"Not only one," the prophetess says. She steps back, giving me some room to breathe. "There are others."

I frown. There can't be others. The Gifted lords of ages past are long gone now. If there were others still alive, Takano Rynn would have killed them, too, like he did his own brother.

"Do not get involved with the likes of Takano Rynn," she continues.

"I wouldn't, he's..." I stop before saying he's dead.

"He's irredeemable."

The words are unsettling. I'd never thought of it that way. Irredeemable seems so final, so hopeless.

But it's true, Takano Rynn is irredeemable now that he's dead.

The finality of it weighs heavily on me.

"I have to go."

I turn to leave then bump into a desk, almost knocking over the lamp with the tentacles. Tears obscure my vision as I run out. I came here to hide from what I'd done, but I can't seem to escape it. If she has another vision or dream, she could tell others!

I run through the front of the store and out into a crowd of people, not caring that I don't have the scissors I came for. I have to get back to Beeps.

I want to look different, to cut and change the color of my hair. Maybe get markings like Star's, and call myself by another name. I don't want to be Rita anymore.

Central is a big city. I won't let them find me.

I keep running until I'm back at the restaurant, and the room I now call home.

CHAPTER 11

"**W**HAT'S WRONG?" BEEPS ASKS. At least I think that's what she's asking.

I slam the door behind me and throw myself onto the bed.

"I killed him, Beeps." I wipe the tears from my eyes and turn onto my side, pulling my knees up to my chest. "I caught him off guard and cut his side open with a metal rod." I swallow hard, taking a moment to catch my breath before continuing.

"Then we fought. I don't think anyone has every openly confronted him before. Who would be that crazy? Me. But I was so scared of him, Beeps, scared of what he would do to the Sisters, but..." I shiver involuntarily. "He asked me to join him. Takano Rynn, the evil leader of the Ruling Order, asked me to join *him*. He was never going to kill me, he wanted—" I stop, not able to finish that sentence.

"Maybe his army had no intentions of killing the Sisters," I say, after a moment. "They were looking for the Gift Stone. But I killed him, anyway." My chest aches and I shut my eyes tight.

Beeps doesn't say anything.

"I dream about his eyes," I whisper. "He looks at me. Through me. He reads my mind."

I take a long, staggered breath, then continue. "In the dream, he reaches out to me with his hand, as he reads my thoughts and searches through my memories. He sees everything, even personal things."

I roll onto my back, remembering the rest of the dream. Takano Rynn reaches for me and I reach for him, too. I look into his thoughts, the way he looks into mine. I see his fears, his memories, hopes and insecurities. I see the power he sees inside of me. He's afraid I can surpass him someday, which makes no sense. *Him*, the fearless Takano Rynn, ruler of the Galaxies.

Then, I became afraid too, in the dream; of being all powerful and of the responsibilities that having such powers would mean. A galaxy of people's lives in my hands. The wars that would need to be fought...

Then, when our fingers touch, a power ignites between us, so strong that it lights up the night sky. And in that moment

I know that we are more powerful together than anything or anyone in all of space and time, even Dukath, the one whom Takano bows down to, according to Parrin.

I shudder at the thought.

"Is that why you wake up screaming?" Beeps asks, pulling me from my thoughts. She projects her words onto the ceiling so I can read them.

"What? I do?" I sigh. "It's only a dream. I have no powers. I'm just a Temple Girl. I mean, I'm just a General Citizen." I cover my face with my arm.

"A human, General Citizen," Beeps replies. "I'm a robot."

"Sometimes I wish I was a robot, like you."

"Do your parents know that you left the Temple?"

I stare at the words on the ceiling for a moment. "Temple Girls don't have parents."

"They don't?" Beeps asks.

"Well, some do, but most of the Temple Girls are orphans, others are given to the Temple by their parents."

"Are you an orphan?"

I frown at the projected words. "I am, but my parents didn't want to leave me behind. And I'm going to find them someday."

"I can help you look for them."

I turn onto my side and smile at Beeps. "Thanks for being my friend, Beeps."

She responds and I don't have to look at the ceiling to know that she said 'you're welcome.'

CHAPTER 12

T HE MARKET SQUARE IS a welcome sight, with all its noise and activity. The festive lights of all colors remind me of High Season at the Village. It was the only time of year when decorations were allowed at the Temple.

With everything that has happened this past week, I'm ready for a distraction. Now that I've become used to the heat, the warm evenings are more of a comfort than a frustration. Back home it never got this hot, even in the summer. But I'd rather the heat, than the cold which would only make me miss home. My heart aches whenever I think of the Sisters. I left without even an explanation or a goodbye.

I understand now why the people in Central love distractions so much. It helps you forget about other things.

I head for the crowds and the lights. My hair weighs heavy on my back, still uncut. I couldn't go through with it. Even the people of Central seem to respect and know the traditions of the Temple. It seems wrong just to ignore them. Beeps tried to help me cut my hair but she couldn't hold the scissors with her tiny retractable arms.

I walk past booths selling interesting things which I long to stop and look at, but already people are silently staring at me, stopping in mid-conversation, pulling small children away, as though I may be a threat.

I try my best to ignore them but then stop when I see a booth selling fabrics. I could get a light scarf to cover my hair. Then I'd be able to shop without drawing too much attention to myself.

Beeps rolls along at my side. "You play with your hair a lot when you're nervous," she says. The words aren't exact but I recognize the word 'hair' and 'upset.' A single beep of a certain frequency means she is talking about herself, two of the same frequency means she is referring to me in the sentence.

I drop my hand from my braid. "I guess I do fidget with my hair."

Beeps stops to pick up a rock with one of her retractable arms.

"Stay close," I say to Beeps.

"Why?" she asks.

"It's crowded here."

We start to walk again, heading to the booths on the other side where the fabrics are.

"Fresh berries!" A man yells in our direction. He smiles at me, holding out a basket of berries; his teeth are lined with gold. Business must be good in this market.

I give him a nod, then continue on.

I check to make sure that my metal fireplace poker is still secure on my back. It was such a useful weapon for fighting Takano Rynn that I bought another one at a shop near the restaurant.

"300 Capital bills for the robot," a large, bearded man says. He steps in front of us, blocking our path.

"She's not for sale." I move around him but he blocks me again. I look up and feel the roots of my hair tingle as my body prepares for a fight.

"It's a generous offer." He crosses his arms. "I usually don't offer to pay for what I want."

"Beeps, go find a scarf for me at the next booth while I talk to this gentleman." I don't take my eyes off the large man as I speak to Beeps. "I've already told you," I say to him. "The robot is not for sale."

"I didn't ask if he was." The man looks over my shoulder and nods to someone behind me.

"Rita?" Beeps calls to me. "There are others."

I turn just as two men cover Beeps with a sack and lift her up. I pull out my metal poker and jump towards them, kicking one in the head and swinging my rod at the other. They drop the sack and Beeps squeals from inside.

The bearded man lunges at me with both arms out. I thrust my rod into his belly and his eyes clench tight as he doubles over in pain.

Beeps' cries become more frantic but I can't get to her. The other two men are back on their feet again. They grab the sack and start running away.

"Stop!" I drop the poker and reach my hand out. The men fly into the air, then crash into a large wagon full of crates. I gasp. Did I do that?

The sack slams into the crates as well, and then rolls onto the floor.

Beeps!

The men scramble to their feet and glance back at me with terrified expressions on their faces. They scurry off and an eerie silence falls over the square as everyone looks towards me. No, not me, but behind me.

A man wearing a gray cloak is standing there, facing the men that have run off. His arm is outstretched to the crates where they were tossed, before scurrying. I look around at the quiet faces watching him. A circle has formed around this man with powers, but the crowd is keeping their distance. He removes his hood and I gasp. His light brown hair, with streaks of gray, seems to glow with the energy that still sizzles at his fingertips.

"Lord Morlin?" I blink. It can't be. Takano's older brother, not quite as tall as Takano or as frightening, yet intimidating just the same. It's like seeing a ghost. His image is painted on a large mural in the sanctuary at the Temple. But he's supposed to be dead, killed by Takano.

He walks towards me and I take a step back.

"Please, don't announce my presence like that," he says when he reaches me.

I look over his shoulder at the inquisitive crowd. They are watching curiously but already starting to return to their shopping. Don't they recognize him? I look back to Lord Morlin. He looks older than the painted image in the Temple, yet still the same. "You're...alive?"

His aged face becomes youthful for a moment as he smiles. "Yes, I believe I am."

I wrap my arms around my stomach, trying to cover the area where my high top has left my belly exposed, so inappropriate in the presence of such a renowned noble. I should be wearing my Temple robes at a moment like this. "But I thought Takano Rynn killed you."

"He tried." Morlin's voice is dry and scratchy as though he's in need of water after a long journey. He watches me curiously and I force myself not to shrink under his gaze. He folds his hands into the long sleeves of his cloak and nods in a direction away from the market.

"Come. We need to go."

"Me?" I glance back to the crates where the men dropped the sack with Beeps in it. The sack moves wildly as she struggles to get out of it. "I'll be right back." I run over to free her. She beeps frantically, rolling around in a circle.

"Beeps, it's okay. They're gone."

I pull the sack off of her and she rolls into my arms.

"We need to go with Morlin," I say softly, glancing around the market square.

The Citizens are keeping their distance from Lord Morlin, who is still in the same place I left him.

"Takano's brother?" Beeps says.

"Yes." I let her go and she finds her balance. "Come on, let's go!"

CHAPTER 13

"**Y**ou can't use your powers, Rita," Lord Morlin says to me. He stops walking, now that we've gone quite a distance from the market.

"My powers?" I say, rubbing dust from my eyes. Why does everyone think I have powers? I don't. For a second I almost believed I did, but it was Lord Morlin who saved us back there. If it weren't for him, those men would have taken Beeps. "Thank you for saving us back there, my lord."

Lord Morlin smiles and shakes his head. "You can call me Morlin. No one has called me lord since I was teaching in the Temple for Boys, before those Temples were all destroyed."

I nod. We are alone now and Lord Morlin watches me with interest, making me nervous. He is nothing like Takano Rynn. There is no hate in his eyes. I would have expected a tormented soul like Takano's, but instead he is full of a different kind of energy, one fueled by life, not anger. Even in person, he seems unreal, like a character from a fairy-tale from my childhood.

Tears swell in my eyes and I blink them away.

Temple Mother always spoke of Lord Morlin with such reverence. She should be the one here to meet him, not me.

"How…"I rub my eyes again, unable to put my words into a sentence.

"It's important that you don't use your powers," Lord Morlin repeats.

"I wouldn't if you asked me not to," I nod. "But I don't have powers." There's so much I want to ask him. How did he escape from his evil brother and why did he stay away for so long? Where was he? Why did he suddenly return now? Is it because…

My chest tightens.

Is it because I killed Takano?

"Did you come to avenge his death?" I say softly, not able to look Lord Morlin in the eyes. I won't run away from what I've done this time. I deserve to face the brother of the man I murdered.

Beeps lets out a tiny sound.

"His death?" Lord Morlin says. "I am not aware of any death."

"I…" the words get stuck in my throat. How do you tell someone that you killed their brother and know where the body lies in the forest?

"I've heard the rumors." He sighs, looking out toward the dust-filled horizon on the outskirts of Central. "You did not kill him, though. I would have known if you had. He is still alive and hiding, gathering his strength. But to what purpose, I don't know. No one knows where he is." Lord Morlin looks back at me. "He'll find you if you use your powers. You must not use them."

"But—" I stop. Now is not the time to convince a Gifted Lord that I'm not actually Gifted. My mind spins with all this new information. If Takano is alive then that means I didn't kill him. It's a bit frightening that he's still out there, but it's a relief to know I'm not a killer. A weight lifts off my shoulders. He's not dead. I didn't kill anyone.

"Dukath has discovered where you are and is sending Ruling Order soldiers to retrieve you," Lord Morlin says.

A chill runs through me, despite the warm air between the buildings.

"Dukath?" I frown. So the all-powerful entity that even Takano fears is not just a myth after all. But if Takano is still alive, wouldn't he be the one coming after me, and not Dukath?

"You must come with me," Lord Morlin continues, "to Antineon. The Ruling Order doesn't know of that planet and you can train with me, like you should have done from the start."

My mind races. Is it because I almost brought Takano Rynn to his last breath, that everyone thinks I have Gift powers? Is that why Morlin wants me to train with him? Would he believe that I'm just good at hitting a target and hiding, and that's how I got the better of his brother? And yet, I can understand why everyone wants to believe I'm a rare Gifted Temple Girl, even though the Gift is passed down only to males, not females. The soldiers must have spread the rumor that I went up against Takano Rynn in battle and defeated him.

I look at Lord Morlin. Does he want to try and join his Gift powers with mine? The same way Takano Rynn wanted to do with me?

"I want to stay here," I say. "In Central. I can train here—"

"It's too dangerous now."

"I won't use my powers, I promise." I hear the desperation in my own voice. I just started my life here. I have my own place, in a city where I can disappear among the crowds. I have Beeps and Parrin, once he returns.

"Takano Rynn is looking for you," Lord Morlin says.

"What does he want from me?" I swallow hard. "Revenge?"

Lord Morlin's eyes search mine. "No, Rita. He wants your Gift."

My dream suddenly comes back to me. Takano Rynn reaching out his hand, our fingers touching, the power igniting between us. I see his eyes, curious about me, not intrusive but inviting, beckoning me to join him. His thoughts are hopeful, like he's found a missing part of himself.

"No!" I cry out, feeling that familiar pull to him, the one I fought against in the forest, the one that tempts me to give in to him.

"The Gift in you is stronger than his powers of influence, Rita. You won't give in to it. You're stronger than that." Lord Morlin sets a hand on my shoulder.

I'm not, I want to say. *I'm not stronger than him.*

"I can teach you to use your Gift," he continues.

I shake my head. Even if I did have the Gift I wouldn't use it. Temple Mother told us that the Lords rarely used their Gift, because use of it eventually leads to evil. Such power corrupts the mind and heart.

I hold back a shudder as I recall Takano's words.

You're just like me.

I shake my head to dispel the memory of his eyes, which I can not seem to escape, both day and night.

"Don't be afraid, Rita," Lord Morlin says. "You can learn to control the Gift."

I don't respond. It isn't the power of the Gift that I fear, it's Takano's desire for me to join him. He was vulnerable for a moment and he was...interested in me, impressed by me. I never knew such interest could be a temptation for me. I saw him not as an evil ruler, but just as Takano. Lonely like me. I swallow hard. If I ever see him again I may not be able to resist this time.

"You're right." I wrap my arms around myself. "If Dukath knows where I am then maybe he's sent Takano Rynn to get me."

"My brother no longer follows Dukath's orders. He's gone rogue," Lord Morlin says.

"Rogue?"

"Yes. He isn't with the Ruling Order anymore. He wants something that is more powerful."

"I don't understand. What could he possibly want?"

"He wants you."

CHAPTER 14

"I'LL TAKE YOU TO the outer provinces, a place we can keep you safe until you're ready," Lord Morlin says.

I hope we're not walking all that way, I want to say, but don't. Lord Morlin reminds me of Takano in some ways, when he's serious, and it's intimidating. He's a Gifted Master. I should be using High Speech, which I learned in Sunday classes at the Temple. But he told me not to call him 'my lord', and High Speech sounds so unnatural whenever I try to speak it.

"Ready for what?" I ask. The heat is now making me agitated. I just want to go back home to our safe little room.

Beeps rolls along beside us, being so quiet that it's making me worry. Does she need anything? Does the heat affect her, too?

"Ready with your training," Lord Morlin replies, as though it's obvious. "Has no one told you?"

I frown. "Told me what?"

"I thought that was why you came to Central."

"I don't know what you're talking about," I snap. "I came to Central to get away from..." I stop, remembering the blood-spattered snow in the hills back home.

Lord Morlin waits for me to finish but I don't.

"We need to hurry," he says.

"No," I cross my arms. "I'm not going back to the outer provinces."

"You can't stay here. I've brought my own flyer. It's on the third tier."

I drop my arms to my sides. Nothing I say will convince him. I'll just pretend to go along with him for now. "Okay. But I need to get some things from home before we leave."

"There's no time, Rita."

A group of soldiers marching past, on a nearby road, head in the direction of the market. Lord Morlin turns his back to them, pulling his hood over his head and shielding me from their view.

"Soon we will be outnumbered."

My throat tightens. I can't just disappear. Parrin will return and be looking for Beeps. Or Star will. And I can't take

Beeps away from them. But I also can't leave her in Central alone. She'd get captured and sold in no time.

"I'll meet you up on tier three," I say to Lord Morlin, then run off with Beeps at my heels.

CHAPTER 15

"WHAT ARE YOU DOING here?" Parrin says, looking at me with wide eyes.

"What are *you* doing here?" I say back.

He gets up from the floor where he was sitting, in front of my door.

"Where did you go? What's—"

"There's no time for all that," Parrin says, grabbing me by the arms. "You have to get out of here. They're going to come looking for you."

"Then come with me."

Beeps says something in agreement.

Parrin sighs. "We need to get out of here." His eyes look tired and he's still wearing the brown jacket despite the heat. It feels nice that he's worried about me. The last thing I want to do is go with Lord Morlin and train with him when I don't even have Gift powers to train with. But Parrin is right, I can't stay here anymore.

"Then you should take Beeps, so she's not in any danger."

Beeps protests at this.

Parrin shakes his head. "I don't know how much safer she'll be with me."

A loud bang startles both of us as a door flies open at the end of the hall. We turn our backs to the person who came in. I catch a glimpse of a large form, silhouetted at the end of the smoky hallway.

I grab Parrin's arm and lead him the other way to the back doors. He hurries along and I notice his limp.

I push the back doors open and we stumble out into the alley way. The street behind the restaurant is abandoned. The only sound is the hissing of steam rising up from grates along the sides of the building.

"Beeps!" I crouch down to her level. "Can you use your tools to lock this back door from the inside?"

"Yes."

"Hurry!"

Beeps reaches up with her little retractable arms and sticks a long metal bit into the door lock. The door handle jiggles wildly and Beeps retracts her arm.

"Done," she says.

A loud bang against the door startles us and Parrin jumps back. Beeps zooms off down the alley and I run after her. They've found me already. That was fast.

We hurry down the street but I slow my pace, waiting for Parrin to catch up as he hops along, one of his legs clearly injured. The shops on the street have all pulled their shades down and the signs have been switched to closed.

I stop when I see the Ruling Order guards gathered at the end of the road. Their dark uniforms and armor seem out of place amidst the colorful flags and lights of this part of the city. They search the area, kicking over stands and barrels to look behind them.

I draw back, ducking behind a large garbage bin. Parrin and Beeps join me and we huddle close. I peek out from our hiding spot. The soldiers' faces are covered by dark hoods and I can't see their expressions. I imagine inhuman faces with sharp teeth and hollow eyes. We'll never get past them. Beeps makes a sound and I quickly shush her.

"Beeps you have to be quiet," I whisper. She responds with more Beeps but I shush her again. "Don't say anything."

One of the guards turns in our direction. I hold my breath. We'd be no match for them. I should have stayed with Lord Morlin. But I had to find Parrin first.

Another guard calls out something and they continue their search in a different direction.

"What should we do?" I whisper, turning to Parrin. But he isn't behind me. I look around frantically. "Parrin?"

"I was trying to tell you," Beeps says. "He left."

"What?"

The alleyway is dark and covered in shadows.

Then I see Parrin, at the top of a fire escape, against the building. He lifts a finger to his lips, motioning for me to be quiet ,then points up.

I look to where he's pointing. The fire escape goes to the roof.

I nod and Parrin continues to climb.

The guards have dispersed, widening their search. One heads in our general direction. I make a run for the fire escape and jump up to grab the bottom of the ladder. How did Parrin do this with his injured foot?

"Stop!" the guard behind me yells.

Shoot! I should have waited. I pull myself up onto the ladder, my shoulder pinching in pain from the sword wound Takano Rynn gave me weeks ago.

The boom of a gunshot echoes down the alleyway. I grasp the ladder tight and stifle a scream. The bullet ricochets off the metal near my ear and I almost let go of the ladder.

"Beeps!" I yell down. How am I going to get her?

She extends two retractable arms up to the ladder, grasping the bars with tiny clasps and pulling herself up. A shot deflects off one of Beeps' metal arms.

"Beeps! Hurry!" I climb up fast, my heart beating wildly. I don't see Parrin above me anymore but I'm glad he's no longer within shooting range.

More gunshots ring out, accompanied by bright streaks of laser beams from other weapons. Weapons used by Ruling Order soldiers.

"Rita!" Parrin leans over the edge of the roof and reaches his hand down to me. I grab it and he swings me up just as a laser beam skims my side.

"Ouch!" I fall onto the roof, doubling over in pain. I grab my side where it throbs. Beeps lets out a worried cry nearby. She made it! The shots continue to streak upward over the edge of the roof and I scoot back farther from the ledge.

"Oh my Galaxies!" Parrin says, looking at the blood on my hand. His face goes pale.

"It's fine, it's just the skin. I didn't get hurt."

Parrin strips off his jacket and pulls his shirt over his head. He tries to tie it around my waist.

"Ow!" I pull it away from him. The shouts of the soldiers below remind me that we're still in danger. They've stopped shooting but are climbing up now.

"Here, take your shirt." I hand the shirt to Parrin. "We need to get out of here."

"Out of here, to where?"

Beeps' head spins around in a circle. "There's nowhere to go!" she cries.

Parrin and I look at each other. There's nothing left to say. The soldiers will either kill us or take us to be questioned, and then kill us when they find out I don't have any real powers or know any thing useful to them.

But for now, they believe I have powers. If the rumor that I'm Gifted brought Lord Morlin out from hiding, and has put Takano Rynn into hiding, then the soldiers must believe it, too.

Parrin grabs my hand, his eyes full of worry. I resist the urge to pull it away.

"It'll be okay," I say. "I'm Gifted." I swallow hard. It's a lie, but nobody knows that.

His eyes widen at my words. There are shouts from below, getting closer. I don't look over to the roof's edge but hold Parrin's gaze instead. "We can defeat them."

Parrin nods, a look of hope crosses his face.

Good, he believes me. Now I just have to make the soldiers believe it.

I look to the roof's ledge and see the soldiers climbing over. I stand up fast, ignoring the pain in my side. They stop. The first soldier to get onto the roof glances down at my blood-stained shirt. I stretch my hand out towards them, keeping my gaze on the first soldier's eyes. He must be their commander or leader.

He stands completely still. The two others behind him hesitate as well, as though unsure.

Suddenly a loud rushing sound and hot wind beat down on our heads and I duck. Parrin puts a protective arm over my shoulders. Beeps cries out and I look up. A large flier hovers above us, preparing to land. The air pressure from the bottom of the flier knocks the guards off balance and they fall backwards, over the edge of the roof.

"Get out of the way!" I yell over the roaring engine.

Parrin crawls over to the side of the building and I do the same, pulling Beeps with us. There isn't much room for the flier and we're dangerously close to the edge. The aircraft makes a shaky landing and the rushing air finally stops.

A hatch opens and Lord Morlin leans out, waving at us, yelling something that I can't hear over the roar of the engine. I get up and run over. Beeps bumps against my leg. I lift her into my arms, ignore the pain, and toss her to Lord Morlin. He grabs her and sets her inside, then offers a hand to me. I take it and jump with a loud grunt, rolling onto the cool floor of the aircraft once I land.

The noise fades off as the hatch closes and the flier lifts into the air. Loud pings hit the outer metal frame as bullets and laser shots bounce off the outer walls.

We rise fast and I struggle to get off the floor as the force of the ship's upward movement holds me down.

Beeps is frantic with all her beeping noises. She's repeating Parrin's name over and over. I look around, but don't see him.

"Parrin!" I crawl to the window in the hatch and look down. We're too high up now to see the roof top anymore. "We have to go back!" I yell.

Beeps rolls left and right, trying to keep her balance on the bumpy ride.

I hurry to the front of the flier where Lord Morlin is seated at the helm. He reaches up to hit some buttons and the ship slows.

"We need to go back for Parrin," I say.

"He'll be fine." Lord Morlin steers the ship to the right and I fall into the copilot seat with a huff.

"They're going to kill him."

Beeps squeals from somewhere at the back of the flier and I immediately regret my choice of words.

"They won't kill him. They were looking for you, not him."

"But—"

"They'll take him for questioning, but he doesn't know anything. And he's a trained Opposition Fighter."

My next words stop in my throat. Did he say Parrin is with the Opposition?

"They have a truth serum to make him talk, so they won't need to hurt him to get information. And he won't have information about you. At least not about where you're going right now."

"Then they'll have no use for him and kill him!"

"They'll hold him for ransom."

I grip my seat on either side so my hands will stop shaking. "We can't just leave him behind."

"It's more important that you didn't fall into their hands."

I frown. Beeps continues making worried noises at the back. I get up to go see what's going on. "Beeps!"

She's stuck under a crate, on her side.

"How in the galaxies did you get stuck under there?" I pull her out and she rolls into my arms. "Sorry girl, it looks like Lord Morlin is taking us somewhere. He was on a rescue mission I think, to rescue me."

Beeps makes a questioning sound and says Parrin's name again.

"I'm sorry, Beeps. But Lord Morlin says Parrin will be okay. They won't harm him because they need him. They want me, not him."

"Why?"

"They think I have Gift powers."

"It's not you. It's me!" Beeps says. "You?"

"Yes!"

"I have..." Beeps continues but I don't understand the rest of her words.

"I don't understand. You have what?"

She repeats her beeps.

"You have something that the Ruling Order might want?"

"Yes!"

I sit in one of the back seats and set my hand on Beeps' head. "Well, then I'm glad we got you out of there just in time. Does Parrin know the Ruling Order is looking for you?"

"No."

"Does Star know?"

"Yes."

I sigh and close my eyes. Everything just got a lot more complicated.

CHAPTER 16

"CAN I ASK YOU a question, Lord Morlin?" I say. He nods and I climb into the copilot seat.

"You couldn't sleep?" he asks.

I shrug, not wanting to tell him that I've been trying everything *not* to sleep. I don't want to dream about Takano Rynn. I don't even want to be alone with my thoughts anymore.

"The bunk in the back is pretty small," I say instead.

"You'll need your rest." Morlin's eyes are glazed over and he looks far more tired than I feel.

"Do you want me to take over, so you can have a rest?" I offer.

Morlin rubs his eyes. He must have flown this ship straight from Antineon, before reaching Central.

"I suppose the flier can auto pilot from here," he says, slowly getting up. "Just keep an eye out for unexpected asteroids or ships."

I nod. "I'll do that."

"If you see a Ruling Order ship on either of these radar screens let me know."

I climb into the pilot's seat and Morlin makes his way slowly to the back.

"Is there any food back here?" he asks.

"There's some bread and cheese..." Suddenly something occurs to me. "Lord Morlin, have you seen Beeps?"

"That little robot? Probably recharging somewhere. And you can call me Morlin."

I nod, keeping my eyes ahead. My hand tightens on the controls. "I thought she was up here with you while I was trying to sleep."

"I'll find her and send her up to the front." Morlin's voice fades away and when I glance back I can't see him anymore.

I maneuver the small ship to the right to avoid a small cluster of rocks, then double check that the autopilot is still running. A small screen lights up.

Please re-enter coordinates.

I frown. What were the coordinates set to again? I punch in the numbers I remember and the ship rises then does a semi-circle.

I relax back into the pilot's seat, keeping my hand on the controls in case I have to manually maneuver around anything else. I never thought about Beeps needing to recharge. She must have a cord that she can connect to an outlet. Maybe she's resting too and powered down.

A sudden thump brings my attention back to flying the ship. We've flown into a meteor shower. There's another thump. I lean over to the copilot's side, trying to reach the shields switch, but can't get to it.

"Are we being attacked?" Morlin runs into the cockpit and jumps into the copilot seat.

"No, meteor shower," I say.

He quickly puts the shields up. "We shouldn't be going in this direction." He stops, looking at the coordinates on the console, then over at me. It takes me a second to realize that I've completely changed our course. "Where are you taking us?" Morlin asks, a curious expression on his face.

I look at the numbers on the console. "I honestly don't know. I thought those were the coordinates you had put in." Or were they? I look down at the numbers again. They're not the right coordinates, not even close. I start to get up to let Morlin take over when a powerful feeling grips me and my muscles tense.

It's Takano Rynn.

I look to Morlin, expecting to see him react to the strong influence I can feel, but he doesn't seem to notice.

It's the same intense feeling I had when I was battling Takano in the forest. When he removed his hood and looked straight at me.

Join me...

He's close. I know exactly where the coordinates are taking us.

Straight to Takano Rynn.

CHAPTER 17

I JUMP UP FROM the pilot's seat, startling Morlin. He's still watching me with a concerned look on his face. He doesn't feel Takano Rynn's pull like I do. But if I can sense Takano, does that mean he can sense me approaching too?

"I'm sorry I put in the wrong coordinates," I say, fighting against the urge to take over the controls again.

He's making me do it.

Morlin, climbs into the pilot seat and recalculates the co-ordinates in silence. I want to push him aside and fly this thing straight to Takano but I grip the back of the copilot's seat with both hands instead.

What is wrong with me?

"Are you well?" Morlin glances at me out of the corner of his eye.

"Just tired" I say. I have to get out of the cockpit.

"Is it about your friend, Parrin?" Morlin asks.

"Pardon?"

"Were you trying to set the coordinates to return to Central, to find Parrin?"

I open my mouth to answer, then stop. It's probably better for Morlin to think that I was trying to head back to Central, than to know where I was really headed.

"I just put in the wrong coordinates," I snap, then realize how disrespectful I sound. "I'm sorry, I'm a little on edge." I hurry out of the cockpit to get as far away from the flight controls as possible. My hands shake as I pace the small area at the back of the ship.

How did I know the correct coordinates for the flight path to Takano Rynn? Is his influence over me really that strong? What else will I end up doing to get to him? Sleepwalk? Will I wake up one day and find myself in front of him with no recollection of how I got there? I shiver at the thought.

Should I tell Morlin? Maybe he'll know something about this strange connection I now have to Takano. Could it be because we looked into each other's minds at the same time, when we first met? Did it create some kind of bond?

I take a seat on the small cot at the back.

I can't tell Morlin now, not yet. I need to figure it out for myself first. Maybe it's no big deal and I'm just overtired.

I fidget with the ends of my hair, itching to take out the braid and get into different clothes. The flier is much colder than being in Central. My thin clothes are not warm enough.

A beeping from behind me catches my attention.

"Beeps?"

I turn to find Beeps huddled in a corner, and them hurry over to make sure everything is alright.

"What's wrong?"

"I'm worried."

"Worried?" I ask, to clarify what her beeps mean.

"Yes."

I pull her out from the corner. "Come and sit with me on the bed. We'll be fine."

I help Beeps up onto the bed to sit beside me.

Takano's pull is dwindling now. We must be making more distance between us and him. But I'm not relieved as I should be. My heart aches, like I've lost a friend. It reminds me of how it felt to lose my parents. I clench my fists. These feelings aren't real, it's just a trick that Takano Rynn is using to get me to go to him.

I lean back against the wall and pull my legs up, hugging them to my chest. All the emotions I've been trying so hard to ignore, rush to the surface; the pain of being abandoned by my parents, the loneliness of feeling different from the other girls at the Temple.

But my parents didn't abandon me, they were taken from me. I don't actually know for certain, but I know they'd never just leave me behind. The Sisters took care of me and I became strong. But deep down, I was still weak with the feelings of rejection and loneliness.

I learned to bury the weakness. I was doing just fine until Star, Parrin and Beeps came along. Now, I can't imagine my life without Beeps. I never intended to open myself up to new friends. It just happened.

I wipe a tear from my face and put my arm around Beeps' small, metal body. She feels warm rather than cold.

"Do you think Parrin is okay?" she asks.

I nod. How could I have left Parrin behind, the same way I was left behind? I left him in the hands of the enemy. I close my eyes and try to imagine my garden and the greenhouse back home, to bring me some comfort, but it only makes me feel more homesick.

My thoughts wander to Takano Rynn. He saw things in my mind I'd never told anyone, how I pretended the girls at the Temple were my real sisters, even though they hardly ever talked to me. He was so curious about all that was inside my head. No one had ever shown that much interest in me before. Morlin is only interested in my Gift powers, that he believes I have, so he can train me to be a strong force against Takano

Rynn. But if he knew I was just an average girl with no powers, he wouldn't even take a second look at me.

I see the snowy forest again and Takano, standing in front of me, the snowflakes falling around us. He's like me, lonely and searching, but pretending to be strong.

"No, no, no." I sit up and climb off the bed. I can't keep thinking of Takano. He's the leader of the Ruling Order. Parrin is my friend. He took a chance on me and helped me out when I arrived in Central. He and Star were my first real friends. They didn't care that I was different than them, but accepted me right from the beginning.

I have to go back for Parrin. I don't care what Morlin says.

I look down at Beeps who's still on the bed watching me in silence. Parrin is Beeps' friend, too. "We need to go back for Parrin," I say.

Beeps' noises don't need a translation. She wants to go back for Parrin too.

CHAPTER 18

"**U**SE YOUR GIFT POWERS," Lord Morlin whispers to me. "The way you did on the rooftop when you paralyzed the soldiers."

I can't—" I whisper back, but then stop. He's right. Powers or not, if the Ruling Order soldiers believe I have the Gift, it will make them worry, and at least provide a distraction, until Morlin can get Parrin out of prison.

The pristine, white corridors inside the Ruling Order headquarters are a stark contrast to the dust covered surface we encountered outside on the planet. We almost didn't find the building which is hidden underground, in a land of only dust and sand as far as the eye can see.

The air is artificially cooled, but my skin still burns with the aftereffect of the sun outside. My cheeks are hot too, but not because of the sun. Morlin doesn't know I'm powerless and it's making me worry. The guards froze on that rooftop out of fear or confusion, not because of anything I did. I feel a lot less confident here, at their headquarters.

Morlin leads the way. He seems unsettled and I can't blame him. He disobeyed orders from the Opposition Base, to bring me here. At least he seems to know where he's going in this building.

He reaches his hand up to the security cameras as we pass by, effortlessly turning them in the other direction with his Gift. I envy his ability.

He'd be a great teacher. It's hard to imagine he's Takano's brother.

Morlin turns right, at the end of the hall. I want to ask questions and go over our plan, but I can tell he is irritated with me, so I stay quiet. I threatened to come on my own if he didn't help me rescue Parrin, so he agreed to come.

The next corner we turn has a large iron door at the end of the hall. It's black and looks out of place among all the white. Morlin turns another security camera away from us and we approach the door.

"You may have to help me with this," he says, running his hand over the front of the door.

I nod. There's no point in arguing. Morlin refuses to believe anything but the fact that I can use the Gift the way he does.

He sets his hand over the security panel near the door then closes his eyes as though to concentrate.

"Morlin? I do want to help but I—"

A heavy clicking sound startles me and I jump.

I push down on the door handle to see if it worked. The door opens and Morlin gives me a smile. I can't seem to return the smile. If anyone is going to be killed on this mission today, it will be me.

When the door is fully open I freeze at the sight. Two guards with large guns stare back at us. They look confused for a moment, and I have no idea what to do. They are blocking the entrance to a hallway lined with prison cells.

The smell in the room is sour and stale. I resist the urge to cover my nose. The guards raise their guns and Morlin calmly lifts his hand towards them.

They lower their guns, again.

"I'll find Parrin," Morlin says to me.

I nod, reaching my hand towards the guards as though to take over for Morlin, while he heads to the prison cells. His gray cloak and light hair seem to glow in the dimly lit prison. The guards don't move. My shoulders relax. I can do this.

A loud clank of a cell door opening sounds and the guards seem to wake from their trance. They raise their guns and point them at me.

"Don't shoot!" I yell with as much authority as I can. "I'm Rita!"

"We know who you are," one of the guards says. He reaches to his side and pulls out a communication device.

"We've got the girl," he says into the device.

"Keep her alive," comes the response.

I look towards the prison cells, hoping to see Morlin and Parrin emerge at any moment. The door we came through is still open behind me. A slight breeze blows across the back of my neck. I need to make a run for it. The guards will chase me and it will create a diversion long enough for Morlin and Parrin to escape.

I turn and run. A laser shot zooms past my shoulder. I scream and duck, covering my head with both hands.

Why are they shooting?

Then I realize my mistake. They're not firing to kill, but to stun. Before I can think of what to do next a burning sensation pierces my side and everything goes black.

CHAPTER 19

"YOU PUT THIS MISSION into great risk," General Anias says with a frown. He's a small man with a big presence. Streaks of gray color his beard and there is a kindness in his eyes, even as he reprimands me.

I'm at the Opposition Base, safe and sound, thanks to the General. His uniform is perfectly pressed, a dark green similar to the other pilots' uniforms, but with more badges and nicer buttons. The shoulder pads make him look authoritative and rigid, but the tired lines around his eyes betray his old age. The Opposition commanders and pilots all watch me from around the large table that they're standing around. A mainframe computer encircles the small room. Its hum fills the silence as the General waits for me to say something.

"I'm sorry," I finally say.

I keep my gaze down on the touch screen surface of the glass conference table. It displays a map of a solar system. At the moment, no one is looking at it. They're here to discuss their rescue mission to get Lord Morlin back from the Ruling Order, who wanted him, not me.

"I didn't think they would capture Lord Morlin," I say. "I thought they wanted me."

"He sacrificed himself in your stead," General Anias says. "The Ruling Order believed Morlin was dead for all these years. And you took him right to them." The General takes a long breath through his nose before continuing. "You must have realized what would happen if they discovered him alive."

I bow my head. I was only thinking of Parrin. It didn't even cross my mind that I'd put Morlin into danger. If anyone was going to get out of the Ruling Order base without any trouble, I assumed it would be him.

The pilots and commanders stand silently in their perfectly pressed uniforms. General Anias clears his throat to address the room. I shrink back from the circle and watch him give orders about what will happen next.

No one looks at me anymore but I can feel their disappointment. The entire Galaxy knows it's my fault the Ruling Order now has Lord Morlin, who just come back, seemingly from the dead, to start a revolution that never had a chance to even start.

Lord Morlin never said anything about to me about starting a revolution. But it's what everyone believes.

I listen to the Opposition commanders talk about a General Randon, who has taken over the leadership of the Ruling Order, now that Takano Rynn is missing. They believe he's planning something big, but no one knows what.

"How many battleships do we have ready?" General Anias asks.

I don't hear the reply from the other end of the table but the expression on the General's face tells me it's not enough. I frown. I've made everything worse. Lord Morlin was their secret weapon and apparently so was I. They'd been searching for the Gifted Girl, a legend that I'd only heard of now, by eavesdropping on the pilots' conversations. They believe I'm this Gifted Girl that everyone's been waiting for and that I will bring an end to the Ruling Order. Nothing could be farther from the truth. I don't even know how they came to this conclusion, but I have my theories.

I told Parrin I was Gifted. I shouldn't have lied about something that important. He's been working with the Opposition and must have contacted them. Then, when Morlin heard of it, he must have come out of hiding to find me first. He had been waiting too, for the Gifted Girl to come along. But it's not me.

The rumors that I was the one who defeated Takano Rynn in battle and sent him into hiding, only further proved their theory that I'm the Gifted one they've been looking for. That's probably why I haven't been properly reprimanded for getting Morlin captured, just frowned upon.

I look around the room at all the serious faces. Now doesn't seem like the right time to convince them I'm not the girl they've been looking for. They've got enough to deal with. Morlin's been captured and this new leader Randon, sounds ruthless, even more ruthless than Takano Rynn. He took no time at all replacing Takano as leader of Ruling Order, and he doesn't even have any Gift powers! But the people follow him and he's willing to do whatever it takes to remain in power.

"Rita?" General Anias says, pulling me from my thoughts. "Are you alright?"

I look up to see that all eyes are on me. "What? Oh, sorry. Yes, I'm fine." My cheeks heat up.

"We were discussing if you should join with the Opposition fighters in the rescue mission to retrieve Lord Morlin. You did defeat Takano Rynn after all."

"Yes! Of course, I'll go." I stand up. "I'll do everything I can to—"

"Now hold on." General Anias holds up a hand. "It may be too soon for you to go out into battle just yet. You need training in your Gift and in our Honor Code, starting with honesty and the greater good. Not to mention self-discipline to keep you from the temptation of the wrongful use of your Gift."

My stomach drops. Should I tell them now that I'm not Gifted? But I want to help in this mission to rescue Morlin. It was my fault he got captured in the first place.

I can't look at the others. Their expectant stares make me uneasy. If they find out I have no powers, it will crush what little hope they're holding onto. As long as both sides believe I'm Gifted, I can use that against the Ruling Order. If General Randon doesn't need the Gift to intimidate people, then neither do I.

"Rita? Are you listening?" General Anias says. He has a concerned look on his face. Was he saying something to me?

"Yes. Sorry."

"You'll report to our training base in the morning. One of the fighters will escort you there."

I'm being given a chaperon? They don't trust me. "Thank you, General."

He nods to me, then dismisses the others. They hurry off to begin their rescue mission, without me.

CHAPTER 20

A TACTICAL ALERT ALARM blares through the speakers in the hallway outside my sleeping chamber. It startles me awake from a sleeping nightmare, and throws me right into a waking one. Alarms are blaring all around and I have no idea what's going on.

I run out from my sleeping quarters to find the Base frantic with Opposition soldiers running around. There is bad news. People are dead. Planes have been destroyed. Opposition Fighters have been captured.

Beeps stays close as we watch the commotion in silence. There's really nothing we can do. I can't be sure how Beeps' class of robot processes emotion, but I worry for her. No one's heard from Parrin yet, after he escaped from the Ruling Order base. He is still missing and so is Star's fighter plane.

"It's my fault," Beeps says.

"What's your fault?" I ask.

"Everything."

I crouch down to talk to her. "It's not your fault. It's my fault this has happened. I didn't listen to Lord Morlin, and I shouldn't have left Parrin behind in the first place. I should have made sure he got into the flier before it took off." I swallow hard. "I'm sorry, Beeps."

Another alarm sounds and people start to rush to their stations.

"We need to help them!" Beeps cries out.

"What do you mean?" I'm surprised by her response. She's just a tiny robot, there's so little she could do to help. She'll likely be destroyed if she tried. And yet she wants to help. I clench my fists. Where's *my* courage? Lord Morlin is in the hands of the enemy and who knows what they're doing to him now.

"Come on Beeps. We need a fighter plane!"

CHAPTER 21

"WE BOTH WANT THE same thing." Takano Rynn's voice comes from deep within the dark hood he wears. I'm dreaming again, but this time it's different. Takano has come into my dream, it's not just a memory of him from the forest, it feels real, like I'm awake.

He stands before me in his terrifying presence. I want him to pull his hood down so I can see his eyes. I can't see his thoughts when I can't see his eyes.

"You don't know what I want," I say. Is he saying we both want to rescue Lord Morlin? Or that we both want to stop Dukath and his new pawn, General Randon? Those are the things I want.

"You want Morlin," Takano says.

"I want him to be safe. I don't want him dead."

"Neither do I."

"But you..." I stop before saying he killed his own brother. He didn't. So then, did he cover for Morlin while he was in hiding? Was he working with his brother this whole time? I want to ask more questions but he tosses me a rock before I can say anything.

As I catch it, I wake.

"Beeps?" I sit up, looking around frantically. Beeps is beside me in the copilot's chair. I look down at the flight console in front of me. How did I fall asleep *while flying* a stolen fighter jet? "How long was I asleep?"

"Six," Beeps says in a few quick beeps, using the numbering system she taught me.

"I'll assume you mean six minutes, not six hours," I yawn. My right hand is balled up in a fist and I open it slowly, half expecting to find a rock in my hand, but it's empty. I check the coordinates to make sure I didn't change them somehow in my sleep. The small aircraft is still on course.

"Beeps, what planet are Tuiperite rocks found on?" I ask.

The rock Takano threw to me, before I woke up was a Tuiperite rock. My favorite traveling merchant at the village sold rocks and he taught me the names of hundreds that he traded.

"Aylvon."

I turn on the navigation screen and search the star maps in the ship's system for coordinates to Aylvon. Then I set the flight destination into the console. The ship rises and turns left. I increase our speed.

We want the same thing, Takano Rynn said in my dream. If what he said was true, then maybe we can work together to make that happen. It wasn't Takano who had Morlin captured. It was Dukath and that new General, Randon. Lord Morlin said himself that Takano has gone rogue. If there's a chance Takano can help me rescue Morlin, then I have to try. I don't have much of a chance of doing it on my own. And desperate times call for desperate measures, right?

"Where are we going?" Beeps asks.

I don't want to tell her. She'll ask too many logical questions, and if I answer them, I might change my mind about this crazy decision. Now that I've decided, I don't want to turn back.

Maybe Takano Rynn has turned away from the Ruling Order and isn't working with them anymore. Even *they* don't know where he is and are searching for him. I might be the only one who knows where he is. But I can't tell the General I 'had a dream' which might lead us to Takano Rynn. I'll find out for myself. I'm only guessing he was trying to tell me where he is, by throwing me that rock. I could be wrong.

The stolen aircraft is fast and able to reach warp speed. I didn't technically steal it. I just told the guards who I was, and they let me take it. The General will probably think I used my Gift Influence to get past the guards. And the guards will probably use that as an excuse for why they let me take a flier, if they get in trouble for doing so.

I smile. I guess it doesn't always take special powers to influence people.

I relax back into the pilot's seat. It's so unreal that I rode in the same flier as *the* Lord Morlin. And now I'm heading straight for Takano Rynn.

I slouch down in my seat. Takano was wounded and went into hiding to recover. Because of me. Lord Morlin came back out of hiding, but then was captured. Because of me. For someone with no real powers, I sure seem to be making big things happen.

I gasp at the sudden stirring inside of me. Takano Rynn's presence seizes all my senses.

We're getting closer.

So my hunch about the rock dream was right.

I am wide awake now. How much of this can I bear, once I actually reach him? Can I trust him? Even if I can't, I can tell the Opposition of his location, and be useful to them, for once.

I look at Beeps beside me. She's quiet and seems distracted, if robots can be distracted.

This would be a good time to tell her all that has been going on with me.

"Beeps," I say.

"Yes?"

"We're flying to Aylvon."

"We are? Why?"

"Because I think Takano Rynn might be there."

"Why are you flying to Takano Rynn?"

I sigh. "Well..."

I tell her everything, about my dreams and the connection I feel to Takano; how I think he can help us, despite his bad reputation.

She listens and remains silent. My heart beats hard in my chest. Am I betraying the Opposition by going to him? Am I betraying Parrin and Lord Morlin by doing so? Or even Temple Mother? I know what she would say. She'd tell me I shouldn't trust him and that I'm following my emotions again, which is always dangerous. She'd say I'm flying straight into temptation.

Beeps turns her little head to me and says, "It's better to go face him now, than to run from him all your life."

I laugh. "Oh Beeps, what would I ever do without you, my smart little robot friend?" I lean over and give her a hug.

"You're right. It's time for me to face my fears and I'm glad I will be doing it with you by my side."

The ship slows and the automatic pilot shuts off.

We've arrived.

CHAPTER 22

I FLY THE SHIP low to the ground, looking for a place to land among the snow-covered treetops. I hadn't expected snow, not on a small planet like this. It glistens by the light of the moons above, reminding me of the forests back home, where I last saw Takano Rynn.

Just when I think the bond that draws me to him feels the strongest it can possibly get, I go a bit farther and the pull grows even stronger, like a magnet tugging at me. I try to focus on landing the plane. There are no buildings, only treetops and snow. The moons bathe the forest in a pink and blue hues.

"When did you learn to fly a ship?" Beeps asks.

"I honestly couldn't tell you," I say to her, trying to keep the ship level as we land. I find a clearing and hover over it. The trees lean away from the ship as the engine blasts snow and jet propulsion winds at them. "My father was a trader and he flew planes. So he probably taught me a few things, before..." I swallow the lump in my throat. "I don't remember a lot from those years."

The ship dips to the left and I pull the controls to the right, but it's too late. I hear the crunching of metal and cringe. The ground beneath the snow must be rock.

Snow billows up all around us as the aircraft finally settles.

"He didn't teach you how to land a ship?" Beeps asks.

I laugh. "I guess not."

My stomach feels queasy and it's not because of the landing. Takano Rynn is near.

I close my eyes to contain the nausea. My rough landing has damaged the ship. I can't tell how badly yet, but even the smallest impact to the bottom of the aircraft could jeopardize its ability to take flight again. What if we can't leave?

Now I really have no choice but to face Takano.

The snow settles around us and I shut off the engine. Everything becomes silent, like we're under water. The only sound is that of my breathing.

A tiny beep makes me open my eyes. "I'm okay," I say to Beeps.

Outside the front view screen, large snowflakes fall; larger than I've ever seen before. They're so big that their patterns are visible to the eye, even from inside the spacecraft. Each one is detailed and different. They slowly drift onto the flier, then melt from its heat, sending steam into the night air.

A shiver runs through me and I wrap my arms around myself. I'm still wearing the sleeping clothes I was given at the Opposition Base.

I turn to Beeps. "Will you be okay? In this weather?"

"Yes, will you?" she beeps in reply.

I jump out of the pilot's seat. "I'll have to be!"

I reach for my new fighting rod, which I picked out from the Opposition Base armory before I left. It was the closest weapon I could find that resembled the iron fireplace poker which proved so useful for fighting in the past. I secure my belt around my waist and tuck the weapon behind me, down the length of my back. I feel better knowing it's there.

"Okay, I'm ready," I say, more to myself than Beeps. It takes me a moment to locate the switch to open the hatch. The hinges creak as the door slowly rises and cold air wafts in.

The pull of Takano's influence returns, as strong as ever, fogging up my mind and making it impossible to think of anything else. I jump out of the plane, landing on the hard ground with my soft soled boots. Beeps waits for me to help her down.

"The snow's not too deep," I say to her. I lift her into my arms and set her down onto the wet ground. The snow near the aircraft is all blown away, but the rest of the forest is covered in a thin layer of white. It doesn't look too deep yet. Beeps rolls around in every direction, as though testing out the terrain.

"Will you be okay?" I ask.

She beeps her agreement and we start moving.

The wet ground soaks into my soft boots, making my feet ache with cold. I look ahead, into the dark shadows of the forest, where I feel drawn. My eyes adjust to the moonlight and I see a parting in the trees. A mountain side rises up high at the end of the tree tunnel, blocking the shine from the moons. At the bottom of the mountain side, there's a dark opening to a cave.

I slow down. This must be it. I haven't seen a ship or anything to indicate there is anyone else on this planet, but someone could be in the cave. Is Takano Rynn really in there? Could I have been wrong? Are these feelings which draw me forward not really a bond I share with him, but something else? A trick to get me captured?

I move closer to the cave entrance. Beeps matches my speed, then we both come to a stop.

A flicker of light bounces off the cave walls from inside. My heart beats faster. Someone is here.

I reach behind me for my fighting rod and clasp my hand around it. Is Takano Rynn waiting for me? I look down to make sure Beeps is still with me.

"Beeps, you wait out here, okay?"

Beeps starts to protest but I don't listen. The last thing I need is for Takano Rynn to use his Gift powers and slam Beeps into a rock and smash her to pieces.

I let go of my fighting stick, leaving it secured on my back. I'll have a better chance walking over the uneven cave floor if I leave it strapped onto me for now.

I make my way slowly into the cave.

The trickling sound of water moving through the passages echoes off the walls. I step around the stalagmites and move further into the cave. Beeps wouldn't have been able to get over all the pointy rocks jutting up from the ground. But I can't leave her out there too long either.

My breath puffs out into the candlelit cavern. I glance back at the entrance to see if I can still see Beeps, but the tunnel has turned a corner and the walls are now blocking my view. I won't be long. I'll see who is in this cave, if anyone, then come back out. Maybe Takano isn't even here right now. But if this is where he's been hiding this whole time, I can let the Opposition know.

I move forward again, toward the flickering light ahead. My toes curl from the cold. Ice cold water has seeped into my boots and my feet burn with the icy chill.

I come across a candle, resting in a groove in the cave wall. There are more set up along the way. I turn another corner and suddenly find myself in a cave room, lit all around with candles. It is much warmer here and the change in temperature makes me shiver.

I stop, uncertain. Could this be Takano Rynn's hideout? I glance around the room. There aren't any high-tech things, just the basics. It reminds me of the Temple; clay bowls, dried meat, a simple bed...

My breath catches when I see him, his dark hair hanging into his eyes as he sleeps. His shoulders are bare above the blanket, which is draped over his long frame. He breathes deeply, in a peaceful sleep.

I remain still, not daring to move. It's definitely him, and he's sound asleep. I could easily kill him if I wanted.

I've found Takano Rynn's hideout.

And he has no idea I've come.

CHAPTER 23

I STAND AT THE cave room entrance, not daring to go any closer to the man asleep in the bed. So this the great Takano Rynn, leader of the Ruling Order. No, the former leader of the Ruling Order, now gone rogue. I study his face. He looks younger while asleep and more vulnerable than I would have ever thought possible.

He stirs and I reach behind me for my fighting stick. His eyes open and he looks right at me.

I tense, ready to fight. His brow furrows in confusion and he blinks, as though he's not sure what he's looking at. He rubs at his eyes and looks at me again. Suddenly he sits up in one swift movement, and the blanket slides down to his waist.

I take a step back. All of a sudden the cold that's been seeping through my feet into my core, hits me and I start shaking violently.

Takano gets out of his bed in and stands to his full height. He's wearing black trousers and no shirt, no socks. My eyes travel down to the white bandage wrapped around his ribs, where I struck him. I slowly pull out my fighting rod from behind me.

"You knew I was coming..." I say, not quite sure if I'm asking a question or making a statement.

Takano runs his hand through his hair, seeming unsure of what to do next. "How would I have known?" he says, his voice raspy from sleep.

It's unsettling, seeing him like this, in such humble circumstances. He looks around the room as though searching for something. Is he looking for his sword or for something else to use to kill me?

"You drew me here," I say. "Your Gift called to me."

Suddenly Takano's hand comes up and I fly back, hitting the cave wall behind me. I collapse to the ground, the impact knocking the wind out of me for a second.

"I didn't call you here!" he yells. "You don't know anything about the Gift!" His eyes flash with anger and he holds me in an invisible grip that I can't break free from. Has he gotten stronger?

He motions his hand up and suddenly I'm standing again. I fly forward and stop right in front of him. He looks me over, curiosity replacing the anger in his eyes.

"You're untrained," he says, the warmth of his breath reaching my face.

I want to deny it, but I can't. He's right, I haven't trained for battle. But I'm also not Gifted.

Takano walks around me slowly, then stops once in front of me again.

"You were foolish enough to come here? Did you think you'd be stronger than me? Without training? Simply because you have the strength of the Gift?"

He reaches up with his other hand and I flinch.

So he believes it too, that I'm Gifted.

"I was weak then," he whispers, "when you fought me at Green Hill. I had just killed my mother. It made me stronger." His eyes search mine. "There's no good inside of me Rita, stop trying to look for it."

My heart hammers in my chest, but I don't speak.

A smile creeps onto his face.

I want to step away but I can't move. How could I have underestimated Takano's strength and blindly decide to come here and ask for his help? Now he's got the better of me.

I look around the room. The candles, the simple lifestyle...he came here to rebuild his strength. But for what? To return as the leader of the Ruling Order once again?

Despite his hold on me, my body continues to shake.

"Let me go," I say between clenched teeth.

"You can't free yourself?" Takano smirks. I don't respond and he frowns. "You're cold."

He releases his hold on me and I collapse to the floor. My metal rod clatters to the stone ground and I pick it up, using it to help me get onto my feet again. I quickly regain my composure and point the rod at him, keeping a distance between us.

Takano turns his back to me and grabs the blanket off his bed, not at all concerned that I may be a threat. He throws it in my direction and it catches on the end of my rod.

"Dry off," he says, not looking at me.

I stand still, not sure what to do. I do need to get out of these wet clothes but...

"Who knows that I'm here?" he demands. "How did you find me?"

Why is he asking me out loud? Why doesn't he just force the answers from my mind?

My eyes travel to the white bandage wrapped around his waist. He's not fully healed from the wound I gave him. But he's much stronger than before.

He moves about the room, putting on a shirt and grabbing another folded blanket. I see other scars on his body and face. I shift the cold rod to my other hand.

My choice of weapon seems pretty pathetic at the moment. I could have at least brought a ray gun or some real weapon, from the base. But he can deflect those shots. I don't even have a plan. What was I thinking? I don't think I was, that's the problem. I came here like a sleepwalker, right into Takano's hands. I just wanted to find him. But now that I have, I'm not sure what to do next.

I lower the rod. "No one knows you're here," I say. "I came alone." There's no reason to mention Beeps. "I found you by following your call to me with—"

"Don't toy with me!" Takano's voice booms. He grips me in a power hold again, so hard this time that for a moment I can't breathe. Suddenly he's in my head, searching everything, going deep into my thoughts.

"Stop," I growl, but he doesn't. I watch him move towards me. His expression changes as he comes closer, his eyes studying mine.

"You didn't bring backup with you." He stops, his curious expression changing to confusion. "You followed this connection you feel to me." His eyes search mine again. "You don't dream of your garden at the Temple at night anymore. You dream...of me."

My cheeks grow hot. "Get out of my head," I say between clenched teeth.

"And you see us together," he says softly. His face is so close to mine now that I can feel his breath. His fingers hover near my forehead as he searches my mind freely.

"Get *out*," I breathe. Anger consumes me, giving me strength. I close my eyes, fighting back. I can't unlatch him from my thoughts but I break from his hold long enough to step back and reach my hand out to lock him in a hold of my own. The action is automatic and suddenly I see his thoughts too.

He's surprised and for a moment considers breaking our bond, to stop me from seeing his thoughts, but his curiosity gets the best of him. He wants to know about Lord Morlin's capture, which he's only now learning of, and he wants to know Dukath's plans, which I don't know about, but he searches my mind for answers, anyway.

He combs through my memories of the meetings at the Opposition Base. Unfortunately for him, I wasn't paying much attention and have no useful information.

I search too, past his surface emotion of curiosity and anger. I find a loneliness, so strong that it's almost frightening. He has dreams with me in them, too, but he doesn't know what they mean. There is also pain, so deep that my heart aches. He didn't want to kill his mother and the regret is killing him on the inside, but he continues to tell himself it was necessary, that it was his choice, the right choice. But in a way it wasn't. It was Dukath's influence. Deep down he knows that.

"Stop!" Takano yells.

He forces his way deeper into my memories, as though in retaliation; me as a little girl yelling for my parents to not leave, as their ship flies off into the sky. I don't want him to see those memories. Yet, the farther he goes, the more he reveals about his own childhood memories. He was sent away, by his father, General Anias, when Takano needed him the most. General Anias is his *father?*

"Let go!" He shouts.

"The General is your father?"

We're facing one another now, just like in the dream I had with our hands reaching out toward each other. I don't want him to see that dream, the one where our fingers touch, but I can't stop him from discovering it. He looks down to my outstretched hand and slowly moves toward me. The energy between us pushes back, but I let him close the gap.

You don't believe you're Gifted, Takano says in my thoughts.

"And you believe it?" I answer him aloud.

Takano steps forward again and his energy pushes me back. "Our Gift powers are repelling. Don't you feel it?"

I shake my head. "I'm not Gifted."

"You've been reading my mind this entire time. Do you think just anyone could do that?"

"It wasn't me." My heart hammers in my chest. "It was you. You're doing it."

"Your Gift is different than mine," Takano says. He stops advancing. "It's untainted. Pure."

"No." I look down at his outstretched hand. I want so badly for our fingers to touch. He wants it too. He's curious about us using our powers together.

My pulse races. It can't be true. I can't be Gifted. I don't want to be. He's just confusing me while he's in my thoughts. His mind races with thoughts of all the power we could have together; his well-developed strength and my new, untapped power.

For a second I see the Gift inside of him, in its purest form. It's still there, the part of him which regrets all the deaths he's caused, the part that yearns to be free of all the killing, the part that yearns to be free from the burden of ruling the Galaxies, a burden he left behind when he went into hiding. Now he believes he can never turn back and that killing his mother has completely turned him over to the bondage of the evil Lord Dukath, leaving nothing but darkness in him.

But just the fact that you have regret means there is still good left in you, I say to him in my thoughts.

"Get out of my mind, Rita," he says. Yet he doesn't pull away from me. He still wants to try using our Gift powers together. All we need to do is close the gap between us, and touch, while we both have an open channel to one another. Am I really using the Gift right now, by reading his mind?

We both step forward as though deciding to at the same time, even as our powers continue to repel each other.

Our fingers inch closer. Sweat drips down my temple and I'm no longer cold. I just need to hold on for a moment longer, then we'll be all powerful, together. rule the Universe. Every Universe. We'll lead nations and armies...

Takano's eyes flicker up to mine, a look of curious surprise on his face.

Yes...he thinks. *Yes, Rita. We'll rule together. And you'll never be alone again.*

His last thought startles us both, and we break away.

CHAPTER 24

I'M NOT SURE WHO breaks away first, Takano or me, but the release is so abrupt that I fall backward. Takano stops my fall, catching me in his arms, in one swift movement. I want to object but I'm too exhausted to stop him.

This was a big mistake, coming here by myself. No one knows where I am or how to find me. I have nothing but an untrained, undisciplined power from a mysterious Gift within me; a Gift I have no idea how to access when needed. So they were right all along. I could have gone with Morlin to train. I could have become as powerful as Takano one day, instead of ending up here, at his mercy.

Takano carries me to the bed and sets me down onto cool sheets.

I protest only with a glare, the rest of my body is traitorously grateful to be lying down on something soft.

I close my eyes. At least Takano isn't reading my mind anymore. If he was, he'd see how embarrassed I feel right now.

The bed is comfortable, making me want to curl up and go to sleep. I fight against the heaviness pulling me down into unconsciousness. Why am I so tired? Is it because I used my Gift for the first time? I have to get up. What am I doing? What is *he* doing? He could just kill me if he wanted to.

I open my eyes to see Takano sitting on the side of the bed, watching me. He could easily restrain me or harm me. But he's just sitting there.

I close my eyes again so I don't have to see his gaze travel over me. But it doesn't help, I can still feel it. I'm no longer cold, just uncomfortable in my wet clothes.

I begin to drift off to sleep but Takano's touch pulls me awake. He touched my foot!

I bring my legs up and hug them to my chest, to move them away from him. He grabs my foot and pulls it back towards him, then takes off my boots, one at a time. Then my wet socks. I can't help but relax at the warmth of his hands. He sets his palm against the bottom of one foot.

"Your feet are very cold," he says.

My foot looks tiny in his large hands. Why is he being so...gentle? Why doesn't he just fight me and be the evil person he's supposed to be? That would be so much easier than...this.

I hug the blankets close to my chest, pulling them into a bundle in front of me. I disobeyed General Anias' orders and I stole a fighter plane. And he's Takano's father!

No wonder he was upset about Lord Morlin's capture, he's his other son! The good son. I really messed up. Now I've ended up here, in Takano Rynn's hideout.

Beeps!

I sit up so fast my head spins and I fall back down onto the bed. I have no energy. I've never been this tired in my life.

How could I forget about Beeps? She's going to freeze her little, metal body out there! The snow will soak through into her circuitry. And her battery...

I try to sit up again but Takano gently pushes me back down.

"I have to go," I say, trying to sound stern.

"You need dry clothes," he replies without a hint of emotion. "I can't have a weak and sick partner helping me rescue Morlin."

"What?" I'm too worried about Beeps to make sense of his words. Did he say he's going to help me rescue Lord Morlin? Beeps is my only link to the outside world and she's also my best friend. Somehow I managed not to think of her at all when Takano was searching my mind. He doesn't know she's here. I don't want him to know she's here. But I can't leave her out there. What if she gets damaged in the snow?

Will she figure out I'm in trouble when I don't return? And then go back to the ship to contact someone for help?

"I'll bring you some dry clothes to change into," Takano says. He sets my foot down onto the cool sheets then gets up and disappears behind a curtain.

I wait until he's out of sight then get up, a little more slowly this time so my head doesn't pound. My muscles feel cramped up, but I have to make a run for it, before Takano comes out from behind the curtain.

I get to my feet, but I don't get very far. Takano captures me in a hold from the other end of the room. I hate this advantage he has over me.

His footsteps sound behind me as he walks over to the bed. He sets down some folded clothes, all black, on a small table in front of me. My pulse races. I need to get to Beeps. What if she's worried and tries to follow after me into the cave? She could get stuck somewhere between all those pointy rocks and the flowing water on the cave floor will get into her circuitry.

I try to fight against Takano's hold, but I can't. He hardly uses any effort at all this time and it's embarrassing. He waves his hand and I instantly get tossed into a prone position on the bed.

"Please," I say, clenching my jaw. "Let me go." I can't stop a wayward tear from rolling down my cheek, more out of frustration of my weakness, than anything.

I should have left Beeps at the Base, in someone else's care, instead of getting her involved in all this. Parrin entrusted me with her.

"Where would you go?" Takano asks, sitting down near me. "If I let you?"

When I don't answer he reaches his hand up to my forehead and gathers the information he needs. I want to hate him for this invasion of privacy but his fingertips caress my forehead so softly that the mix of emotions inside of me battle in confusion.

"The robot." He says, standing. "I'll go get it, while you change."

"Wait!"

The hold on me loosens and then he's gone.

CHAPTER 25

MY ENERGY BEGINS TO return after Takano leaves. I have to stop him from hurting Beeps!

But he said he'd go get her, not go destroy her.

I look at the clothes on the table. My thin night clothes are still soaked through and sticking to me now. A breeze from the cave entrance makes me shiver. I'll get sick if I don't warm up soon. Maybe I should change, fast, before Takano returns.

I grab the clothes and quickly duck behind the curtain at the back of the cave. Inside, I find a make-shift bath and toilet, both cut into the rock and both with small streams of water coming out from tiny holes in the cave walls.

I look into the tub. The water flows through, but can be stopped on one end. I shiver at the thought of an ice-cold bath.

Maybe after filling the tub with water, it could be warmed up with some hot coals from the fire...

Stop it! I need to get out of here. There's no time for baths.

I pick up the clothes Takano gave me, a black long-sleeve shirt and a pair of black pants, both made of a soft material. The pants look like they were made for a female, and would be quite form fitting, once on. I pick up the shirt again. Is this what the Ruling Order soldiers wear under their armor?

I toss the shirt aside. I'll never wear the Ruling Order armor. I'd rather freeze to death.

I look down at the shirt again. I guess it's not technically Ruling Order armor, it's just a black shirt and a pair of pants. I curl my toes as I try to decide. The cave floor is damp and wet. Maybe I'll wear the soldier boots, if I have to. But not the armor.

A cool breeze blows up from underneath the curtain. I hold my breath and listen for Takano, worried that he's returned already. There are no other sounds so I hurry to get dressed.

I quickly pull off my shirt, my teeth chattering, then put the black long sleeve on. I struggle to get the dry clothes over my damp skin. The shirt feels soft and warm around me. It has some fur lining on the inside for warmth. I pick up the pants, and a pair of black socks fall to the ground. I quickly grab them before they can get wet.

Pushing the curtain aside, I see that I'm still alone. The gentle breeze continues to blow through the room, making the candles flicker and extinguishing some of them.

The cave grows darker, and the air now smells like rain. There's a storm coming.

Could it have been my Gift this whole time, whenever I sensed a storm coming, or sensed danger? The premonitions, the sixth sense that always came so naturally to me? I always thought I was different than everyone else. But I never imagined I was Gifted.

I sit down on a chair beside a table. It still seems like a mistake. Maybe Takano wants it to be true and is projecting his abilities onto me somehow.

I pull the socks on. They feel warm over my feet, also lined with a soft, artificial fur. I sigh, reminded of Takano's large hands on my foot when he removed my boots earlier. He just wants to use my powers for his purposes, I remind myself. If I was a regular girl showing up here he'd have killed me without a second thought.

I rub my face with both my hands. It would be so much easier if I actually believed that Takano was nothing more than the evil, merciless ruler of the Ruling Order who killed countless, innocent people in senseless battles.

My breathing becomes heavier and I look around the cave room. It suddenly feels too small and I want to get out from beneath this mountain.

Should I go see where Takano and Beeps are? The cave floors outside this room will be wet from the trickling water between the rocks.

I walk over to the bed and grab one of the blankets to wrap around me. I'll wait a bit longer, then I'm stealing a pair of Takano's boots and going out to find them. I'll just rest my eyes for a minute. The blanket quickly begins to warm me. I'll rest just for a moment. Then I'll go after Beeps...

***

I wake to the smell of food and my stomach rumbling. My muscles feel stiff and tense, like I've been sleeping a while. I stretch and look up at the ceiling, a rock ceiling. Where in the Galaxies am I?

"Beeps!" I cry out, remembering suddenly.

I fell asleep! And Takano was going after Beeps!

Her now familiar beeping sounds fill the cave room and I look down to see her on the floor beside the bed. My shoulders relax.

"How did you..." I look around the room. "Did Takano bring you here?"

"Yes," she beeps in response. "After he chased me for a while."

"What?" I grin at the image it creates in my mind, even though it was probably not funny to poor Beeps. "Oh no! Sorry, I guess you didn't know why he was coming to get you and bring you here."

"No. It was so scary."

I climb out of bed. I'm wearing black clothes that I don't recognize. Then I remember that too. I lean down to look Beeps over. "Did Takano hurt you?"

"He didn't hurt me. He left you food."

My stomach growls again. I get up to look at the food left on the small table beside the bed. A bowl of something that looks like a bread pudding steams beside a cup of water and rustic looking spoon. I sit on the bed and take the bowl. It's still warm. "Where is he now?" I ask, grabbing the spoon.

"I don't know."

I nod, then start eating. The thick pudding is soft and melts in my mouth. I close my eyes, savoring the mildly sweet taste.

"He left you boots and that." Beeps opens one of her tiny compartments and points to a pair of black boots and a sword on a nearby counter. I finish the bowl of soft food quickly. I could definitely eat more, but I'm not about to ask Takano for a second helping, even if he were here. I toss the bowl aside and rush over to the sword.

It's a really nice sword. I reach for it but before I can pick it up Takano steps into the room and I pull my hand away. He's fully dressed in his dark armor and cloak.

"Get dressed," he says. "We'll begin our training today." Then he leaves.

I'm left blinking and confused. Training? I don't remember agreeing to any training.

I look at Beeps.

"I didn't agree to train with him," I say to her, as though defending myself. She twists her little body in a small movement but doesn't say anything.

I pick up the sword. It has engravings on the handle, like the vines of one of my favorite plants in my garden back home. I run my fingers over the carvings then grasp the handle, lifting the sword into the air. It's lighter than it looks. The metal glistens in the candlelight. I touch the edge to see how sharp it is.

"Ouch." I stick my finger in my mouth to stop the bleeding. "I'll have to be careful with this sword," I say to Beeps. She nods her head. "I'm so glad you're okay." I lower the sword and crouch down to her level. "I'm sorry I left you behind." My words catch in my throat. Once again, I left someone behind.

"You didn't leave me behind. I was your backup."

I smile. "Thanks."

"Are you going to train with Takano?"

I look down at the sword in my hand. "Well, a little training couldn't hurt, right?"

BRANDI ROWLAND

CHAPTER 26

"**M**AYBE I'LL PUT ON some armor first, then go outside," I say to Beeps. "But we're not going to hang around here much longer. We need to get back to our ship and fly the heck out of here."

Beeps agrees. I push down the thoughts of the ship possibly being too damaged to fly. It wasn't that rough of a landing. I hope.

"But first, I need to freshen up a bit and..." I gather my hair and twist it up into a bun. Did Takano take out my braid last night? I don't remember him doing it.

Beeps swivels her head around as though searching for something. She gives a reply but I don't understand, then goes over to the table and grabs something from it.

"My elastic! Thanks Beeps."

"Takano put it there."

"Hmm." I pick up the boots left for me and slip my feet into them. They're a little big, but they'll do. What I need to do is get back to the Opposition Base and tell them where Takano is. General Anias will be relieved that his son is safe...Or will he?

I pick up the sword again and it reflects the light of the few candles left dripping.

"We need a plan, Beeps."

"Our ship is not far from here."

"Maybe I should agree to train with Takano, then we can make a run for it when he doesn't expect it."

Just as I finish my sentence Takano returns. He frowns and crosses his arms. Did he hear what I said?

"Is it because you're a female, or because you're undisciplined, that preparing in the morning takes you so long?" he says.

I spin the sword in my hand to ready position. He did *not* just say that.

"Not here," he says, uncrossing his arms. "You'll destroy the place." He turns and walks off, his cape trailing behind him. Does he expect me to follow?

I take my time looking over the armor laid out for me on the bed. It's not Ruling Order armor, but similar. Why does everything have to be black?

I try on the breast plate then the belt, which has some buttons on it I can't figure out.

I leave the rest of it. I don't want to be bogged down with armor when I make a run for it. When I return to the Base, with information on where Takano Rynn has been hiding, I'll be a hero.

I slide my sword into the sheath on the belt.

"Takano probably has a ship, too." Beeps says, patiently waiting beside me as I prepare.

"You're right. He might follow us and shoot us down. Or he'll leave this planet and not be here when we send the Opposition back for him," I whisper.

"We can go at night, when he's asleep. We can send a transmission to the Opposition base."

"Good thinking, Beeps." I glance over my shoulder in case Takano has come back. "Maybe we can shoot out the engine of his ship, if we find it."

I lift Beeps up into my arms. The sleep and food have made me strong again.

Now I feel ready to face Takano. He's not going to get the best of me today. Before I leave tonight, I'll get some answers out of him.

One thing is for sure, I have no interest in joining the Ruling Order or being his partner in some galactic war that I know nothing about. I have one goal and only one. The same goal I've had all my life. To find my parents. And now it's time to get back to that goal. Once I'm out of here, that's all that matters.

CHAPTER 27

I SET BEEPS DOWN on the ground with a grunt and look out across the forest. It's muddy from the snow that is now beginning to melt. Beeps will get all dirty.

The sun shines bright above us. It's a clear day. If it stays this way until nighttime, I should have no problem flying right out of here.

I take in a deep breath of fresh air. I've missed the clean air. It reminds me of the outer provinces, but here, it's even more pure and undefiled, unlike anything I've ever smelled before. The plants and trees add a sweet scent to the crisp smell of snow.

A loud crack, like a tree trunk breaking, startles me and I turn around. Takano is slicing a heavy branch off of a large tree with his sword, then before it lands he catches it with his

Gift powers, throwing it into another tree. The crunch of the thick branch on impact sounds like human bones shattering. A shiver runs through me. I don't think I could ever use my powers to hurt anyone or kill them.

I watch Takano practice. He's really good with the sword, and he's also very good on his feet. His cloak swings behind him as he jumps up onto the thick branch of a large tree. He can jump high by using the Gift. I suddenly remember when I jumped down from the top of the Temple gates and was able to slow my landing enough not to get hurt. And when I was falling from the tree and time seemed to stand still for a moment. Was that my Gift abilities too?

I frown. There's so little I know about all this and I'm still not sure if I fully believe that I have the powers inside of me that everyone seems to think I have.

Takano stops suddenly and looks over at me. He jumps down from the branch he's on, landing with a soft thud.

"Are you going to try out your sword?" he asks, walking towards me. "Or just watch me?"

My cheeks flare up and I look away. "I was just studying your moves." I groan inwardly. Did I really just say that?

"Then let's see if you've learned anything." He twirls his sword in his hand to get a better grip on it. "We don't have time to build up your physical strength." He looks me over. "But you seem fit enough."

"Is that your way of giving me a complement?" I ask, just to pester him.

He doesn't answer but stops to stand right in front of me. I look up and in a split second he's got his sword at my throat. I put my arms up in front of me and push against him. The fear of being caught off guard is quickly replaced by anger. So he wants to play dirty does he?

I push his arm away just enough to give me room to drop down and do a back somersault. He falls forward when I'm suddenly no longer in front of him, and stumbles into the mud. By the time he gets up again, I've got my sword at his throat.

"I could have struck you down while you were still getting up," I say, breathing hard now.

"Why didn't you?" Takano wipes mud from his cheek.

I frown. A twinge of fear stirs in my belly but I ignore it. "Because we're only training, right?" I can't read his expression. What did he have in mind for the day's training? A battle to the death?

I lower my sword. He's right though. If we train as though we really will harm one another, then we'll learn better and try harder.

He swings his sword at me and I jump back, trying to get my footing. I swing back at him, catching him off guard, then slash my sword down. He raises his sword just in time to stop me from slicing his body in half.

We spar for a moment but he's physically stronger than me. I won't be able to fend him off for long. I hop up into a nearby tree, the energy of my Gift boosting my efforts. Now that I've unlocked it somehow, it's easier and easier to access, especially when I'm defending myself.

I push off the branch and jump back down again in an aerial attack on Takano. He's agile and quick, despite his height, but I'm faster. I duck beneath him. He grunts, swinging his sword with more anger now, but missing each time. His body is lean and strong. For a second I lose focus and suddenly his sword is at my neck again. I cry out.

"What are you doing?" he asks, releasing me.

I reach up and wipe the spot of blood at my neck. It's just a tiny cut but I can tell Takano hadn't intended to actually draw blood. My heart pounds. I got distracted watching him fight.

I ready my sword and attack him again, with more vengeance this time. I hate him. I hate that he can distract me like that; I hate that I let myself be distracted by his form, in a way that I've never had happen before. I don't even want to entertain the idea of why I'm caught off guard by his physical appearance.

I catch a glimpse of a smile on his face as he fends off my attacks, which are sloppy now and less calculated, because I'm so angry. I'm angry because I'm embarassed. He's not even really fighting back.

"What are you doing?" I breathe heavily, lowering my sword. "Why aren't you fighting back?"

He reaches out his hand to me, palm up, as though he expects me to take it. I step back. Is this a trick? His sword is still ready in his other hand. This must be a lesson in gullibility.

I swing my sword around from behind me and slice down at his outstretched arm. He moves it just in time, but not fast enough to avoid a cut to his arm. He cries out and I jump back, confused. I remain in my fighting stance, just in case.

"You're not wearing armor?" I ask.

Takano clutches his forearm, blood seeping through his shirt.

"How are we going to fight together, if we can't trust each other?" he says.

"Fight together?" I lower my sword but don't put it away. "What do you mean? We're not fighting together, we're fighting against each other."

"Yes, but we stopped, and I gave you my hand."

Now I'm more confused. "I don't know what I'm supposed to do, be on my guard for an unexpected attack, or..." Or what? Or trust him?

He stretches his hand out towards me again, palm forward this time, and I know what he's about to do. I block his attempt at reading my mind and he blinks in surprise, lowering his hand.

"You're stronger today."

"Yes. I've rested." And I also have some important thoughts to protect, like my planned escape tonight. I have to keep him out of my thoughts. "Like you said, we can't waste our strength reading each other's minds. So we should just communicate the old fashioned way, by talking...And trusting each other."

He nods, agreeing all too quickly. Does he also have something to hide in his thoughts, that he doesn't want me to see? He returns his sword to its sheath. I relax my stance and put my sword away too, keeping my eyes on him in case he does something unexpected.

We stand in silence for a moment, still breathing heavily from our fight. Wisps of snow circle around us. Takano offers me his hand again.

What is his game here?

"Aren't you going to do something about that cut?" I say, avoiding his invitation for me to take his hand. It reminds me too much of Parrin for some reason.

"Take my hand," Takano says firmly.

"Why?"

"Are you always this distrusting?" He finally lowers his hand and I feel a twinge of disappointment at how easily he gave up.

"Yes, always." I cross my arms.

He nods then suddenly grabs my hand. I start to pull away, then stop. I'm not in the mood for games. Takano holds my hand firmly, watching me. He runs his thumb slowly over the back of my hand.

"What are you doing?" I ask, my stomach fluttering. "There's no power between us. Not just by touching."

"I thought there would be."

I shrug. It's a lie though. There is definitely something powerful flowing between us. And it makes me very nervous.

CHAPTER 28

"WE NEED TO FIGURE out how this works," Takano says, still holding my hand in his.

"Why would I want to work with you?" I resist the urge to pull my hand away, trying to sound calm even though I can barely able to catch my breath. "You're working for the Ruling Order."

"I was never working for Dukath. I just wanted him to think I was. Randon and I had different ideas, different purposes for the use of the new Mass Destroyer."

"There's only one use for that weapon and that's to destroy planets and civilizations."

"That's not true." Takano's hand tightens over mine. "I wanted to use it to intimidate, as a threat to the space pirates and the—" He stops. "I didn't plan to destroy entire planets."

"Maybe not. But you still did. You used your powers for evil." Does he seriously expect me to believe he's never had anything but evil plans for the Galaxy? I've heard all the stories. Everyone knows what an evil leader he is. Or was.

"You have the same Gift as me inside of you," he says softly. "The Gift isn't evil."

"No, but how you use it can be."

We're standing closer to each other now.

"There was disorder within the Temple and amongst the Gifted Lords, and everywhere that the Gift was being used," Takano says. His fingers loosen their grip on my hand but I don't pull away. "My brother saw it too, that's why he left. He knew things weren't right and he went to search for answers."

"I don't understand."

Takano drops my hand and it feels cold without his warmth.

"Why did you kill your mother?" I ask, watching him.

"She wouldn't have lived for long. Dukath would have killed her anyway, if I hadn't." Takano stops a moment, then continues. "I had to prove to Dukath that I could be trusted. He was beginning to doubt me, beginning to wonder if I had other plans. I didn't want him to discover that."

"So you killed your own *mother?*"

He looks right into my eyes. "She was nothing but a Drifter, making dishonest trades. She will do more good for the Galaxy dead, than she ever would have while alive." Takano turns abruptly, his cloak swinging around. "I did what I had to do."

"You don't ever *have* to kill someone," I challenge.

"You're not familiar with the Temple Vows, are you?"

His question doesn't deserve an answer so I don't say anything in response.

"We believe in..." Takano frowns. "*They* believe in eternal life. The Gifted Lords weren't obsessed with mourning for those who died, like others are." Takano turns to face me. "And they also believe in the good of the many outweighing that of just one person."

Again I don't respond. The soft chirping of some creature in the forest circles around us as it flies by. Takano walks off and I stay where I am. The chill in the air pinches at my cheeks. I let out a breath I didn't even realize I was holding. Takano isn't at all who I believed he was.

His words swirl around in my mind, confusing me. He had a greater purpose to all the evil he was doing? The greater good outweighs that of just one person, but what greater good? Was his plan to get Dukath to trust him, then take down Dukath and the whole Ruling Order? Does that justify killing a family member?

Is everything I heard about Takano wrong? I was told he killed his brother, but Morlin is alive. But he admitted to killing his mother. Could I ever trust someone who killed his own mother?

A loud bird call from the trees brings me from my thoughts. The forest animals are getting restless, planning their evening meals. This planet turns faster than what I'm used to.

I suddenly realize I'm standing alone in the forest.

Where's Beeps?

I turn to look around, then spot her a little ways off, near a tree. She must have heard everything. I wave and give her a smile. The poor little thing. She's a big muddy mess.

"Come on, Beeps. Let's get you cleaned up."

CHAPTER 29

I WATCH AS TAKANO wipes a small cloth gently over Beeps' tiny doors, cleaning the more difficult spots of mud that I missed when I washed her off earlier. I did a quick wipe down with a towel after Takano carried her into the cave for me. Then he left, returning soon after with an animal for us to eat. I couldn't tell what he was thinking or feeling when he stormed off.

I found three sets of extra women's clothes tucked away in a high shelf, cut into the stone wall. I threw my muddy clothes into the tub for cleaning later and changed into another pair of clean clothes before Takano returned.

I glance over at him now. Did he bring those extra clothes for me? But he said he didn't know I was coming. So then why does he have extra women's clothes?

He looks relaxed as he cleans Beeps, in an almost meditative way. The candles flicker around the cave, warming the air and making the room muggy. The scent of wax reminds me of home. It's getting late but I don't want to fall asleep while Takano is still awake.

I blink, sitting up straighter. I ate too much food for supper and now I feel heavy and sluggish. Takano cooked the animal over a fire. I didn't ask what it was, not wanting to imagine it alive. It was food and I was hungry.

His muscles flex in his arm as he continues cleaning Beeps. He's removed his cloak but left his shirt on, sleeves rolled up. I don't think he can see me sitting on the bed, in my shaded corner, watching him take his time with Beeps. She doesn't make a single sound and I can't help but smile. I don't know how robots think, but I can't even imagine being Beeps right now. I close my eyes, forcing myself to stop thinking about Takano's hands cleaning mud off of me.

"Are you going to sleep?" Takano's voice makes me jump.

"No. I was just resting my eyes."

"You should lie down. It's late." He gets up, having finished with Beeps.

"What about you?" I ask. "I slept for a long time last night. Did you sleep?"

"No. I kept watch." He picks up his sword from the table. "I'll keep watch again tonight."

"I can do it," Beeps responds.

I'm still not sure if Takano knows her communication sounds but I've told her to be mindful of what she says in front of him, just in case.

"Beeps is offering to keep watch," I say to Takano. "She doesn't need sleep and she can see and hear farther than we can."

"No." Takano slides his sword into its sheath. "I can sense when things are approaching. A robot can't."

"Yes and you can also get weak if you don't sleep for two nights in a row," I say.

He gives me a confused look and I groan inwardly. Now he thinks I *care* whether he's weak or tired. "Or you can stay up all night if you want," I shrug.

"You can both sleep," Beeps says. "I can keep watch. I don't need to sleep." She turns to me and then I suddenly remember our escape plan. Shoot! I need time to talk to her because...maybe I don't want to escape, yet. Or do I?

I rub at my forehead. I need more time to think.

"Take the bed," Takano says to me. "I'll rest in a chair. The robot can keep watch at the entrance."

"No." I slide off the bed and stand up. "This is your bed, you sleep in it."

I'll never get past him if he stays awake in a chair all night, guarding the cave entrance.

"I took the bed last night," I add, grabbing a blanket and a pillow off the bed. "I'm an orphan, I can sleep anywhere."

I look around the room for a comfy nook to settle into. I could move the plates and bowls off the wide shelf in the kitchen area. I'd fit up there, I don't need much room. It's better than the wet, cave floor.

I walk over to the counter. I'll just rest for a bit, until Takano is asleep. I want to have my strength when Beeps and I make our next move.

"You'll take the bed," Takano says and walks behind the curtain into the bath area, without waiting for a response.

I hug the pillow to my chest. I don't care what he says, I'm not taking the bed. I need to be closer to the entrance.

I hear Takano dropping his muddy clothes into the water in the tub, where I put mine. I frown. Will he sleep with his shirt off, the way I found him when I first arrived?

I shake my head to dispel the image. Curse him and his well-built body. I've never been attracted physically to anyone before and it's disarming. It was always something that never came to my mind at the Temple. It didn't matter then because Temple Girls don't get married. It wasn't a part of my life.

I sigh. Now isn't the time to be thinking about physical attraction. Suddenly I think of Parrin. He was a great guy. He *is* a great guy, and he's still out there somewhere, missing.

Beeps rolls up beside me. "Are you okay?"

I nod, then lean down close to talk to her. She's as clean as a brand-new robot, after Takano's meticulous attention to detail. "Let's talk about this after he falls asleep," I whisper to her.

Just then the curtain moves aside and Takano steps out, looking taller than ever.

And shirtless.

I look away. Great. How am I supposed to avoid looking at him now? He's going to notice something is up with me. And if he 'reads my mind' I won't be able to hide my interest in his physical appearance. Why are my hormones betraying me like this?

I get up and move about, trying to keep busy so I don't have to look at Takano, shirtless. I blow out a few candles so there is less light. If I am going to sneak out tonight then I will need as much darkness as possible. I keep a couple candles burning though. I still need to keep my eye on Takano after all, and what he's up to at all times.

I make my way to the large shelf with the plates and move everything off of it, then lay out my blanket. Not bad. It actually looks pretty cozy. The shelf is cut into the cave wall; a little cave itself. I don't hear Takano approaching until suddenly he's right beside me, grabbing my wrist.

"Hey, let go!" I yell at him, turning around.

"I offered you the bed."

"I know, and I told you to take it," I snap.

"There is enough room for two people," Beeps interrupts. We both turn to her.

"*No,* Beeps," I say in a harsh whisper, frowning at her and shaking my head. Her human socialization software should be sophisticated enough for her to understand why we would *not* want to be using the bed together, no matter how much room there is!

"He's right," Takano says, his hand still clasping my wrist.

"Beeps is a *she,*" I say, using my anger to hide the other emotions coming on strong at his closeness without a shirt on. "How can you understand her?"

"Robots don't have a gender."

"I *asked* her."

"*She's* right then," Takano says, looking down at me. It's hard to stand up to him when he's so much taller, and so unclothed from the waist up. "It's a basic robot language, not that difficult to understand."

My heart beats wildly. Is he saying he wants to share the bed, then? I yank my wrist out of his hand then turn and walk to a dark corner of the room. "I'm not going to be your fighting partner and I'm not going to become evil like the other Gifted Masters that used their powers. I'm just going to be myself, and not use my powers at all."

Takano goes to the bed and sits down on it. He runs his hand through his hair. "You won't be able to keep from using your Gift."

"I went my whole life not using it," I say from my corner of the cave. "I was just living and existing and—"

"And waiting," Takano adds.

I wrap my arms around myself, wishing he didn't know so much about me. He's seen my thoughts. He knows how long I've been searching for my parents, waiting for their return. I stand quietly in my spot, waiting for him to say something, or for him to lie down and fall asleep already.

A candle wick flickers, making little popping sounds, then dies out as the last bit of its wax drips down the side of the cave wall. The room grows darker, but I can still see Takano's slumped shoulders as he sits on the bed, hunched forward.

"I didn't plan on using my Gift for evil," he says. "I trained, hard..." He stops a moment then continues. "But the higher I went in my training, the more I saw the disorder in the Temple and everywhere. They needed order."

"Let me guess, they needed the *Ruling Order*," I say, with more menace than I intend to. All I really know about the Ruling Order is that everyone says they're evil and are trying to take over the Galaxy. Everything I know about them is second hand, through stories which made their way to us at the Temple; and what Temple Mother told us.

"People needed order and I wanted to give it to them," Takano continues. "I began to understand what Dukath was trying to accomplish. I could see the wisdom in having one ruling Galactic authority…" He stops again, looking in my direction. "Are you going to stand there in the dark all night?"

"No." I step forward into the light. Takano waits and I finally give in and walk over to the bed, sitting down as far away from him as possible. I don't fully trust him yet, but he's being open and I want to encourage him to keep being open. Sitting down is better than standing anyway.

He looks down at his hands and I wait for him to continue. My heart beats loudly and I realize that it isn't him that I don't trust, it's myself.

CHAPTER 30

Takano crosses his arms, his broad shoulders lifting. "Parrin was in the Ruling Order army before he left with his friend," he says softly. "They were both in the Ruling Order."

"What?" I look over at Beeps but she doesn't say anything. "How do you know about Parrin?"

"I've seen your thoughts, remember?"

I takes me a moment to grasp what Takano is saying. Parrin was in the Ruling Order? That makes no sense. He is with the Opposition, the good guys.

I glance at Takano's uncovered body then quickly away and focus on a nearby candle instead, waiting to hear what he has to say next.

"He was different than the others," Takano says after a moment. "He didn't follow my orders."

"Can you blame him?" I say, unable to help myself. "Who would want to follow orders to kill people?"

"When he escaped from our base, he killed other Ruling Order soldiers. I don't think he has any problems killing people."

I shake my head. "Parrin's a nice guy."

"Is he? He didn't tell you he was once in the Ruling Order." There is silence for a moment, then Takano continues. "He's a coward and a liar."

I grab my sword from the bedside table, where it was sitting beside Takano's, and point it at him. He leans away, but doesn't seem afraid.

"Parrin was the first person that was nice to me when I went to Central," I say. "He doesn't kill innocent people for *sport*," I add, between clenched teeth.

Takano's eyes glow in the reflection of the single candle still burning. "I don't either," he says. "It's always for a purpose."

"A purpose? Is there ever a good enough purpose for killing someone?" I keep my sword up.

"Is one person escaping his responsibilities with the Ruling Order, a good enough reason to kill his fellow soldiers on his way out?"

My hand wavers but I don't lower it. "You're lying."

"Everyone's good, in their own eyes."

"The bad buys are bad, in my eyes." I say it with confidence, but he's confusing me.

"And the good guys are bad in my eyes," he says, his gaze locked on me.

I shake my head. "No. You kill innocent civilians for no reason."

"So does the Opposition. Ruling Order soldiers aren't robots, Rita. They're citizens too, fighting for the side they think is right, the side that they believe will keep order in the Galaxy. They have faith in the Ruling Order, enough faith to fight and die for it."

I shake my head. "No! They're soldiers against their will." I swing the sword at him but he blocks my attack with his Gift powers, stopping my hand from coming down. He can only predict my moves for so long before I get my chance to slice him.

"You're a liar," I say. "And you're evil."

The words feel false as I say them, like I'm just repeating something I was told. I tighten my grip on the hilt of my sword, ready to defend myself from Takano's anger at my hasty words.

"I may be evil," he says, his expression growing dark, "but at least I'm honest about it."

"What's that supposed to mean?"

"I've seen your thoughts, Rita."

I break from his hold and thrust my sword at his chest. He moves out of the way just in time, leaving me to cut the bed sheets instead. I get up quickly and go after him, but he's now got his sword in hand, and easily blocks my attack.

"You had no right to go through my memories," I yell, knocking down bowls and plates as I swing at Takano. He fends off my blows but doesn't attack back.

"Nor you mine," he says calmly.

"I hate you!" I scream, swinging harder.

Takano grabs my wrist, holding my sword away from him. "I don't need to read your mind to know that's not true," he says, forcing me backwards until my legs hit the edge of the bed. I fall back onto the makeshift mattress. He pins me down, holding my wrist above my head. My sword drops from my grasp, clattering to the ground. He loosens his grip, but I can't get away.

Tears of frustration swell in my eyes.

"Maybe how I feel about you has changed since you last read my mind," I say, my voice trembling despite my efforts to keep it steady. "Did you ever think of that?"

"Changed since yesterday?" he says. He's so close that when I take in a deep breath my chest pushes up against his. He seems to notice this at the same time as I do, and rolls off of me, lying down beside me instead. There isn't much room and our knees touch. I push my palms against his chest to keep him from coming any closer. His skin feels warm beneath my fingers.

"I was clear about my mission and how I would bring it about." He sets a large hand onto my shoulder, his eyes searching mine he says. "But then you came along."

"I don't understand."

"When we fought outside your village. I never saw anyone look at me with so much hate."

I doubt that, I think. "How could I not hate you? You were trying to kill me. You threatened the Sisters!"

"I needed the Gift Stone, to help me fulfill my plan to destroy Dukath."

I wait for him to continue but he doesn't, his hand still resting heavy on my shoulder.

"So did you find it?" I finally say.

"I did," he says softly. "And it wasn't a stone."

I look at him, confused. He found the Gift Stone? Was it in the Temple after all?

"If it's not a stone, then what is it?"

Takano hesitates a moment, then says, "It's you."

I try to pull away but there's no more room for me to back up against the wall. I shake my head. I want to deny it, but I'm not sure what to think anymore. All those years knowing I was different but not sure why. Was that why my parents abandoned me? Did it have something to do with my Gift or me being different?

"I removed my hood to get a better sense of you," Takano continues. "I felt your power. I didn't know there was anyone else Gifted like me, other than my brother."

"What about your father?"

Takano tenses, his eyes growing dark. I shouldn't have asked.

"He isn't Gifted," he says. "Not like us." I can't look away from his eyes.

"They knew about me," I say. "The Opposition, even before I knew about myself." I'm whispering now, though I'm not sure why.

"There were a lot of different legends. Dukath was certain it would be a stone; one we could forge into my sword."

I sit up. "Did you tell Dukath you found the Gift Stone then? That you found me?"

"No."

Takano doesn't say anything more and I settle back down onto the bed, not wanting to climb over him to get out of the bed. I have to admit it's more comfortable than sleeping on a stone shelf.

I listen to the sounds of the cave; the soft trickling of water from the tiny streams throughout the tunnels, the crackling of the few candles left burning. A warmth radiates from Takano beside me. I shouldn't so near to him. I don't even know his true intentions. But I can't deny the Gift connection we have. Do all Gifted people have this connection? But I didn't feel it with Morlin. Maybe it isn't a Gift thing at all, but something different.

"Is this connection…" I begin to say, not sure how to ask. "I mean, when two people are Gifted, does it draw them closer together, the way ours does?" I groan inwardly at my words. Maybe he doesn't even feel it at all, the way I do. Maybe his influence is just really strong and everyone feels it.

"Not usually," Takano says, looking up at the ceiling. "It's a forbidden thing."

His words hang in the air between us. He turns onto his side again and brings his hand up to my hair. I tense. Is he going to read my mind again? He rests his palm lightly onto the side of my face and I close my eyes at the unexpected gentleness of his touch.

"I won't read your mind anymore," he whispers, "if you don't read mine."

My shoulders relax, but I don't reply.

"We have to start being honest with one another," he continues.

"What's forbidden?" I whisper, my eyes still closed. "Using our power together?"

Takano's fingers brush the back of my neck, sending a tingling sensation down my back. "Two Gifted people becoming too close, is forbidden."

I open my eyes to find him looking down to my lips. His thumb brushes lightly over my bottom lip and I shudder.

My heart beats wildly and I try to push him back with my palms, but not with much effort. Then suddenly I'm surrounded by his arms. His hand runs down my back in a soothing motion over my shirt, and all my tense muscles relax at his touch. The gesture takes me back to another time, long ago, an old memory I'd forgotten until this moment.

I was young, maybe four or five years old, and my mom would rub my back and sing to me at bedtime. I see her smiling face, details about her that I'd long forgotten suddenly come back like it was only yesterday. Then the image is gone and a familiar fear creeps in, the fear that I'll forget what she looks like. The image of her face begins to slip away and I can no longer recall it.

A sob catches in my chest. I'd completely forgotten how my mother used to sing me to sleep. A lump forms in my throat. How many other things have I forgotten without realizing it?

I can no longer hold back the tears and they finally escape down my cheeks. I don't want Takano to know I'm crying, but he still has me pulled tightly against him and they slip down onto his bare chest. His hand on my back balls up into a fist, gathering the fabric of my shirt tight. His arms tighten around me.

I take a few deep breaths to get a hold of myself, then push out of his arms. He lets me go this time and makes room for me to climb out of the bed.

I take the candle holder, with the last burning candle in it, and hurry into the small bathroom. Thankfully there are no mirrors to reflect my shame. It's just a moment of weakness. It won't happen again. Ever. I won't let it.

I splash my face with cold water from the small trickling stream that runs into the makeshift sink. The icy coldness of it wakes me from my sadness. I hear a soft beep from behind the curtain.

"I'm okay, Beeps."

Beeps' shadow slowly retreats from the curtain and I grab a towel to dry my face.

Am I okay?

Yes. It was just a sad childhood memory which caught me off guard. But I'm grateful to have remembered it.

I set the towel down and walk back out of the small bathroom.

Takano is sitting up on the bed now, leaning forward with his elbows on his knees, fingers clasped together. He looks up as I approach.

"Would you like to be alone?" he asks.

I don't answer but simply climb into the bed and lie down on my side, pulling my knees up to my chest. I face the wall so I don't have to look at him.

There's no movement behind me and yet I can't fall asleep, despite how tired I am. My heart squeezes in my chest. It's been so long since I've cried about my parents like this and it only reminds me of how weak I am. Now that I'm older, I know there could be so many reasons they had to leave me behind. Yet it doesn't make the feelings of abandonment any less painful.

"I'll go keep watch," Takano says behind me, getting up from the bed.

I turn and grab his hand. "Stay."

He hesitates only a moment then climbs into the bed again, pulling me into his arms. No sooner are his arms around me than I drift off to sleep.

CHAPTER 31

I'M BACK HOME IN my dream, but everything is different. I walk through the Temple grounds. Everyone is gone. The only movement is that of the sand blowing across the abandoned courtyard. Then I see the bodies on the stone floor. It's the Sisters in their Temple Robes, lying on their sides, unmoving. The sun is too bright but I don't want to look down at the bodies below, so I keep my gaze up.

A glint off a metal catches my attention. The fighter plane I took from the Opposition Base is sitting just outside the Temple gates. Waves of heat rise from its hull plating, beneath the blazing sun.

Where's Takano? Did he come back here with me?

Where's Beeps?

I run to the ship and look inside. Beeps is not there. Then I remember, I left her on Aylvon. I left her in the cave! My heart hammers in my chest, beating harder and harder, until I'm unable to catch my breath. I told Beeps to wait for me in the cave and that I'd go back to carry her out once I was done packing things into the plane. But I forgot to go back!

"Aylvon is gone," a voice says behind me.

I turn. It's Takano. He's fully dressed in his black cloak and armor, his hood covering his face so I can't see his eyes.

"What do you mean, gone?" I say. I don't like the hood hiding his face. It reminds me of when I first saw him; when the sight of him terrified me and I thought he was going to kill me.

"The Opposition destroyed it," he says, not sounding like himself.

"No," I shake my head. "No, they wouldn't do that. Why would they destroy Aylvon?"

"Because you told them I was there."

"They can't do that!" I yell. "We have to go back for Beeps. She might still be there. We have to try." My throat closes up and I can't speak anymore. Beeps has to be there somewhere, even if the planet is gone. She could have survived it. Maybe she's floating in space, waiting to be rescued. She can survive in space, she doesn't need air.

I run to Takano. "Please, we have to go back and look for her."

He lifts his hand towards me and I'm thrown back, tossed upward into the air. I land hard on the cobblestone floor of the Temple courtyard. It knocks the wind out of me and I can't even cry out.

Suddenly the ground gives way beneath me and I fall into a hole.

"Takano!" I yell, scrambling for the edges and trying to crawl out, but my attempts only make me sink faster into the wet sand below. "Takano, help!"

I see him standing nearby. He turns and walks away, towards the hills.

An army of Ruling Order soldiers materialize in the heat waves. They turn in perfect unison and follow after Takano as he goes to his ship.

"No! Come back!" I yell. Suddenly I'm not sinking into the ground anymore but standing in front of my childhood home, looking up at the sky.

"Mommy! Dad!"

I'm a child now, watching our family ship leave without me. A hand grasps my arm, holding me back. I want to run to the top of the hill. I can wave to the ship so they'll see that they forgot to take me! But I can't get away from the strong grip. I woke that morning to the sound of the ship lifting off.

Mom probably told me to get up and get dressed, but I must have fallen back asleep. I was probably not paying attention as usual. I really messed up this time. It's my fault.

"Mommy!" I yell one final time, but I know it's too late. My voice hurts from yelling and they can't hear me anyway. Hopelessness washes over me as I watch the ship get smaller and smaller. I give up. They can't hear me. Mom must think I'm on board already, playing with my toys at the back. She would never leave me behind without her. She gets too worried about me.

Soon she'll realize I'm not on board and they'll come right back. Then she'll hug me tight and cry, saying how they thought I was with them the whole time and I should listen when she tells me to get up and get into the ship. And I'll know she's right, that I'm not a very good daughter and I never listen.

I still can't get free of the man gripping my arm. I turn to see who it is. The hollow eyes of a hooded figure stare back at me.

I wake with my heart pounding and my body covered with sweat. Where am I?

Then I remember. I'm in Takano's hideout. I look around. He isn't here.

"Beeps?"

She's gone, too.

I kick off the blankets, almost knocking over a bowl of warm bread pudding that's been placed on the bedside table. Beside it, there's a note, written with what looks like fireplace soot scratched onto a thin cloth with a stick.

We went to search for food.

I'm surprised to see Takano's writing. It calms me. I'm not sure why I'm surprised to see that he can write. He probably went to school as a kid, a nice school. I smile at the scratchy writing, but then I frown again.

Where are they? They could have woken me up. Why did Beeps leave without me? What help would she be anyway, in catching animals?

My dark mood from my nightmare makes it hard to have an appetite. I take the bowl of sweet, bread pudding and start eating it anyway. I'll need it for my strength.

I eat fast, wanting to get up and do something so that I can get my mind off my dream. I left quite a mess from the fit I threw last night, when Takano said Parrin was a liar and a coward, and I fought with him.

I start picking things up off the floor and my mind wanders back to last night and Takano's arms wrapped around me before I fell asleep. My cheeks flush. It's a good thing he wasn't here when I woke up, screaming and sweaty.

How am I going to face him today?

I make the bed, then use a dried up bush to sweep up. Hopefully it isn't some kind of important medicinal herb or Takano's favorite dried leaf tea or something.

When I'm all done, I look around for more to do but the cave is spotless. What's taking them so long to get back? Should I go out and look for them? But then I'd have to see Takano and it will be so embarrassing, after last night.

I run my fingers through my hair. I can't believe I cried in his arms. I groan as another wave of embarrassment washes over me.

My hair feels sticky. I need to wash up.

I head into the small washroom. Our clothes hang from the bar that holds the curtain. Takano washed our muddy clothes from yesterday. I smile. The tub is cleared of the muddy water and the small stream runs along the bottom again.

I reach down and let it trickle past my fingers, thinking of how difficult clean water is to find back home. Here, it flows freely past my fingers, an endless supply.

I plug one end of the tub and let it fill with water. If I could heat it up somehow, I could take a bath.

I head out of the washroom to see if the small fireplace in the corner is still burning wood. There are some black pieces left, glowing red at the bottom. I look up to see where the smoke is going. A narrow tunnel in the cave ceiling runs up into the darkness above. I can't see the top, but it must open up to the outside.

I'll heat some water and pour it into the tub. If Takano and Beeps return before the tub is full, I won't have a bath. If not, then I will have a bath.

One thing's for sure, I can't spend another night here with Takano. In fact, I don't want to ever fall asleep and dream, again. I'd once heard of deep meditation practices that are equivalent to a full night's sleep, without the actual sleeping part. Maybe I'll do something like that and stay awake for the rest of my life.

I grab the only pot in the place and return to the tub to fill it with water. The tub is already full so I plug the other end to stop the flow of water, then scoop up a big potful.

I take it to the fireplace and grab what's left of the firewood to start the flames up again.

The simple task of getting a fire going and warming up water is relaxing and helps get my mind off of everything. Maybe I can do some running later today. The thought of being free to run to my heart's desire, makes me feel better.

Once the water is boiling, I add it to the cold water in the tub. I dip my hand in it. It's not as warm as I would have wanted, but warm enough for a quick bath. I'll just get cleaned off as fast as I can.

I pull the bathroom curtain shut.

It's no big deal, I tell myself. I'm just going to get in and out. No one is here anyway.

I take off my shirt first, then climb out of my pants quickly. Somehow, there's always a slight breeze blowing through the cave, even in here. I shiver and climb into the tub.

The water rises as I lower myself down. The feeling of water all around me is unfamiliar, and exhilarating. It's colder than I thought it would be, now that I'm in it, but not un-pleasant.

I close my eyes. The gentle splashing sounds that accom-pany every movement I make, are calming. This isn't so bad, in fact, it's really nice. The Temple didn't have a bath house. We used buckets that were only big enough to stand in, with ankle deep water, and we'd wash ourselves from head to toe with a sponge. Now I understand why stories in books speak so fondly of swimming or bathing. Surrounded by water, I feel lighter, and it's only a small tub of water! Imagine how light I would feel in an entire ocean of it! I'd float away...

The sound of the curtain drawing back startles me and I open my eyes wide. Takano is standing there, looking as surprised to see me in the tub as I am to see him standing there. I let out a choked squeal, crossing my arms in front of me. Beeps rolls in after him. She lets out a high-pitched sound then quickly rolls backwards, out of the bathroom.

"Get out!" I yell at Takano. He just stands there and opens his mouth, as though to say something, then seems to think better of it and turns to leave instead. He stops with his hand on the curtain and his back to me.

"You're wasting training time," he says, then drops the curtain and walks away.

CHAPTER 32

WHEN I FINALLY WALK out of the musty cave, I'm greeted by sweet, mountain air. I stretch, feeling more alert and awake than I've ever felt in my entire life. I'd grown too used to living in Central, where the heat makes everyone walk around half asleep all day.

I look out across the forest. The day is clear and bright with the morning sun. The scent of rain still hangs in the air from a recent rainfall, which has left the ground muddy and smelling like roots and freshly dug up dirt. It reminds me of my garden back home. I take a deep breath, then start walking.

Where did Takano get to? Just when I didn't think it was possible to feel any more embarrassed than I already did, Takano had to walk in on me while I was having a bath. But I'm passed the point of embarrassment now. He didn't gawk at me in the tub, but simply left. And he didn't try to get intimate with me when we were in the same bed together last night. He isn't interested in me in a romantic way, it seems, so I don't have to be self-conscious or embarrassed about the things that have happened.

I cross my arms. Where's Beeps anyway? Is Takano really so much fun to hang out with that she'd rather be with him than wait for me? If she wasn't a robot I'd swear she had a crush on him.

I head out into the forest, following a narrow path through the trees. Then I see them, near the stolen ship that I flew here in.

I stop to watch them playing some kind of game where Beeps tries to outrun a wooden log that Takano throws through the air. Should I join them? They seem to be enjoying themselves just find without me. If Takano wants me to come train with him then he'll come find me.

I take out my sword and give it a twirl in the air. I like the feel of it in my hand.

Might as well break it in a bit. I slash at a large leaf and the sword cuts right through it, hardly moving the leaf at all. I look at the sword's metal edge. How can it be so sharp? Is it special somehow?

I try slicing a tree branch and the sword has no trouble cutting straight through it. I try other things as well and there isn't one thing the sword can't slice through. I swing down at a rock and it cuts into the rock, surprising me. I check to see if I've dulled the blade, but it seems fine. Takano's armor must be made of a metal that can stop this sword.

A series of beeps catches my attention and I look over to Takano and Beeps. They're no longer playing their game but watching me now. I pretend not to notice and continue experimenting with my swords abilities. Neither of them comes over to greet me, so I stay where I am. Takano said I was wasting training time, yet he's wasting time playing with Beeps. He hasn't even asked me to start training yet. I continue doing my own thing and Takano does his.

The rest of our morning 'training session' consists of Takano and I ignoring each other while we slice and dice the trees with a vengeance. I practice my jumps and somersaults. Takano practices forward lunges and blocking moves. I watch him when he isn't looking. He relies too much on his strength. I like to use my agility in a fight, which gives me an advantage with larger and stronger opponents. I've had experience fighting off forest animals and aggressive travelers at the market square in the village. They were stronger than me, but I was quicker. I learned ways of taking care of myself, way before I knew I had Gift powers.

I continue practicing with the sword. As long as I can keep this sword out of my enemy's hands, I will win any fight. Beeps rolls around nearby, doing her own thing as well, but no longer with Takano. I stay close, keeping her in sight.

Last night's dream still has me on edge. The thought of losing Beeps scares me.

I stop swinging my sword to take a breath. Something doesn't feel right, like there's a disturbance inside of me that I can't escape. Maybe it's the left over embarrassment from crying in Takano's arms last night, or him walking in on me while I was in the bathtub this morning.

"Aren't you going to train with Takano today?" Beeps says, rolling towards me.

"What?" I slip my sword into its sheath. "I am training Beeps," I say. "Can't you see?"

"It looks like you're trimming a tree," she replies, or something similar, like 'preparing' the tree.

I grunt, looking at the poor tree that got the worst of my frustrations today. She's right. I'm just wasting my energy.

"Wouldn't it better to train with Takano?" Beeps continues. She rolls closer to me and her beeps become quieter. "Are we going to escape tonight? Is that why you are avoiding him?"

"Avoiding him?" I ask, to clarify her words.

"Yes."

Nothing gets past Beeps.

"You're right. I'm avoiding him. But he's avoiding me too."

I look over at him now. He's swinging his sword around, spinning and ducking as though following some routine he learned at a fancy fencing school.

He stops suddenly, like he can feel me staring at him. I quickly look away. He's in great shape and he moves well. Why am I disappointed that he stopped his fencing moves? Because now I can't continue to watch him? The image of him with his shirt off from the previous night flashes through my mind. I shake my head to dispel it.

"What's wrong?" Beeps asks.

"Nothing!" I say a little too loudly. I look over at Takano again and our eyes meet. I quickly turn away. Why am I letting myself get so distracted by him? Am I betraying the Opposition by being here? Betraying myself somehow? Why does Takano have such a strange effect on me? When he's around I'm too confused to even figure out how I feel. Am I still scared of him? Do I trust him now?

Takano starts to walk towards me and I walk away.

I'll head back to the cave. I'm not ready to face him yet.

"Rita," he calls after me.

I don't stop, but keep going.

"Rita!" he calls louder and I walk faster. I smile, despite myself. If we had a race I think I'd win. Let's see if he can catch me.

I start to run, but don't get too far. Takano lifts me off my feet with his Gift powers and tosses me into the air. I cry out, more from anger than anything. Did I think he'd play fair? Even in a race?

I'm flung towards a large tree and brace myself for impact. Then, at the last moment, I remember I have powers too and can use them to stop myself from crashing into the tree.

I push the energy forwards and spin myself around, landing on the ground in a crouch position. Takano walks up to me, then hesitates when he sees my expression.

With a loud cry I lunge forward, hands out in front of me. Takano goes flying back. I can't stop the forward force before he slams into the large tree behind him.

Takano's back hits the trunk and I hear a cracking sound. I cringe.

Oops.

There must be some way to control the amount of force I use. It seems the angrier I am, the stronger the energy force.

Takano gets back on his feet, his expression menacing.

"Rita, come here," he commands, dusting off his cloak.

I clench my fists. Is he trying to make me obey him? I could walk away again, but he'll just toss me into the air from behind, like last time. I must have flown over ten feet. I'm not turning my back on him this time.

"Rita," he says again, his voice no longer angry. "Start walking and come here."

I start walking. Then stop. What am I doing?

I shake my head to clear it. My body feels strange, all limp and tingly inside like I laughed for too long and my muscles are weak. I cross my arms. There's no way I'm taking orders from Takano right now. I'm not one of his soldiers or his slave.

"You want to walk to me," he says, calmly. His deep voice drifts into my mind, distracting me from my thoughts. There was something I was trying to remember, but it keeps slipping away. I blink and squint my eyes towards the sun. What was I doing again? Oh yeah, walking to Takano.

I start moving again. Why was I heading towards him? Probably to give him a piece of my mind about him ignoring me all morning. Especially after he made that comment about me wasting training time and then when I came out, he didn't even train with me at all!

When I stop in front of him he has a grin on his face.

"What?" I say.

"You came." His eyes flash.

"Of course I came, I wanted to come here and tell you something."

"You did?" He smiles even more. "What is it?"

Then I remember. I *didn't* want to walk over here!

I pull out my sword and hold it up to Takano's chest.

"You used *mind control* on me?"

"Manipulation." He sidesteps me, unfazed by my sword. "You should learn how to use it."

"You don't want me to learn how to use it," I growl.

He nods. "You're right. I don't."

I want to be mad at him but another thought is brewing in my mind. "When you threw me from behind," I say, an idea forming. "I flew really high."

I lower my sword.

"Enemies won't wait for you to be ready and facing them before they attack," Takano says.

"I know, but I mean, I *flew*."

Takano gives me a questioning look.

"And," I begin to pace, swinging my sword around as I talk. "If I needed to get up high, to get away from an enemy or escape from a trap, or to get to the top of a cliff—"

"I understand," Takano says. He steps back and puts out his hand. "Go ahead." He nods towards my stolen ship in the clearing. "Run to the ship and I'll boost you to the top of it."

"I don't think so," I say, putting my sword away. "I need to be ready. I don't want to be blasted into the air from behind when I don't expect it."

Takano considers this for a moment. "We can use hand signals," he says, turning his palm up and raising it. "Up..." he demonstrates the hand movement. Then he sets his palm forward. "Stop..." He curls his fingers towards himself. "Forward."

"Forward? That doesn't work—"

Suddenly I'm pulled forward right into Takano's hand, clasping my throat. I grab his arm with both hands and he lets go.

"That's forward," he says.

"Don't." I push him but he doesn't even budge. "I think you need to work on 'forward'," I say, rubbing at my neck. Would I be able to pull him forward like that, if it was necessary for some reason? I can't imagine when it would ever be necessary, nor can I imagine Takano ever needing my help in battle. But he thinks that together we could take down Dukath. If he's right, I would be a hero. We could rid the Galaxy of the supreme leader of the Ruling Order. No one else even stands a chance going up against Dukath and his army. If it isn't us, then it will be nobody.

"You're weaker than I imagined," he says, looking me over.

I glare at him. "My throat's fine. Thanks for your concern." I decide to let him off easy this time. "Just give me a boost. But *wait* for my signal."

Takano crosses his arms and gives me a bored look.

"You're seriously the most impatient teacher ever," I say. "Just don't boost me before I give the signal." I jog over to the ship, then stop far back enough to give myself room to run.

I turn and look back at Takano. He's still got his arms crossed, with that bored expression on his face.

I sigh. I'll just expect the boost when I give the signal, then ride it into the air. I should have more control since I know it's coming.

I prepare to run and jump. My stomach tingles with anticipation. Will I get tossed into the sharp edge of the ship's wing and get sliced in half at the waist?

No. I have Gift powers too. I can control what I slam into.

I glance back at Takano. His arms are uncrossed now, his hands outstretched and ready. I start to run, then give the 'up' signal with my hand at just the right moment. The boost comes sooner than I expect and I'm thrown high, much higher than I would need, to get to the top of the small ship. My stomach flutters as I look down at the treetops below me.

The forest stretches out in every direction, towards a horizon of blue misty mountains in the distance. A laugh bubbles up inside of me as the wind blows over my face. I bend my knees and arch my back, suspended in the air for a magical moment. Then I do a twirl, feeling weightless. But it doesn't last long and I start to fall. My stomach drops.

The Gift, use the Gift! I look down and my muscles tense. There's not enough time to focus my Gift as I fall fast towards a tree. I tumble down into the leaves. My shoulder and hip snap branches, slowing my fall just enough to give me a second to orient myself and grab onto a strong branch. It's a large tree and when I look down I get dizzy from the height.

Beeps is rolling around frantically on the ground, beeping all kinds of things I can't figure out.

Takano looks up, a smile on his face.

"Not funny!" I yell down at him.

He raises his arms. "Jump."

"No way! You'll let me hit the ground."

"Jump, Rita," he says again.

My hands begin to sweat and my grip loosens on the thick branch. I don't really have a choice but to jump.

"Takano Rynn, you'd better catch me!"

My hands slip and I fall. Takano uses his Gift to slow my fall, lowering me into his arms.

"Why couldn't I use it?" I say, trying to push myself out of his arms.

Takano sets me down. "You were scared."

"So? Shouldn't I be stronger in my Gift when I'm scared?"

He shakes his head. "You have to be confident. You have to believe. Fear is the opposite of that."

Suddenly I don't want to train anymore. I wipe my scratched-up palms on my pants. "Well, I'm sure I'll figure it out eventually," I say. But I don't mean it. I can't do this. I don't want to. I don't have the power, or the desire to go up against Dukath. I need to get back to Central.

"You've lost your confidence," Takano says to me.

I frown, turning away from him. "I've got a lot on my mind." I start to walk away but he grabs my arm.

"Let's try it again."

He's so close I can feel warmth radiating from him, behind me. I turn to face him and square my shoulders. His hand rests on his side and I remember that he's still recovering from his injury, the one I gave him.

I sigh. "Fine, I guess I don't have any other plans for today."

CHAPTER 33

AFTER THE TREE INCIDENT, Takano is a lot more careful with how high he throws me, even though I ask to go higher each time. I practice my landing and using my powers with each jump.

He was right. Confidence is the key to using the Gift. I toss him too, which isn't any harder or easier based on weight, but rather it's tied to concentration and how alert or tired I am. We make it into a game, getting better and better at responding to each other's hand signals.

I don't even feel hungry when the sun begins to set. I just want to keep jumping and flying through the air. But as the temperature drops with the sun and darkness sets in.

I have no idea what kind of animals live on Aylvon. The larger ones may be waiting for the covering of darkness to come out. The thought sends a shiver through me. I know how dangerous forest animals can be. I look between the trees where it's dark and imagine hidden eyes of unknown creatures watching me.

I wrap my arms around myself. It's time to head to shelter, but the thought of going back to the cave only reminds me of my bad dreams and the embarrassment I felt when Takano found me in the tub.

"One more time?" I say, turning to him.

It's harder to see in the fading light, but I can still make out his form. He shakes his head no and starts to walk away. There's a sinking feeling in my stomach when I think of going back to the cave. I never liked going to sleep, after my parents left, and would sometimes avoid it until the sun came up.

"Please? Just once more?" I run after him and grab his arm. "I want to try jumping together."

"We tried that. It doesn't work when we jump at the same time."

"Let's try it again. I'm more confident now," I insist. Maybe if I make myself tired enough, I'll fall asleep quickly tonight and not go through the nightly battle I normally do. "I'm sure I can stop my fall, without landing on you this time."

Takano runs a hand through his dark hair, looking up at one of the moons. The sky has gone dark so quickly I'm reminded again of how fast this planet actually turns. His eyes catch the starlight and I want to freeze time, right here, forever. I never want to forget what he looks like right now in the moonlight. I close my eyes, saving the image of him in my mind.

"Alright, one more time," he says softly.

I smile and open my eyes. "Great! In the clearing. Come on."

I start to run and Takano follows. We've got it practiced now. We're not quite there yet but I can now see how our powers could become an extension of each others' Gifts, if we worked together.

Takano catches up to me and takes my hand. He's a fast runner and it feels like my feet barely touch the ground as I try to keep up.

"Ready?" he says.

"Yes!"

He squeezes my hand and we jump, using our opposite hands to release a burst of energy towards the ground. We're in sync this time and I'm not too early or too late, too high or too low, alongside Takano. The downward blast of energy pushes us up high.

The wind rushes over me as we rise and I tilt my head back to a sky full of stars. It's the highest we've gone yet. I reach a hand up as though to grab a star. I've never felt so free.

Takano's wraps his arm around my waist suddenly and the movement throws us into a spin. He pulls me against him so I don't fly out.

I laugh, throwing my head back and watching the stars spin. Millions of stars and planets, and then there's us, here, on this one tiny planet, alone.

Our twirl slows and I close my eyes. We'll never have this moment again. I feel a shift coming, one that will change everything. It's an ominous feeling that I can't explain, but I recognize. It's the same intuition I would get from my Gift powers in the past, when something bad was coming. I just didn't know that's what it was. When I was young, I always knew when trouble was on its way.

I clench Takano's cloak in my fists, holding him tight. Does he feel it too, this unknown turn of events that is looming?

The spinning comes to a stop and I rest my cheek on his shoulder. Thunder rolls in the distant hills and I look out across the land. The moons bathe the treetops in soft colors. We're suspended, in a moment of weightlessness that stretches on and on. Is Takano doing this? Keeping us suspended in the air?

A cool breeze circles around us, but Takano's arms keep me warm. The Gift inside of me feels alive, like water moving around inside my body, awakening sensations that I've never known before. I feel truly alive. I feel free.

This invisible river flows through me to Takano, then back to me again. Our energies swirl, like two different colors mixing to create a new one. There are no forest sounds up here, so high above the trees; only the sound of Takano's heartbeat and his cloak flapping in the breeze. A flash of lightning lights up the sky. Then another, followed by claps of thunder.

I smile at the colorful display of lightning flashes on the mountain side.

"Wow," I breathe.

"That's us, Rita," Takano says. His voice is thick with emotion and his eyes reflect the lightning as he watches it.

"What is?"

"The lightning. We're making it happen." He takes my hands and interlaces our finger together, palms touching. My hands look small in his, like a child's.

"That's impossible," I say, and yet I know he's telling the truth. I can feel it, too. Our energy is flowing through the life of this planet, all the way to the electricity in the sky.

"I could never control its power," Takano says, setting our clasped hands against his chest. "But with you, it's easier."

His eyes search mine and I hold my breath.

"The Gift is lighter to bear, with you," he continues. "It always felt like a bondage I couldn't escape. But maybe now, I don't have to." He looks down at my lips, then back to my eyes again. "Who are you?" he whispers.

"I'm Rita," I say. "Who else would I be?"

Takano closes his eyes and an emotion so strong, unlike any pain I've ever felt, grips my heart. It's not my pain, but Takano's. His thoughts and memories flow freely to me.

"What are you doing?" he asks, tightening his grip on my hands.

I shake my head, because I'm not doing anything. I don't know what he means. Yet I can't seem to stop what is happening. Takano's memories flood my mind. I close my eyes to see them better. He's in a room, as a boy. It's a classroom. He's the only one not outside playing at recess. He's being held in, punished for another outburst of anger.

There are stares from the other kids, fear in their eyes.

He can't control his Gift powers, the energy inside of him that is tearing him apart, fighting for control of his will. It acts out when he's excited, hurting others by accident.

He's an outsider, not included in conversations; feared and unwelcome. A hush falls over the room when he enters. They whisper about him. He's strange, weird. Always untouched and always lonely. His mother doesn't understand. He is nothing like his older brother, who has excelled in every way. She frowns whenever she looks at him, trying to figure him out. His teachers have lost their patience with him. The kids have alienated him at school.

There are conversations behind closed doors. "He's too much like his grandfather."

The only way to help him is to send him away from home, to the elder Temple Masters who would better understand what is inside of him and how to control it. It is a power different than the one his brother wields. Takano's Gift is uncontrollable. He's different than the other Gift-sensitive boys.

Even the Masters fear him and cannot help.

More images come and Takano doesn't try to stop me this time, from seeing them. I see him finding his grandfather's sword, or maybe it found him. His grandfather, a servant of Dukath's, is the only one that could really understand all this. Takano believes it's his destiny, to follow in his grandfather's footsteps. I want to tell him that I was different growing up too, and the images pass between us. My home at the Temple, with all the letters I'd written to my parents. I don't want Takano to see the letters, but I can't choose what he sees. The endless days I marked in my journal, symbolizing how long I've been waiting for my parents to return. Always surrounded by others at the Temple, yet still feeling alone.

"Not alone," he whispers.

He lets go of my hands and I open my eyes. His arms lower to my waist and my hands slide up behind his neck, into his hair.

"Rita, what are you doing?" he asks again. His breath is near my lips and I pull him forward. He touches his lips to mine and in a moment of lightheadedness I begin to fall. I look down and my heart stops when I see how high up we are.

"Don't let go!" Takano yells, trying to keep hold of me. But it's too late. I'm falling, and he tries to help me, but I only bring him down with me. Takano's Gift is stronger than mine and he saves us from falling to our deaths, but we land hard. I do a tuck and roll somersault to help absorb the landing. Then I stop rolling and settle onto my back, on the wet ground, looking up at the tall trees. My heart grips tight in my chest, too tight. The pain is making it hard to breathe. Takano appears beside me. He kneels down to help me up.

"Something's wrong," I say.

Am I having a heart attack? No, it's the Gift, telling me something.

"There's been a disturbance," Takano says, his expression intense as he looks down at me. "I sense it."

I recognize the feeling now. It's the same shift I felt earlier, only stronger. The one I've been feeling all day. Something is coming.

And now, it's here.

And there's nothing I can do to stop it.

CHAPTER 34

"**W**HEN DID YOU LEARN to fly a ship like this one?" Takano asks. His dark hair hangs into his eyes as he watches me maneuver the controls. Is he impressed? Or just worried that I don't know what I'm doing?

"They're all pretty much the same," I say, trying to concentrate.

The ship tilts to one side, then the other. My cheeks heat up as I scramble to level out our take-off. I've never flown a ship like Takano's before, but I know the basics of flying and how the controls are supposed to work, except now I'm apparently doing the worst take-off in all of pilot history.

"And why am I flying *your* ship again?" I ask.

The ship finally levels off and we lift higher.

Takano gets up from the copilot seat. "I never fly my own ships," he says, about to walk away.

"Who flew you here?"

I look behind my shoulder when he doesn't reply. I don't think he even heard me, he seems so deep in thought.

"Wait," I say, not wanting him to leave yet. "What was the disturbance we felt tonight? We never really talked about it." I turn to look ahead. We're not far enough from the planet yet to turn on the auto-pilot. "Does it have to do with Lord Morlin?"

Takano rests a hand on the back of my seat. "Either someone strong with the Gift has been killed, or a planet was destroyed."

"But who would destroy an entire planet?"

"I have some guesses," Takano says, then leaves.

I focus on the flying. In a few seconds I'm going to switch to light speed, then set the coordinates for warp speed. Then, hopefully I can get this thing running on autopilot. I flip a switch and the ship blasts forward, pushing me back against the seat. I watch Aylvon disappear in the view screen. We didn't even go back to the cave to gather some things to bring with us, before leaving.

I reach for my belt. My sword is still with me. I don't know how many times I checked for it before boarding, but it was a lot. So why do I have this feeling that I've left something behind? Beeps is with us, on board.

She is. I'm sure of it.

"Beeps?" I yell over my shoulder, unable to let go of the uneasy feeling. The ship shakes with the impact of a loose flying meteor and I turn my attention back to flying.

There are more meteors ahead and I can't get control of the ship fast enough to stop us from hitting a pile of them. I fly up and around a large floating rock at the last second. I just need to find the warp drive controls and activate it. Once I have the autopilot turned on, it will detect meteor showers far in advance and fly around them.

I find the warp drive controls but can't reach them from my seat while still piloting the ship.

"Takano!" I call. There's no response. I grind my teeth and look down at the dashboard. There are two buttons which have to be hit at the same time to activate warp drive, a safety feature where both the pilot and copilot have to consent for it to be turned on.

Seriously? How did Takano fly this thing to Aylvon alone?

I stretch as far as I can but still can't reach the second button. If my arms were just a bit longer...

I give up with a heavy sigh. Should I leave the bridge and go find Takano? We'll probably crash into something if I do. Beeps could push the button for me if she were here. Why is she always running off?

I don't want to go into warp drive anyway, not until I know for sure Beeps is on board. I check the course we're on. It looks clear enough, for the next 10 minutes at least. I put the shields up in case we do run into some debris. That should deflect any objects in our way without wrecking the hull plating. But it also wastes energy, so I can't leave it on for long.

I jump out of my seat and rush to the bridge doors, nervous about leaving the controls without the autopilot activated. I run down the long hallway outside of the bridge. I'm totally unfamiliar with the layout of Takano's ship, but so far there's only one direction to go. I turn a corner and collide into Takano's chest, as he is also rushing in the opposite direction.

"Ouch."

"Why are the shields up?" he asks. "Are we under attack?"

"No. I need help getting into warp drive."

Takano gives me a questioning look.

"There's a comm device you can use to contact—"

"Where's Beeps?" I say. "I need to see her."

"I don't know."

"What?" I push past him. "You'll have to fly this ship yourself then."

I run down the long corridors and around corners, looking into rooms that open or have no doors. I've all but lost my mind by the time I find Beeps. I don't know whether to be mad at her or just be happy to see her. She's in the interrogation room of the ship. At least it looks like some sort of interrogation room, with a chair that has straps to tie a person down, placed at the center of the room.

Beeps' little head is tilted down towards the ground in a way I haven't seen before. She's usually alert and full of energy, with her head always level. I rush over to her and kneel down.

"I was looking for you! Is everything okay?"

I feel the ship jump into warp drive and lose my balance for a second. My stomach tightens. We're on our way now.

Takano's plan is to pretend he has captured me and is turning me in, to the Ruling Order led by General Randon who is working with Dukath.

They don't know why Takano left or where he went, but he is saying he left to find and capture me. The whole plan makes my stomach uneasy, and we haven't had time to properly talk about it in detail yet.

I frown, looking down at Beeps. "What are you doing here Beeps?"

She raises her small head, then lowers it again. "I was looking for a place to recharge," she beeps quietly.

"Recharge? Oh, I'm so sorry! Why didn't you tell us you were low on charge?"

"There was no place to charge on Aylvon. So I didn't want to worry you."

I rest my hand on Beeps' little frame. She feels cold to the touch.

"What kind of power conversion do you need?"

Beeps opens one of her small compartments, the door moving slower than usual.

I look at the tiny cable inside.

"I can open up a panel in this room and use a wire from under one of the control panels," I say, thinking out loud.

"Okay," Beeps replies softly.

I get to work. Beeps rolls over to join me and help unscrew a panel with one of her tiny screwdrivers, which makes a slow gear-grinding sound. I want to help, but don't have tools.

Once she's taken the screw off, I lift the metal sheet aside and pull out a mass of wires. One of them should be the right current. But I'll need a knife. I look around the room then remember my sword.

Before long, I've got Beeps hooked up. Just as she begins to charge a ringing sound startles the both of us. I look down at the wires. Did I trigger some kind of alarm?

"It's the communication system," Beeps explains. "An incoming call."

"Oh." I stand and look down at the communication console. It's a bunch of zeros and ones. "Can you read this Beeps?" I lift her up so she can see the screen.

"An incoming call from General Randon," she says.

"What?" I almost drop her in surprise. "We have to get Takano!"

CHAPTER 35

I SET BEEPS DOWN quickly and run over to the intercom port near the door, to contact the bridge.

"Takano?" I say, pressing the button.

"Rita, get into the interrogation chair. I'm on my way," comes the response.

"What?" I push the button again. "Takano what's the plan?"

There's no response this time. I look around the room. There's a view screen set up high, on the wall in front of the interrogation chair. Takano said for me to get into the chair. Will Randon do a video communication to see if I'm really here?

"Beeps, just stay out of sight, okay?" I say.

Beeps rolls back into the open panel just behind the interrogation chair, hiding. She remains quiet as she charges among the wires. Is she afraid?

The door slides open and Takano barges in. It only takes him a few long strides to reach me. He picks me up like I weigh nothing at all.

"What are you doing?" I say. Without even slowing his steps, he carries me to the interrogation chair and plops me down into it.

"Don't say anything," he replies as he fastens me in.

Our eyes meet for a moment then the comm system turns on and Randon's face appears on the big screen. Takano turns to face him.

"Rynn," General Randon says, looking down his nose at Takano from the view screen above. "You say you've been hard at work while you've been away. I find that hard to believe."

"I've got the girl," Takano replies.

"I see that. When we heard the Temple Girl had gone missing from the Opposition Base we assumed you took her, so that *we* couldn't get her."

"She's here," Takano says, clasping his hands behind his back and standing straight.

"We hadn't heard from you in a long time." A grin forms on General Randon's face. "We could only assume that you were planning to work against us. So we took the liberty of destroying your little Alma Mater."

Takano's fists clench at his sides.

"A little planet called...Orusk, I think?" Randon continues.

I gasp. They destroyed Orusk, the planet with the very first Temple of the Gifted Lords? They destroyed the *Orusk Temple*?

General Randon has a smirk on his face as he watches Takano. "Your old Gifted friend, Master Kra'an was it? He was living out his final useless years on Orusk, was he not?"

Takano's hand moves to his sword. His back is turned to me and I can't see his expression. General Randon clears his throat.

"Did you think we didn't know about him? Now that we have Morlin, we can find Antineon too, and do the same thing to it, that we did to Orusk."

Takano doesn't reply. My wrists ache and I realize that I've been pulling on the restraints, my hands clenched into fists. I force myself to relax into the chair.

"High Leader will be happy to know you're bringing the girl," General Randon continues, seeming bored now with the conversation. "He was beginning to lose faith in you and I told him I will be the new leader of the Ruling Order."

"How did you destroy Orusk?" Takano asks. His voice is calm, yet I can tell he's angry.

Randon cuts off communication and there's silence.

Takano doesn't move and I'm not sure what to say.

This is far worse than I ever imagined.

"Takano?" I say, after a moment. He lifts his head and walks over to me, unclasping my restraints without a word. I sit up when he's done and rub my wrists.

"How could they destroy all of Orusk?" I ask.

"They didn't just die instantly," Takano says softly. "They suffered. I could feel it, back on Aylvon." He tightens his grip on the arm rest of the interrogation chair. I want to put my hand on his, to comfort him somehow. But I don't know if he'd want me to touch him right now, so I don't.

He's right. I could feel it too, something terrible happening. But I didn't know what it was.

I hug my knees to my chest. I don't even want to think about how it happened.

"Who was Master Kra'an?" I ask Takano.

He draws his sword suddenly and slashes the control panel below the comm screen, sending sparks flying. I cover my face, turning my head away so the sparks don't burn my cheeks.

Takano stops the destruction, his shoulders moving with his heavy breathing.

I shouldn't have asked. I don't know what to do now. Should I go over to him? Comfort him? No, that's probably a bad idea, his sword is still in his hand.

Beeps has burrowed all the way inside the open panel where she's still charging, buried in wires. I want to tell her it's okay to come out now and that she doesn't need to be scared, but I'm not sure what Takano will do next.

"Master Kra'an was a mentor of mine when I was a teenager," Takano says. He rests his gloved hands onto the charred control panel in front of him and leans forward, clenching the edge in a death grip. "He was the first person to ever tell me to let go of my internal battle, to stop fighting against my own nature, against the power within me; the anger, and pain…and regret.

"He told me those things aren't bad, they are a part of me and a part of the Gift. He told me to embrace them. But I was afraid to. I didn't want to hurt more people or kill them by accident."

I wait for him to continue but he doesn't.

"What changed?" I ask quietly.

"He said, 'if they die Rynn, then they die. They will continue on in eternal life, and will help you in your mission to bring back order to the Galaxy with your Gift. The Gift connects all of us, whether alive or dead.'" Takano sighs. "He told me the Temple on Orusk will stand forever and when I am in a position of power, I can ensure it will never be destroyed."

I wrap my arms around myself. "Takano, I really don't think—"

"I failed him," Takano whispers. "I should have been there. I should have stopped Randon. The Temple was where all the Masters lived. I got distracted..." He stops a moment, as though thinking.

Another incoming transmission interrupts us and Takano straps me into the interrogation chair without asking. He keeps his eyes down but I can see that they are red from tears, or anger. His hands are more rough this time as he tightens the restraints.

I lean my head back in the chair and look up at the ceiling.

I hate the metal ceiling above us. I this metal chair. And I hate Randon.

I need more time to talk to Takano. We didn't have enough time to train with using our Gifts together, or to plan our attack on Dukath. We just knew something bad was happening in the Galaxy and we had to go stop it. But it's too late.

There's a bleep and the comm unit switches on again.

I look over at the cracked screen, which is surprisingly still working after Takano attacked the panel. A hooded figure appears, which isn't General Randon.

"High leader," Takano says in a commanding voice. "To what do I owe the honor?"

"I wanted to see the girl for myself."

Dukath's voice makes my skin crawl. His face is a sickening shade of gray, aged with evil. He stares at me with black eyes. I look away.

"You've done well," Dukath continues, his words slow and unhurried. "I was certain you wouldn't succeed."

Takano takes a deep breath then says, "I'm taking her to Randon."

"No. Bring her to me." Dukath grins. "I want to watch you kill her in my presence. The Temple Masters are all dead now, except for your brother. And this one," he nods to me. "As long as she's alive, the Opposition will still have hope."

"I can kill her now, your High Leadership," Takano bows slightly.

"No. I don't trust you. Bring her to me, or Morlin dies."

Takano nods.

"The Gift Stone. Did you find it?"

Takano opens his mouth to answer, then shuts it again.

"Never mind," Dukath says, sounding irritated. "Come directly to me."

"I will," Takano says, and the transmission ends.

CHAPTER 36

I START TO SIT up, forgetting I'm strapped in, then fall back against the interrogation seat.

At least Lord Morlin's not dead. That's a relief.

My shoulders relax and I let out a breath. "Takano?" I try to lift my neck, to see where he is and how he's dealing with all this, but he's somewhere behind me. "Can you please let me out now?"

I hear Beeps moving around on the ground but I can't see her either. Is she stuck in all those wires? Did she finish charging?

"The Masters are all dead," Takano says.

"Not Lord Morlin."

"Morlin?" Takano yells. "Does he matter more than the others who died?" He steps in front of me, anger flashing in his eyes. My words catch in my throat and suddenly I can't breathe.

"You're hurting me…" I whisper, the sound barely audible as my throat tightens painfully.

Takano releases his invisible hold and blinks a couple of times. "Rita?" He takes another step back. "I'm sorry." He turns away, rubbing his face with his hands. "It's my fault," he says. His words are so quiet I can barely hear them.

"It's not your fault—"

"Orusk was destroyed because of me, and Master Kra'an—"

"Randon did it, not you. You're not evil, like him."

"You don't know me!" Takano shouts at me.

The tightness in my throat returns and my eyes burn as he grips me in an invisible hold again. This time I fight back with my Gift powers and Takano loosens his hold, not bothering to fight back. "Just because you've seen my thoughts once," he continues. "It doesn't mean you know me, Rita. You think I have some good inside of me, but I don't."

The room goes silent. Even Beeps stops moving about in her jittery way. I want to check on her. She must be scared that Takano and I are fighting like this.

I pull on the arm restraints again, trying to channel my Gift powers to help me, but it's no use. The interrogation chair was obviously built to hold a Gifted person.

"Please let me out," I say to Takano, finally giving up the struggle with the chair.

He ignores me and begins to pace. "I have to take you to Dukath."

I rest my head back. "Yes. And we'll…" I stop. We'll what? Attack him with our swords?

Takano stops pacing, his back turned to me.

"The Temple Masters believe that it is better to sacrifice one for the good of the whole."

"What do you mean?" My heart pounds and I swallow hard. "Takano? You're scaring me. Please let me out."

In one swift movement he's beside me. I try to pull away, but the arm restraints hold me in place.

"Convince me to let you out, Rita," he whispers.

"What?"

His eyes are alive in a way I haven't seen before. Is it Dukath? Does he have some sort of effect on Takano? I close my eyes, trying to focus on my Gift of influence.

"Let me out, Takano. You want to let me out," I say, feeling stupid in my attempt. I haven't practiced mind manipulation yet, but I really do want to get out of this blasted chair.

Nothing happens.

I open my eyes again and Takano has a grin on his face. I clench my fists.

"You *want* to let me out of this chair," I say between clenched teeth.

His gaze travels over my body. "You look good in black, Rita. It suits you."

I tense as he moves in closer.

"Takano, stop. Please." I try to pull away but there's no room to move back. Takano looks down at my lips. I shake my head. "Don't. You're not like this."

I blink back tears, confused. Angry. He's so close that I can feel the warmth of his body. I turn my head away from him, pushing my cheek against the cold chair. I just need to relax a moment, control my emotions and use my powers of influence. I close my eyes and focus in on Takano's thoughts.

"Stop it!" he yells, backing away from me.

"This isn't you," I yell back.

"This *is* me, Rita!" Takano's voice booms in the enclosed space. "You haven't seen the thousands I've killed. You haven't heard their cries for help, the fear in their eyes before they died. The mothers with their children—"

"Stop!" I shout, my body trembling.

Hold it together Rita.

I take a calming breath. "I'll tell you what I do see," I say between heavy breaths. "A man who comforted me when I was crying; who was kind to me."

"Why do you think I was nice to you?" Takano says, coming in close again. "So I could get what I wanted."

"You want us to work together, remember? And defeat Dukath." Why isn't he letting me out of the chair? Is he really planning to turn me over to Dukath?

The ship's engine hums as I wait for Takano to say something. We're still headed towards General Randon. Dukath asked Takano to take me straight to him and not Randon, so why hasn't Takano changed our course yet?

"I don't understand," I say. "Why are you doing this?"

Takano reaches up and touches my hair. I flinch.

"Please don't touch me."

Suddenly Beeps comes rolling out fast, in a cry of hectic beeping sounds, from somewhere beneath the broken panel. She rams into Takano's foot, her little body colliding with his large boot. He looks down. She does it again, and again until he finally shoves her hard across the room with one kick. She rolls uncontrollably, her little face scraping against the floor. Her body slams into the wall, sending sparks flying.

"Hey!" I shout and Takano goes flying back through the air. He hits the door and seems startled for a second.

"I'm sorry, Rita." He shakes his head, regaining his composure. "I'll let you out." He heads towards me again and the ship comes to an abrupt stop, causing him to lose balance.

"What happened?" I pull against the arm restraints and the skin at my wrists burns.

"I don't know," Takano says, rushing over to one of the consoles. He pushes some buttons.

"Takano?"

"Someone's locked a tractor beam on us." "Takano, please get me out."

"It's Randon. He's found us first."

He glances over at me then runs out of the room.

"Wait!" I yell, but he's gone.

CHAPTER 37

"**I** DIDN'T BELIEVE HE could do it," General Randon says, striding into the interrogation room with a big smile on his face. He rubs his hands together and looks me over. "I don't see anything particularly special about you."

"Nor I, about you," I say, unable to help it.

Randon smirks. "Tell me..." He walks around the chair slowly. "How did he get you into this chair? I know it wasn't by force." He stops, then whispers near my ear. "Morlin told us who you are, or shall I say, we found a way to coerce him into telling us."

"I don't know what you're talking about," I reply between clenched teeth.

Randon straightens and begins to pace again. "You're in this chair willingly. Why?" He's on my other side now and reaches a gloved hand to my lips. I turn my head away. "You like him, don't you?" His fingers travel down my neck. "How cute."

"Don't touch me," I growl. His eyes go wide and he begins to choke and sputter.

Ruling Order soldiers stand at attention by the door but don't catch on to what I'm doing, right away, as Randon struggles for air.

Now that I'm locked onto him I do a quick search of his thoughts. He has a strong mind, and there are details he keeps well hidden, details about Morlin and what they're doing with him. He seems familiar with this type of mind search, trained to protect certain secrets. I don't have time to force that information out of him. But I do see that he is planning to betray Takano. He wants to kill him and take me to Dukath himself, so he can become the official leader of the Ruling Order.

Two of the soldiers rush over to me and zap my arms with an electric shock.

I cry out. The current seizes every muscle in my body at once. They don't stop, even when I release Randon. My body shakes as I try to clench my muscles tight against the pain.

Randon raises a hand. "Dukath wants her alive," he says.

They stop and pull away.

My head pounds and my vision blurs. But I can still see Randon rubbing his neck, looking down his nose at me. All humor has left his face now. Then I see that Takano is standing silently behind him.

"Takano?" I blink a few times. He's wearing his hood over his head now and I can't see his face.

How long has he been in the room? How long did he watch them hurt me?

Randon steps out of the way and Takano comes forward. He removes his hood and stands before me. My heart squeezes at the sight of him. His eyes are now devoid of the emotions I saw during our time on Aylvon, as though it's not even him.

"What's the plan Takano?" I whisper. This has to be part of his plan. He said sorry after hurting Beeps. He's still on my side.

He avoids my eyes, looking over my shoulder as he leans down close to my ear.

"I'm sorry, Rita," he whispers, then unlatches my sword from my belt. He straightens and hands the sword to Randon, putting his hood back over his head.

Randon gives me a wink before they both turn and walk out of the room. The soldiers march out after them.

Then the doors slide closed and I'm left in silence.

CHAPTER 38

I STARE UP AT the ceiling, my mind blank as the silence stretches on. The electric shock has left me exhausted and I can't think of what to do next.

The automatic lights shut off suddenly and I'm left in the dark; blind, like the day I watched my parents' ship fly off into the noon-day sun. I couldn't see anything indoors for a while after staring at that sun that long. Now, I can no longer see the metal ceiling above me. Even the lights from the consoles have gone dark.

I breathe, and wait.

My wrists burn at my sides. My heart beats slowly.

Go to Orusk.

The thought is so potent that I hear it as an audible voice in my head. Was it just my imagination? I can't go to Orusk, it was destroyed...

Gather your strength, young one.

The words continue and I don't fight them or question them, I just listen.

The time is now, to rise and fight.

Prepare your sword, for comes the night.

Your heart make ready,

Dwell not on sorrow.

For no longer is this day today,

But now it is tomorrow.

Your mind is strong, Your heart will know,

You will lose only that

Of which your heart does let go.

A tear glides down my cheek.

I don't want to let go. *Give me strength not to let him go,* I plead.

Will Takano and I be allies in this fight, or enemies? I won't let him go, without a fight. I won't give him over to Dukath so easily.

Go now, take Takano Rynn's sword, the voice continues.

Within it lies the strength of the Gifted Lords,

But do not use its power

Do not use its strength

Do not by its might
Allow it, to you tempt.

Then the voice is gone, yanked from my mind.

There is only silence left. A peacefulness settles over me. My ears wake to a beeping sound, my eyes to the bright overhead lights that have come on.

"Rita, are you okay?"

It's Beeps. I can't see her but she's near the base of the interrogation chair.

"Beeps? Did I fall asleep? How long was I out?"

"You were still for three and a half minutes. I thought you died." Her beeps are high pitched and I can tell she's scared. "It was dark. I was hiding. I wanted to see if you were okay, so I came out and the lights turned back on. But you didn't say anything when I talked to you. You didn't move at all."

I swallow hard. "I'm sorry. I'm okay."

The words I heard come back to me, *you will lose only that, of which your heart does let go.*

"I will never let go of you, Beeps. Okay?" I try to look down at her from the chair. "Ever."

She stops moving around but doesn't respond. Then a moment later she says. "Does that mean you will carry me all the time?"

I laugh. "I mean, I will never let us be apart, okay?"

"Okay."

"Can you help me out of these restraints?"

"I'll try." Beeps extends one of her tool extensions towards the chair arm restraints. "Are we going to run away?"

"Yes, but not yet."

"I can't undo it." She withdraws her extensions then takes out a tiny screwdriver.

"Brilliant!" I say. My heart beats faster. I can't shake the feeling that Randon or Takano will walk in at any moment. "Hurry, Beeps!"

Beeps unscrews the hinges on my right arm restraint and a piece of metal clatters to the floor. I flinch, worried the sound might alert Takano. Beeps hurries to the other side of the chair so fast that she loses balance and scrapes the side of her head on the shiny floor.

"It's okay, it's okay," I say to her. "I've got this one." With my free hand I unlatch the other arm band and then bend down to free my feet, too.

"Rita, are they going to hurt you?"

I climb down from the chair, my muscles stiff and my wrists burning.

"No." I wrap my arms around her small metal body. "We'll be just fine. I promise." I pull back to look at her. She's got skid marks on the side of her head and one of her doors is dented in. I run my fingers over the markings on her head. I know she doesn't have pain sensors but I blink back tears anyway. "How's your head? Can you move it around just fine?"

"Yes." Beeps drops her head down slowly. "I don't understand. I thought Takano liked me."

"He does." I pat her little body. "He's just dealing with a lot right now, being back again with Randon. And I think Dukath has some kind of influence over him."

"He was yelling at you."

I frown, not sure what to say.

"If we leave Takano here," Beeps continues, "will Randon kill him?"

"No. I don't think they'll kill Lord Morlin either. I think they need him alive, and that they need all of us who still have the power of the Gift to be kept alive, to do whatever they're planning."

"What are they planning?"

"I don't know, but I know what we have to do. We have to go to Orusk."

"But Randon said Orusk was destroyed."

"I don't think it was. I think Randon is lying."

"So, we won't see Takano again?"

"Well, I have to get his sword from him first, before we leave."

Beeps lets out a worried beep.

"I just need you to stay close to me, okay?" I say. "And out of sight and out of the way so you don't get hurt."

Beeps nods.

"We need a plan and I'll need your help."

"I found a way to connect myself to the ship's computer while I was hiding under the control panel," Beeps says. "Will that help?"

"Brilliant girl!" I say. "That will definitely help."

CHAPTER 39

I LOOK DOWN FROM my hiding spot in the ceiling, where the metal tiles open into a ventilation system. Beeps leans her head back to look up at me from down below.

"Ready?" I say to her.

"Yes," she beeps in reply. She rolls into the open panel with the exposed wires.

I see a few sparks fly and then the alarm sounds.

I close my eyes and take a slow breath. I can do this.

I have to try.

A moment later the door flies open and Takano strides in. Randon follows in after him. They stop in front of the interrogation chair.

"She's gone." Takano's voice is monotone.

Randon turns to the two soldiers who were likely guarding the door from the outside.

"You weak minded fools!" he yells at them.

"But she didn't leave the room, Sir," one of them says.

"No, of course she didn't," Randon says with calm sarcasm. "She used mind manipulation on you so you'd forget!" he yells, making them jump. "Now go find her!"

They hurry out.

"We don't need to tell Dukath just yet," Randon says to Takano. "We'll find her soon enough." He turns and walks out of the room. The door slides closed behind him. The green light on the door access panel turns red, locking the doors.

Beeps did it! She locked Takano in. But it was too easy. He didn't even try to leave the room. Why?

My palms feel clammy and slippery against the metal bars I'm holding onto. I watch as Takano walks around the room, then stands by the interrogation chair. He removes his hood and stops pacing.

"I know you're in here, Rita."

I hold my breath, my heart pounding in my ears. Takano pulls out his sword and begins to walk again, looking around as he does.

"You're only just beginning to understand your powers," he says. His cloak moves behind him as he takes slow steps.

I wait.

"I can feel you. I know you're here."

He stops, almost directly below me. My legs tremble with the effort of keeping the position I'm in. Just a little further...

Takano takes another step forward.

Now!

I jump, landing on Takano's back.

He falls forward and we tumble to the floor. His sword flies from his hand and slides across the room.

I jump for it but Takano pulls me back by my foot. I kick him away and he pushes me hard with a burst of his power. I fly forward but stop myself before hitting the wall.

I do a quick spin in the air, turning to face him. He reaches for his sword and I lock him in a hold before his hand clasps around it.

"Beeps!" I yell.

She comes rolling out from beneath a panel and slides the sword over to me. I have to release Takano, to pick it up. A second is all he needs to lock me in a hold, too.

"Let me go, Rita."

"You let *me* go," I say.

The muffled sounds of blasters hitting the outside of the interrogation room door catches both of our attention. Randon and his soldiers are trying to blast through. Beeps has locked the door, but it won't hold for long.

I lift up Takano's sword.

"Stop!" Takano yells. The intensity of his voice makes me drop the sword. It lands between us. Our eyes lock.

"Don't use it," Takano says. "Please."

I can't get to the sword now, with Takano's energy pushing me back, and he can't get to it either. We circle around the sword.

"Randon is going to betray you," I tell him. "He's going to kill you."

"Don't you think I know his plans?" Takano sneers.

"You said we'd destroy Dukath together and rule the Galaxy."

The banging on the other side of the door gets louder. I close my eyes and focus on Takano's thoughts. He'll either release his hold on me, so I don't read his mind, and then I'll be free to grab the sword, or he'll keep locked onto me and I'll be able read his mind with the open channel between us. I can find out what's really going on in his head.

His hold on me wavers for a second when I push into his thoughts. I prepare to lunge for the sword, but he doesn't let me go.

You promised you wouldn't read my mind, he thinks.

I instantly start to back off. But then I notice something unfamiliar inside of him, it seeps into my mind like black oozing oil.

Join us, Rita, and we'll rule together. I recognize the slow forming words from the view screen earlier.

It's Dukath.

Use the sword. It will make you strong and combine our powers.

"No," I struggle to pull out of Takano's thoughts, but now I can't. His dark eyes don't look like him at all.

I have him under my power, the voice continues, *and now, I will have you, too.*

No... My strength wavers.

All of a sudden the doors blast open and the spell over me breaks. Debris from the blast flies at us and a large piece of metal knocks Takano down, freeing me from his hold. Soldiers pile in, shouting and firing their weapons. I grab my sword and deflect the shots as fast as I can, sending them back from the direction they came. They hit the soldiers in the chest, making them fly backwards. There are too many blaster shots to stop. One shoots past my ear.

I scream and duck, waiting for the inevitable. But it doesn't come. The shots aren't firing at me anymore. I look up. The soldiers are being shot at, getting hit from behind. Some turn to fight back, but they're overtaken by the surprise attack and a moment later they're all down.

The ones shooting at them are wearing Opposition solider uniforms. One of the soldiers looks familiar.

"Parrin?"

Parrin steps over the pile of Ruling Order soldiers on the ground. "Rita!" He runs over to me, a look of relief on his face.

I get up but then a force pulls me backwards. My back crashes into Takano's chest and a second later a strong arm is wrapped around my chest from behind, holding me firmly. I grab at his arm, but I can't break free of his iron grasp. His chest is like a brick wall against my back.

Parrin and the others point their blasters at Takano and he stretches his free hand out towards them.

"*You...*" Takano growls from behind me.

Parrin begins to choke, his hands grasping at his own throat in surprise.

"Parrin!" I cry out. "Stop! Takano! Don't hurt him!"

One of the Opposition soldiers shoots his blaster at Takano and he releases Parrin long enough to deflect the shot back at them. It flies towards Parrin instead.

"Watch out!" I yell.

Parrin ducks and I drop all my weight down, somersaulting forward. The unexpected move catches Takano off guard and he's left exposed to weapons fire.

Parrin shoots at him and Takano cries out. He tosses Parrin into the wall with an invisible blast of his power. Beeps has become frantic, rolling in circles. I look from Parrin to Takano. They're both hurt.

More Ruling Order soldiers arrive, firing at the Opposition fighters, who turn to defend themselves.

Takano is on the floor, bleeding. Another shot hits his shoulder and he jerks back. It's Parrin firing. He's moving in on him.

"Stop!" I yell, tossing Parrin back with a burst of energy. He slams against a control panel behind him and cries out in surprise. He blinks, stunned, and gives me a look of betrayal.

A Ruling Order soldier fires at him and I deflect the shot so he doesn't get hit. I fend off the shots as Parrin pulls himself together and runs over to me.

"Come on!" he yells over the blaster shots. He reaches his hand out to me and I take it. My hip jerks backward and I look back. Takano is pulling on my belt. I slide backwards and Parrin grips my hand tighter, pulling me in the opposite direction. Takano struggles to put my sword back into its sheath. He's hurt.

Beeps zaps Takano's leg with a live wire that she has dragged out from under the control panels. He cries out and lets go of his hold on me, sending Parrin and I flying forward.

The Ruling Order Soldiers are dead all around us. I no longer have to defend myself and Parrin. Apparently there weren't enough soldiers that came with Randon, to fight win against the number of Opposition fighters who came to rescue me.

They continue to shoot at Takano and he holds them off as best he can, but there are too many of them.

Parrin pulls my arm. "Let's go, Rita! This is a rescue mission to get you." He gives me a confused look.

The Opposition fighters finally stop shooing and retreat, leaving Takano for dead. They run down the hall. I run with them.

But I know Takano's still alive. I can sense it.

He's badly hurt. I want to go back, but I let Parrin pull me after him. Tears blur my vision and I don't see where we're running.

I can't reason with Takano anyway. Dukath is in his head now, bound to him in a way he wasn't before, not when we were on Aylvon.

Is that why Takano was hiding out there? To get away from Dukath's reach?

We stop running and the air changes. It's cold now. The shouting fades off and I try to blink my tears away to orient myself. I don't know where we are. Parrin shoves me forward, into a small shuttle pod. He gets in beside me, pulling the heavy hatch down and shutting us in.

The muffled silence in the shuttle pod is so devoid of sound that it's deafening and painful to my ears.

There is a rapid pressure change as Parrin straps me into the seat, then secures himself. He takes the controls and the ship lifts, so fast that my stomach lurches.

We blast into the darkness of space, leaving Takano behind. I'm shaking violently and still catching my breath. Parrin is speaking but I can't understand his words. All I hear are Dukath's words, over and over in my mind. *I have him under my power and now I will have you, too.*

CHAPTER 40

"**B**EEPS?" I WHISPER. SHE turns her little head towards me. I'm glad she's here. If she didn't have important data inside of her, would the Opposition have even bothered to save her from Takano's ship?

"Yes, Rita?" she says.

"I just got scared for a second that you weren't here." I sigh and lie back onto the most comfortable bed I've ever been in. Yet, I can't seem to relax.

A breeze blows sheer curtains in through the large archway windows, which have no glass to shield the room from the wind. Outside, I only see sky, making it look like the stone room I am in is hovering above the waters below, rather than a being a part of the castle we are at.

The many shades of the setting sun break through the clouds and fog, in colorful streaks. The planet is covered in water, except for the many stone islands jut out from the raging ocean waters. This is where the original Temple was built. This is where the Ancient City once was. A few of the islands are now being used for the Opposition base, headquarters and living quarters, where troops can rest between missions.

The Ancient Temple is not on this island, but near the Base Headquarters. This one holds all the living quarters of the Temple Monks of long ago, according to Parrin, and has been preserved for the Opposition living quarters. The Monks are no longer here, but their spirits seem to haunt the hallways.

I look up at the ceiling. The castle is made of white sandstone and pillars, with archways and open rooms built into the sharp mountain side of a rock island. There's no escaping the sounds of the waves crashing against the rock, below. It fills the hallways and rooms like a rushing wind. It lulls me to sleep. I sit up, trying to fight off the drowsiness. I don't want to sleep. I don't want to have another nightmare.

"I can't lie here anymore," I say to Beeps. "I'll fall asleep if I do."

"Isn't that what General Anias wants you to do?" she asks.

"Yes, well..." I swing my bare legs over the side of the bed. "He's not the one who has to dream my dreams."

Beeps does her questioning sound but I don't feel like explaining it to her.

The marble floor feels cool and smooth beneath my bare feet. It covers all the floors, in the rooms and hallways, and is also used for the archway bridges that connect the gathering space to the dining hall and the residence area.

"I guess the sun just doesn't want to set," I say, squinting towards the horizon, where the orange sun still persists.

"It doesn't fully set on Antineon," Beeps explains. "It circles around the horizon."

"Oh." I smile. "This planet understands me then. It doesn't let nighttime ever come."

Beeps does her questioning beep again but stops mid beep. She's beginning to understand that I don't always want to explain my comments.

"Want to go explore this castle a bit?" I say to her.

She does a little spin and I take that as a yes.

CHAPTER 41

THE TALL PILLARS IN the main hall cast long shadows across the marble floor. Fog spills in through an open balcony. I walk towards it, my bare feet sticking to the smooth marble. The sleeping gown I was given to wear flows around my legs. It is made of a light material, like the sheer fabric of the curtains on the windows, so light that I feel undressed.

The entire monastery is a combination of old and new. Old pillars and crumbling white stone walls, new marble floors and large potted plants set in various places. The earthy smell of the dirt and roots from the plants in the main hall, reminds me of being with Takano in the forests of Aylvon.

My chest aches and I turn my attention to the sound of the ocean waves crashing on the rocks far below. My mouth tastes salty with the moisture that hangs in the air. The stickiness mattes my hair to my face.

I refused food when we arrived, but now that everyone has finally gone to their rooms, and no one is looking at me or asking me questions, I'm ready to eat something.

My stomach grumbles and I crave a spoonful of the sweet bread pudding Takano made for me during our days together.

"Beeps, can you take me to the dining hall? I don't remember the way. Maybe there's still some food left over on the tables, that we can eat."

Beeps zooms ahead, spinning in one spot first before finding some traction on the smooth floors. I follow after her, my feet slapping the marble as I go. Now that we've made some distance between us and the sleeping area, I don't have to tiptoe around and be quiet.

The dining hall faces away from the never-ending sunset, towards the cloudy side of the island, which sits in dark shadows. The long, dining room table has two large bowls at the center filled with some fruit I'm unfamiliar with. I grab one of them.

"You couldn't sleep either?"

The voice startles me and I drop the fruit back into the bowl, which clatters on the table.

"General Anias," I gasp. "I didn't see you there."

"Don't worry." He smiles at me. "I'm glad you're here. Please, have a seat." He pats the chair beside him and I sit down.

"You're not sleeping well?" I ask, smoothing out my nightgown and sitting up straight. It's strange to think the General is Takano's father. He seems nothing like him, in temperament at least.

He has kind eyes and a frail form in his old age. Yet, I can tell he is a determined and courageous person, which I also see in Takano.

"Go ahead and eat." He gives me an encouraging nod. Now that we're both sitting close to one another, I can see the tiredness in his eyes.

"You're worried about Takano?" I ask. He frowns and looks towards the windows. I shouldn't have asked. "I'm sorry. It's none of my business."

"It is your business," he says, then sighs. "I won't bombard you with questions this late at night, but tomorrow we'll talk about Bryn. Or perhaps I should say, Takano Rynn, as he is called now." He looks out at the sunset and takes a slow breath. "And we'll discuss strategy with the others."

I nod and he gets up.

"I'm boiling some water. How about some tea?"

"Sure, yes. Thank you." I return his smile as best I can. My stomach is already in knots at the thought of a long conversation over tea with Takano's father. And he called him Bryn, instead of Rynn. Is that the name he was born with?

The stillness all around is eerie as I wait for General Anias to return. The only movement is the leaves of the nearby plants, when a breeze wafts up from the ocean below.

I begin to imagine shapes of cloaked monks in every pillared corner. My tired mind is playing tricks on me. I rub at my eyes. Surely the ghosts of all the murdered Temple Monks haunt these white castle walls. I push the strands of my hair, damp with moisture, away from my face. Would a place like this have any hair accessories, or even a comb? How do the female Opposition fighters keep their hair out of their faces?

"Here we are," General Anias says, returning with two clay mugs of tea. I take one gratefully, wrapping my chilled fingers around its heat and breathing in the exotic aroma.

"Where's Takano's sword?" I ask, trying to sound nonchalant, but realizing too late that the question is a bit abrupt. I take a sip of tea to avoid the General's eyes. I have to get the sword. The voice that spoke to me when I was tied up in the interrogation chair was clear about my mission. I don't know where the voice came from, but my Gift sense tells me I can trust it.

The General takes a seat beside me and clears his throat. "It's locked away safely in a chamber. It's dangerous. No one should ever use it, especially not someone who is Gifted." He glances pointedly at me then continues. "Bryn could barely contain its power, and he was trained by the masters."

I nod. Now definitely isn't the time to get into what I intend to do with the sword. He's right, it is dangerous and I'm glad it's locked away. It would be easy for anyone to justify using it, for self-defense or to win against evil. But its power is dangerous to the one who wields it.

I blow on my tea and close my eyes at the delicious scent. "He still has goodness left in him," I say softly, clutching the clay mug even tighter.

General Anias doesn't respond, so I look up at him. He's blinking back tears. I shouldn't have said anything. "I'm more tired than I thought," he says, clearing his throat. "I think I'll take my tea back to my room."

"Of course." I get up when he stands. "Thank you for the tea." I give him a small bow and he sets a large hand on my shoulder.

"Tomorrow, I want to celebrate your safe return. We can discuss your insubordination of stealing a ship later. But for now, go rest, gather your strength." His words remind me of the words I heard when I was in the interrogation chair:

Gather your strength, young one.

The time is now, to rise and fight

Prepare your sword for comes the night

The General leaves and I sit back down. How will I ever be able to tell when it's morning, with the forever sunset on this planet? If I stay in the dining hall too long, the early risers will soon find me and stare at me, or worse, ask me a questions about Takano and my time as his 'prisoner,' as everyone is calling it.

I finish off the tea quickly and get up from the chair.

I have to get out of here.

The sound of trickling water echoes lightly all around me in the dining hall, bouncing off the stone walls. I imagine a fountain nearby, like the one back home. I suddenly want to find the water that I hear. Whenever I would need to think in peace, back home, I would go to the fountain in the Temple courtyard. Watching the sunlight or moonlight glistening off the tiny waves, always calmed me.

"Come on, Beeps." I get up and stretch. "Let's continue our exploring."

Beeps spins around and follows me as I walk. My legs feel weak and my chest heavy.

"Are you okay?" Beeps asks, rolling alongside me.

"I just need to sit down a minute," I say. "But first we need to get out of the dining hall."

My eyes burn and I sniffle, feeling dizzy and unlike myself.

We leave the open dining area and enter a smaller hallway that leads to another part of the castle. I spot a bench a little farther down. It faces the foggy archway windows. The ocean's crashing waves against the rocks below sprinkle water up onto the balcony.

I take a seat on the bench with a heavy sigh.

"Beeps, something's wrong with me."

"Maybe you're sleepy from the sleep tea the General gave you," she says.

I groan. Sleep tea? Shoot.

I want to be angry. I want to tell Beeps to hurry and get me some kind of strong morning drink, but I'm already drifting off. I down onto the bench.

My damp nightgown sticks to my body, but I'm too tired to pull it away from my skin. My bare feet are cold but there's no blanket, no warm fire like back home. The cool breeze over my exposed skin and the sound of the crashing waves lull me to sleep.

"Just like you imagined it would be," a low, familiar voice says. I sit up. "Before you'd go to sleep each night, back home."

A tall figure materializes from the fog.

"Takano?"

CHAPTER 42

I STAND UP SLOWLY, my muscles aching. Where's Beeps? She's not by the bench anymore. I look in every direction, my tiredness completely forgotten. "Beeps!"

"She's not here," Takano says.

His presence fills my very being, even though I don't turn to look at him.

"You can't be here," I say. "And what do you mean Beeps is gone?"

"Robots don't dream," Takano says.

I look up at him. "Dream?"

He smiles and my breath catches. He looks different, happier somehow and calmer than I've ever seen him. He comes closer, the fog moving around his cape as he steps out from the shadows. He's not wearing his black clothes, but dark blue instead. The color contrasts with his pale complexion and dark hair, and makes him look like a wealthy ruler of a kingdom.

His glance travels over me and suddenly my sleeping gown feels invisible. I hug my arms around my chest and look down to see if the light fabric is still sticking to my skin, in a revealing way. But I'm not wearing my sleeping gown anymore. Instead, I've got a long evening gown on, also a midnight blue color like Takano's royal outfit. My gown reflects the dim light from the fading sun, making the fabric sparkle like snow under moonshine.

I run my hand over the front of the dress. "I don't understand," I whisper. "I'm awake, I'm not dreaming. And I wasn't wearing this gown before I sat down on the bench."

Takano closes the distance between us and takes my hand in his. It feels warm and familiar.

"This is a different kind of dream," he says, his eyes searching mine. "We're in it together."

What does he mean? I have to know more. I have to know what he's thinking.

I close my eyes and center my focus on the Gift inside of me. My eyes fly open. It isn't there! There's no Gift, no power, nothing...

Takano rests his hands on my shoulders and leans his forehead against mine.

"I can't read you," I say, my voice shaking.

"You don't need to," Takano whispers. "You're already inside my mind."

"Or you're inside of mine," I say.

Takano straightens and looks around the spacious room. "You could be right. I've never seen this place before."

I blink, trying to imagine a reality outside of this one, but nothing could be more real than this moment. I've never felt more awake. Am I really dreaming?

"I'm not going to tell you where I am," I say. If I'm really in Takano's mind, then Dukath will find out where I am, and where the Opposition Base is.

"I won't ask you to." Takano holds out his hand to me and I take it. He's not smiling anymore. He leads me to a curtain that wasn't there before, with bright lights behind it. I squint as we near it. He moves the curtain aside and I look in.

It's an operating room. The doctors are frantically working on a patient in a bright and sterile looking hospital room. They don't take any notice of us as they operate. I gasp.

The patient is Takano.

I turn away, shutting my eyes tight.

"It looks worse than it actually is," Takano says beside me. The bright lights of the surgical room fade away behind my closed eyelids and a darkness settles in around us again.

I open my eyes again. We're in Takano's cave now, on Aylvon. Candlelight dances in the cool breeze wafting in from the cave entrance, carrying with it the sweet, earthy smell of the forest outside.

I glance around the room. Everything is exactly the way I remember it. Even the bowls have leftover bread pudding in them. I'm wearing the black clothes I had on during my time here.

"Takano?" I turn and find him sitting on the side of the bed, shirtless, just like my first night on Aylvon.

"Is this a memory?" I ask.

Takano's eyes dance in the candlelight.

"No." He pats the bed. I walk over and sit down, close enough that our arms touch. "This cave is in both of our memories," Takano continues. "But we're making a new memory now."

"Have we met in dreams before?"

"Maybe."

I try not to stare at Takano, sitting in the soft candlelight, without his shirt on.

"If you would ever sleep," Takano gives me a sideways glance, "then we could meet in our dreams more often. How did they finally get you to go to bed? Did you faint from exhaustion?"

I laugh, then quickly stop when I see Takano's eyes have gone dark. "Or is Parrin holding you in his arms so you're not scared?" he asks.

My cheeks flare up. I press my lips together tight. I will not even dignify such a ridiculous question, with a response.

"They gave me a sedative," I say, finally.

"Same with me," Takano's expression softens.

I look away from him. How could he imply that Parrin and I would be sleeping in the same bed? It's like he doesn't know me at all.

I sigh, remembering how Takano held me the second night I was here in this cave. I guess I did lay down with him after hardly knowing him at all. But does he think I would let just anyone hold me at night, so that I won't have nightmares? Maybe he does.

I glance over at the bedside table where both of our swords lie, side by side. The cave feels incomplete without Beeps. I need to get away from Takano, not just because he hurt my feelings, but because I want to wake and make sure Beeps is okay. And maybe also because he is shirtless. It shouldn't have such an effect on me when I'm mad at him, and yet it still does.

"I want to wake up," I say firmly. "I need to make sure Beeps is okay."

"She's guarding you as you sleep," Takano says. His hair hangs over his eyes and I resist the urge to move it off his forehead. Instead I grip the edge of the make-shift mattress tightly with both hands.

"You seem different," I say. "More relaxed."

"I am," Takano replies. "Dukath doesn't have influence on me in my dreams. That's why he doesn't let me sleep."

"What?" I look up to see if he's serious. He is.

"He knows that in my sleep he has no stronghold on my mind, so he keeps me from dreaming."

"But, you're dreaming now."

"I'm also on the operating table. So it couldn't be helped."

My shoulders tense. "You're actually in that operating room right now?"

"I'll be fine. They're fixing some shattered ribs." Takano's hands are also gripping the edge of the mattress like mine are, and I smile. In some ways, we are similar.

His gaze travels down to my lips. "I don't know how long the surgery will take," he continues. "But afterwards, Dukath won't let me fall into any more deep sleeps like this one, again." He swallows, looking away. "I don't know the next time I'll see you. I don't know where you are right now."

I gather my hair into a ponytail, lifting it off my neck, using the distraction to take time to think. Should I tell him where I am? Will he ever be free of Dukath, when he's awake?

Takano hands me a hair elastic and I smile, taking it from him.

"Where did you find this?"

He reaches his hand up and touches my hair, setting it gently to rest on my shoulder. The unexpected gentleness breaks my resolve not to cry and my eyes fill with tears.

"You left me in that horrible interrogation chair." My lips quiver and the tears begin to fall. "You hurt Beeps…"

"Rita." Takano's eyes turn sad and my heart aches.

What am I doing? Why am I blaming him when he was just under Dukath's influence?

"Why can't you break away from him?" I whisper.

"Because if I do, I'll die."

"What?" My breath catches.

Takano rubs at his eyes, his shoulders slumping forward. "Promise me you won't use the sword."

"Your sword? It's locked away."

"Good. Leave it there."

"But I need to take it to—"

"No," Takano booms. "Don't put it in your hand. Don't touch it."

"But—"

"Promise me." His expression is so serious that all my words catch in my throat and I simply nod my head in agreement. "You need to kill Dukath. *You* need to do it."

"Me?"

"Yes."

"But you said if Dukath dies, you'll die, too."

Takano nods, looking down at the ground.

"While you were here," I motion around the room, "you were separated from Dukath, weren't you?"

"Not entirely." Takano rubs his face with both hands. "He knows my thoughts when I'm awake. I'll remember this dream. There's just no way to escape him. It's better if I die, than be Dukath's pawn forever."

"No!"

Takano grabs my shoulders. "Rita, look at me!"

I press my palms to my ears to block out his words.

Takano moves my hands away. I try to resist, but he's stronger.

"I thought I'd be more powerful with you," he says. "I thought I could break away from Dukath, because your hold on me seemed stronger than his was."

"My hold on you?"

"Yes. But I was wrong. And I almost took you to Dukath—"

"Don't." I shake my head, not wanting to think of how betrayed I felt when Takano turned on me. "Please."

"Rita, listen to me. I've seen a vision." He lets go of my arms and runs his hands through his hair. "I saw you, turning to the evil side of the Gift." He frowns. "Don't let that happen."

"I'd never."

"Don't say never." Takano takes my hands in his, interlacing our fingers.

"Then you shouldn't say that you'll never break away from Dukath either." I grip his hands tight.

Takano gives me a questioning look. Then his expression suddenly changes. "You should wake up now," he says, looking down at my lips.

"Why?"

He lets go of my hands.

"Takano?" I reach up to touch his face. Did he see another vision?

"Just wake up." He grabs my wrist.

"No, not yet."

"Why don't you ever *listen*," he says, his jaw clenching tight.

"Because you can't mind-control me while we're in here, remember?"

"Attachments are forbidden, Rita." Takano's eyes search mine. He lets go of my hand and we sit in an awkward silence.

I pull at the ends of my hair, twirling the strands with my fingers. I was worried he'd seen another vision of some horrible fate, but now I understand his urgency of wanting the dream to end. He's afraid of how attached we're getting.

Takano moves closer, taking my hand away from my hair and running his fingers through the strands instead. His touch makes the roots of my hair tingle. The sensation moves down my spine and into the small of my back. I arch forward and Takano pulls me against him in response. He presses his lips to mine, stifling my gasp of surprise.

I push against his chest but he holds me tighter, lifting me into his lap. My legs wrap around his waist.

"Rita..." His hand clenches a fistful of my hair and I tilt my head back.

A loud crash startles us both and we jump away from the bedside table where our swords are now vibrating with energy. I can feel the heat radiating off of them, on the side of my face. All of a sudden, Takano's sword flies through the air, almost hitting us. I scream and Takano pulls me out of the way.

We spin around to see where the sword flew to. A dark figure has it in his clutches. He's standing in the corner of the room, dressed in a Dark Master's cloak. His eyes glow red. He holds up the sword, anger and hate flashing in his eyes...In *her* eyes.

I gasp. The Dark Master...is me.

CHAPTER 43

"W AKE UP!" SOMEONE SHAKES me by the shoulders. "Rita, wake up!"

"Parrin?"

"Are you okay?" he asks. I throw my arms around him and hold on for dear life.

"I don't want to turn into a Dark Master or join the Ruling Order! That's not me. It won't be me!" I cry and my body trembles uncontrollably.

Parrin sets a hand to my back, as though to hug me, but then lets go, as though unsure.

"You'll never be a Dark Master," he says. "Or join the Ruling Order."

I release him, pulling myself together. Takano said Parrin was once a soldier in the Ruling Order. I glance at him now.

He seems too timid to be one of those soldiers. "I'm sorry," I say, wiping at my eyes. "I had a bad dream."

"It's okay," Parrin reassures me. "I get them too."

I look down at my hands. They're still shaking. "I killed soldiers..."

Parrin doesn't reply and I look up to see his reaction. But he only seems concerned for me.

"On Takano's ship," I continue, "when you guys came to rescue me. I deflected their shots right back at them so they'd stop. But I could have deflected the shots into the wall or—"

"But then they would have kept shooting," Parrin says.

I can't look at him. What if one of those soldiers was an old friend of his?

"I already have that evil inside of me," I continue. "Since I started using my Gift, I've hurt people. Killed people too." I cover my face with my hands.

"So have I," Parrin says softly. "But we're stopping the Ruling Order from destroying entire planets and civilizations, from taking away all the peace in the Galaxy, so children can live safe lives, without fear of their planet being blown up for no reason at all."

"So the good of the many, outweighs sacrificing the few?" A chill runs through me.

"I suppose."

I stare at Parrin for a moment. Does he realize his philosophy is the same as Takano's?

"You're not Gifted," I continue. "If I kill, I choose a path which will lead to a lot of deaths in the future, because it's so much easier for me to kill. And I'll become like Dukath."

Parrin shakes his head and smiles, like what I've said is silly. But my heart races in panic. I can't escape the vision of me as a Dark Master in my dream, my eyes filled with hate and rage.

"It doesn't work that way." Anias' voice startles us both.

Parrin and I turn to see him approaching. We slide apart from each other on the bench. He's dressed in his General's uniform now. His long, gray hair is tied back and he has a serious expression on his face.

He looks intently at me. "The evil path isn't something you simply fall into," he says. "It's not something you catch like a virus. It's a conscious choice. You have to choose it, freely and of your own will."

"But Takano doesn't." I stop, realizing what I've just said to Takano's *father*.

Beeps rolls up to my feet and bumps my leg gently. I rest my hand on her head, instantly soothed by her presence.

"Maybe he doesn't actively choose it anymore," Anias says. "But he did choose in the beginning. He chose to become a Dark Master and to follow Dukath. And he chose to kill the rest of the Gifted Lords so he could harness their power, for Dukath."

"So now he's trapped under Dukath's spell forever?" I ask.

Parrin stays quiet, listening. I must sound crazy to him, being concerned about Takano, and afraid that I will turn into a Dark Master against my will.

"Rita..." The General gives me a tired smile. "You'll never be like Bryn. I know the Gift is a powerful and scary thing but—"

"Don't say never," I say softly, remembering Takano's words.

"Granted, you will need practice controlling your emotions," Anias continues. "So they don't control you and make your decisions for you. That's the danger of the evil side of the Gift, and the lure of powerful weapons like this new one the Ruling Order is building, or of Bryn's sword, which is also full of power. These can tempt you. But in the beginning it is always your choice; a series of choices, up until the point where you've made too many bad ones and are no longer in control of them."

"Unredeemable." The word slips out of my mouth before I realize what I've said.

Anias frowns but doesn't answer. Parrin looks down at the ground.

"Enough of the heavy talk," Anias says. "Breakfast will be an informal gathering this morning, but this afternoon I'll be giving an announcement in the outdoor amphitheater before our afternoon meal. I think we've had enough of battles for the time being."

He looks from me to Parrin, then back again. "You two take a break. The Galaxy wasn't built in one day, and neither will it be saved in one day."

Parrin and I both nod and then Anias leaves.

The hall is bustling with people now, Opposition fighters dressed in their plain civilian clothes, carrying bowls of food as they take their seats and chatter.

"Are Opposition fighters always so cheerful?" I whisper to Parrin.

He laughs out loud and it startles me. Has it really been so long since I've heard a heartfelt laugh?

"They're just happy to have won a victory," Parrin says. "A small victory in a big battle, but still a victory."

Does he mean rescuing me?

"I'm sorry," Parrin continues. "Everyone's celebrating when you've just recently been kidnapped and held hostage by an evil Lord. It must seem weird that they're happy."

"No."

"Would it help to know that Takano's probably dead by now?"

"What?" I gasp.

"We don't know for sure." Parrin shrugs, his leather jacket moving with his shoulders. "But two of our fighter planes hit the warp core reactor on Randon's battleship early this morning and blew the whole thing up."

My eyes go wide and I wrap my arms around myself. There would have been so many soldiers on that ship, so many lives lost. Could Takano have been on that ship with him, too? No, I saw him in my dream. That had to be real, I couldn't have made it all up. We talked...

"There are reports," Parrin continues, "of escape pods, but we know Randon wasn't on any of them. Takano may have escaped, using his Gift powers or something, but Morlin wasn't on that ship, thank goodness. We think he might be with Dukath right now."

A chill runs down my spine and I feel exposed in my sleeping gown. "Parrin, I have to go get dressed."

"Oh." Parrin gets up quickly, offering me his hand. Such a strange gesture, considering there's no reason for me to need help standing up from a bench. I almost don't take it, but then I look up and see the expression on his face, full of kindness. He wants to feel he's being of some service. I give him a smile and take his hand.

"Let me walk you to your room," he says.

"Thanks," I nod and walk close to him to hide my nightgown from the others in the dining hall.

Parrin smiles, seeming to enjoy my closeness.

"Let's hurry," I say, walking faster.

Parrin nods and picks up his pace beside me.

CHAPTER 44

T HE AMPHITHEATER IS CROWDED with Opposition fighters, pilots and officers, all discussing strategies for the next battle plan. I look out across the waters. A beam of sunlight streams down through an opening in the clouds, like a spotlight shining onto the neighboring island. I pull my shawl tighter around my shoulders.

That is where I want to be, under that sunbeam and away from all these people who think Takano is the enemy. They're here to celebrate his possible death.

I close my eyes and see him sitting on his bed beside me. He said he was okay, but hurt. They were operating on him. I try not to focus on the worry that creeps in. He'll be fine. The Ruling Order must have some of the best doctors in the galaxy.

"May I please have your attention?" General Anias' exclamation breaks through the chatter, and the voices quiet down as everyone begins to take a seat on the steps.

At the front, sits a wide archway covered in thriving green vines. Three, throne-like seats sit under the archway, where Anias is standing to address the group. He waits until the chatter dies down, then speaks again.

"Today," he begins, "we're gathering not to discuss a battle, or mourn our dead, but to celebrate a victory."

Cheers erupt from the fighters and a chill of excitement runs through me.

"Rita," the General says, looking at me. I tense. "Will you please come up here?"

All eyes turn to me.

I quickly rise, stepping around those sitting on the step below me. Thankfully I chose to wear an Opposition fighter's Plain Clothes to this assembly, and not the dark green dress with the embroidering, that was laid out for me in my bed chamber. I don't know who left it there but I asked Parrin to find me a size small in Plain Clothes and bring that to me instead.

I wrap my arms around myself and keep my eyes down as I walk up onto the platform. When I look up, Anias is smiling at me. He gestures for me to stand beside him.

"Tonight, we celebrate the destruction of General Randon's battleship and the safe return of a young Gifted One, the last of her kind, Rita."

Everyone cheers again and my cheeks flush. I clench my jaw. The vision of Takano being operated on is still fresh in my mind from last night. I can't smile or celebrate at that moment, so I settle for a tight-lipped grin instead.

"Food is being prepared in the dining hall," Anias continues over the chatter. "And tonight there will be a feast." He raises his hand to stop everyone from cheering again. "At least, it is the best we could do under the circumstances. The festivities will take place at the Ancient City town square on the Main Island. Shuttles will leave here in a few hours. I'd also like to remind everyone that tomorrow we plan our attack on the Ruling Order's new Super Weapon, and on Dukath. So I expect you all to be up bright and early tomorrow."

There is a hush over the crowd and Anias smiles.

"But tonight, we celebrate!"

Applause breaks out and Anias pats my shoulder before stepping down from the platform to join the others. I step down too, hoping to get lost in the crowd and avoid attention. But the friendly faces single me out; looks of awe, respect and pity for my hostage situation, even some tears. They nod and smile at me, as though I've done something great. My stomach tightens.

I push through the crowd, wanting to get away from them. A young Opposition fighter stops me and shakes my hand. What do they think I did, that would deserve all this recognition?

I smile anyhow, and shake hands, not wanting to ignore anyone. They need to believe in this victory. And in a way, it was a victory. It would not have been good for me to be taken to Dukath and been put under his spell as well.

I spot Parrin sitting on a step nearby. My shoulders relax and I wave to him. His face brightens when he sees me. He waves back and gets up, hurrying down the steps to meet me. He has no trouble pushing through the crowd, in his determination.

"Want to get out of here?" he says.

I nod. "Yes please."

* * *

"Wow, thank you." I take the plate of food out of Parrin's hands. There are so many colors and it all looks so pretty that I don't want to ruin it by eating it. I carry the plate over to the small table at the corner of the bedroom that is now currently mine.

"I brought you a little of everything," Parrin says, smiling proudly.

"You didn't have to," I say, smiling back. "But, thank you."

There are no chairs so I stand, picking up a tiny sandwich with a small marine animal between the bread.

"That one's great," Parrin says. He grabs the edges of the stone table the plate is on, lifting it with some effort. "Parrin, it's fine..." I start to say but he's already carried the table over to the bedside.

"Here, come sit down and eat," he says. I walk over, still holding the tiny sandwich.

"Aren't you going to try it?" Parrin takes a seat at the other end of the bed, giving me room to sit at the table.

"I wish I had your energy." I plop the sandwich into my mouth and take a seat. The meat is chewy, then crunchy in the middle where the bones are. It tastes salty, but has a sweet aftertaste. There's another one on the plate.

"Do you want the second one?" I ask Parrin.

"No, no." He puts up his hands. "I'm full. I tried every piece of food in the dining hall, twice, to make sure I picked the good ones for your plate."

I'm not sure how to respond to that so I play around with my food, trying to decide what to eat next.

"Oh, I didn't get you a drink!" Parrin gets up.

"No, it's fine..." I start to say, but he's already gone. The tiny fish sandwich I ate has triggered my appetite, so I pick up the second one and shove it into my mouth. There are desserts on the plate too and I eat them one by one, trying the different flavors, leaving the chocolate covered dessert for last because chocolate is my favorite. We weren't allowed desserts at the Temple but once a year we got to buy chocolate at the local market for the High Season celebrations. It wasn't sweetened, but Brianne knew how to melt it with milk and honey to make the perfect dessert.

I finish off everything on my plate then pick up the chocolate dessert.

Parrin returns with a mug of water and I set the dessert down. He's out of breath but I pretend not to notice.

"Thank you." I take the mug and drink all the water in seconds. I was more thirsty than I thought.

"Should I get you some more?" Parrin asks.

"No," I shake my head. "I'm fine. Thanks for helping me avoid the crowds earlier."

There's a moment of silence and I twirl a strand of my hair around my finger. I never did end up cutting it. But I'm glad. What if something bad would have happened to me? Now that I know I'm actually Gifted, I don't want to cut it. My powers could be connected to my hair, if the legends are true about Gifted girls.

I look down at the chocolate dessert, still sitting on the plate in front of us. I don't want to eat it in front of Parrin for some reason. I'll save it for later.

Parrin rubs the back of his neck. He is wearing Plain Clothes with his brown leather jacket over top. It suits him.

"How's Star?" I ask.

"Star?" Parrin smiles wide. "She led the flight crew on your rescue mission."

"Really?" I turn to face Parrin. "I'm glad she's okay. Is she here?"

"She likes to keep to herself sometimes, especially after a mission."

Parrin looks like he's about to say more but then stops. He watches me carefully. Our talk of friends makes me think of Beeps and I suddenly want to see her again.

"Do you want to take a nap?" Parrin asks.

"No!" I answer a little too loudly. "Sorry. I just don't want to fall asleep right now."

Parrin nods. "Okay. Do you want to go down to the ocean then?"

I shake my head. "I think I'm going to go see how Beeps is doing."

"She's having some repairs done, I heard," Parrin plays with the cuffs of his jacket. "You really care about that little robot, don't you?"

I nod and my throat clenches with emotion. I don't even like the fact that Beeps is away from me right now, having repairs done.

"Star asked Beeps if she'd like to join her again," Parrin continues. "In one of the fighter planes on our next mission. But Beeps said no. She wants to stay with you instead."

I smile and get up, needing to move around. Last night's dream of Takano, and the vision I had, have left me feeling raw and vulnerable. There's no one I can talk to about it. I don't feel like I know Parrin well enough yet to open up.

I want to talk to Beeps. She hasn't said anything to anyone about our time with Takano on Aylvon, and I think she understands now that there's a difference of opinion among the Opposition, concerning Takano Rynn.

I start to twirl my hair again, pacing the room. I don't like not knowing where Beeps is exactly.

"I need to go find Beeps," I say.

Parrin stands. "Would you like me to go with you?"

I shake my head. "I'll just check in on her. I can meet you at the transport shuttle for the party."

"Sure," Parrin gives a curt nod, no longer smiling. I bite my lip. Did I hurt his feelings?

"I'll see you tonight," he says, then walks out of the room.

I close my eyes and sigh. The last thing I feel like doing is going to a party.

"Oh, you're alone."

I open my eyes again.

"Star?" I gasp. "What are you doing here?"

"I came to rescue you, again!" Star steps out from the shadows in a pilot's uniform. She pulls her helmet off and shakes her blonde head of messy hair.

I laugh. "You mean rescue me from Parrin?"

Star laughs. "I thought he'd be here. I wanted to see him, too."

"He just left." I try to stifle my over-zealous smile. There's no reason why I should feel so happy to see Star, but she feels like family already.

"So, you're on first name basis with Takano Rynn, I hear?" Star winks and my cheeks heat up.

She couldn't possibly know the details, that I spent a night sleeping in Takano's arms. That we almost kissed...

"Come on," she says, nodding her head towards the door. "I'll show you around."

CHAPTER 45

I TUG ON THE green embroidered dress, trying to see my reflection in the hull plating of Star's aircraft. The dress fits a little tight in the hips, but General Anias insisted I wear something other than military sanctioned Plain Clothes, to the party tonight.

Star stops at the copilot's side of the fighter plane.

"Thanks for offering to give me a lift to the party," I say to her.

"Of course!" She smiles and opens the hatch for me. After she showed me around the base, we searched for Beeps and found out she is in the repair warehouse. The bay doors to the warehouse were locked for the day, and there was no one around to open it for us.

"Ready?" Star says, offering me a hand up. She's still in her pilot's uniform and I feel overdressed in my dress. I take her hand and climb up into the plane. She gives me a thumbs up then walks around to the pilot's side and hops in.

Once we're inside, Star hands me a helmet and I put it on. There's so much I want to ask her, but she's been kind of quiet and solemn, as though she's got a lot to think about, and I don't want to be annoying by asking her questions. "I didn't even know they were having a party," Star says into the headset.

"And I didn't even have a choice not to go."

Star starts the engine and we lift off into the fog. We rise so fast that my stomach drops.

"So what happened out there, with Takano Rynn? If you don't mind me asking." Star keeps her eyes on the screens that show her which way to go.

"I discovered he still has some good left in him," I say.

Star keeps her focus on flying and doesn't reply.

We fly in silence for a short while, then the plane drops down again.

"That was quick," I say as we lower gently onto a rock surface.

"It's just two islands over," Star says, leaning back in her seat.

"You seem about as excited as I am for this party." I unlatch my safety belt and sigh. We remove our helmets and I smooth back my braids.

"I don't plan on staying long," Star says.

"Me neither. I want to find someone here who can help me get to Beeps tonight."

"You've really warmed up to her, haven't you?"

I shrug. "She shouldn't have to be in that warehouse all alone all night. Why would they do that?"

Star shrugs. "They probably have her turned off. She won't even know."

"Turned off?" I grip my fingers into a fist, my heart hammering in my chest. They better not have turned Beeps off, or I'll turn *their* lights off with a punch to the face!

Star opens the hatch and jumps out. I follow after her. She waits for me at the steps leading down into the ruins of an ancient city. The fog has lifted a bit and the sun shines onto Star's face, illuminating her short blonde hair like a halo.

"I hate celebrations," she says, crossing her arms.

I sigh, letting go of my anger and worry for Beeps. Robots get turned off sometimes. It's not the same as their entire systems being deleted.

"Why is that?" I ask.

"Because celebrations build camaraderie and friendships. Then you miss those who die even more, when they're killed in battle. I don't want anyone to miss me if I die. I don't want that to distract them in battle and get them killed, too."

I nod, not sure what to say. The sound of a flute playing in the distance drifts up from the ruins below. Star heads down the steps and I follow after her.

We pass by crumbling walls and pillars covered in vines. It reminds me of a graveyard and I shiver.

Star walks fast, like she's on a mission. I hurry to keep up with her. The crumbling city is eerie and I don't want to be left behind.

She reaches the courtyard first and waves at someone in the crowd. The place is filled with people laughing and talking, adding to the festive atmosphere. My shoulders relax and I smile. The ruins don't look so ominous, with all the people around.

"Over here!" Star yells, waving to someone.

I look to see where she's waving. A large man waves back, the tallest in the crowd.

"Charlie!" Star runs down the steps and the tall man named Charlie makes his way to us.

"Star, it's been too long." He says when he reaches us. He gives Star a big hug. "It's great to see you."

Star breaks away from their hug first. "I heard you flew in on the Eagle," she says.

Charlie lets out an excited hoot and nods his head. "We did! The one and only Eagle Ten!"

I laugh at the large man's childlike enthusiasm.

The lively flute song changes to a different tune with a fiddle joining in. I glance around at all the happy faces. They begin to clap along to the beat and a circle forms around us.

"What are they doing?" I ask Star.

"Rita!" I hear my name and look around to see who's calling me.

Parrin waves to me and I wave back.

"Go, dance with Parrin," Star yells over the music.

"What?"

"He wants to dance."

I hesitate for a second then run over to Parrin.

Everyone begins to sing.

Good and pleasing it is,

For friends to dance together

In unity we gather to sing

Our unity will last forever

Everyone joins hands and Parrin takes my hand in his.

"I don't know how to dance," I yell over the music.

"It's simple," he says, looking down at our feet. "Step left, left, right, then left again. And repeat."

I follow along with the others. The circle does a slow turn as everyone steps in the same direction at the same time.

We continue on until the chorus, when suddenly everyone switches places. Before I can figure out where I'm supposed to stand Parrin lifts me off my feet and sets me down on his other side. I laugh in surprise, my skirt spinning around us.

The singing continues and we start the steps again, all moving together.

"I don't think lifting me up is part of the dance," I say to Parrin.

"Sure it is." He winks. "The guys lift the girl in the air."

I look around the circle. Most of the Opposition fighters are men and I don't see any women, except for Star. She's standing outside the circle watching the dancing, with Charlie. They both have silly grins on their faces. For all her talk about not wanting any attachments, I'm glad to see Star has at least one close friendship, with Charlie.

I look back to Parrin, who is dancing with a smile on his face. I already feel like we're friends. It's difficult *not* to be friends with Parrin.

The song comes to the chorus once again and I try to escape before Parrin can lift me up again, but I'm not fast enough though and he grabs my waist, lifting me into the air as high as he can. I laugh out loud, hearing the hoots and cheers around me.

Parrin sets me down but leaves his hands on my waist for a moment too long. His palms feel warm and unfamiliar through the fabric of my dress.

"I have to go," I say over the singing.

A look of surprise crosses over Parrin's face, but I run off before he can respond, leaving him calling after me. I can't stop the tears and I don't want anyone to see them.

This always seems to happen when I'm having too much fun. It makes me feel like I'm disappointing my parents all over again; playing around when I'm supposed to be serious and pay attention. When I'm having fun, they're being taken away from me. It's happening again with Takano. He's hurt and fighting for his life on an operating table, and I'm out here having fun and laughing.

You will lose only that, of which your heart lets go.

I'll lose Takano if I let him go.

I won't let him go.

But I've already left him behind, like I left Morlin. And my parents left me.

I don't look where I'm running, I just run. The familiar movement is a welcomed distraction. If I run long enough, will I fall off the edge of this island, into the ocean below?

I stop when I reach an abandoned fountain with a statue at the center. It sits in the shadows of the stone city and reminds me of home. There are no torches lit here and the air is cooler than it was in the courtyard filled with people. The sounds of their singing and merriment carries on the breeze.

I take a seat at the edge of the fountain and look down at the dry bottom. Where there was once clean water, there is now only dirt. My heart beats wildly from my run and doesn't want to calm down.

I close my eyes and count slowly, the way I used to back home whenever I felt this way.

They didn't come back for me...

I clench my fist to my chest, squeezing my eyes tight. No. They're coming back. They will return, just like I will return for Takano.

I can't seem to breathe. I need more air. But I'm already outside. Where would I go for more air?

When you have the Gift, you are never alone.

The voice startles me. It's the same voice that spoke to me in the interrogation room.

A gust of wind blows my hair away from my face and I breathe freely again.

I look up and see a massive bird, similar to the forest eagles back home, but a lot bigger and a different color. This one is gray with blue feathers, like the colors of the ocean below. It lands on the fountain statue, grasping the head of the stone figure in its large talons.

I get up and step away from the fountain. The bird folds its majestic wings down onto its back, then turns its head to the side, eyeing me.

The ocean waves crash below as we watch each other.

Come... the bird beckons me.

I reach my hand towards it and close my eyes, focusing on the eagle's thoughts, knowing that it wants to communicate.

The eagle lets out a cry that startles me. I open my eyes and see it flap its large wings down in one dramatic movement that raises him into the air and kicks up a cloud of dust from the bottom of the fountain. It hits me in the face and I close my eyes again.

Suddenly I'm weightless, rising up with the effort of heavy wings flapping at my sides. I look down. The fountain is below me now, growing smaller as I rise. I am the eagle. I lift higher and higher, above the clouds. The air catches beneath my wings and I float on the wind.

My mind is one with the eagle. We fly above the fog where the sun sits on the horizon. Its heat warms my wings. There is only the sound of the wind this high up and I no longer hear the celebration below.

The eagle's thoughts are not in words, but visions. I see his memories of the islands on this planet; some lush and green, others made entirely from rock. I see visions of Temple Monks walking on the steps of the monasteries in ages past. There are animals too, which once thrived here; large sea creatures jumping up from the waters below and falling back down with a splash so big that the water reaches to the eagle's wings. The voice of the sea creature's cry pierces my heart.

Then there is only the sound of the wind again and a slow drumbeat deep within me, the eagle's heartbeat.

The vision changes and battleships descend from the sky. They lower down into the fog, firing, destroying. The castle walls crumble into the ocean. They don't look like Ruling Order spaceships, but I can't be sure. The eagle watches as the trees at the top of the islands burn and the rocks crumble. The animals try to flee but have nowhere to go.

> *While evil reigns, the planets die*
> *The forest trees, the sea and sky*
> *No wind for eagles on which to fly*
> *No land for the creatures on which to lie*

With a blast of torpedo fire, another island crumbles, disappearing entirely beneath the waves. The heat from the blast disrupts my flying pattern and I plummet. My heart races and I try to flap my wings, but I'm trapped beneath the rush of hot air. It finally passes and I catch a new pocket of cold wind just in time, leveling out again.

My wings ache with the burn left from the blast. I've got no energy left to flap them. I look for a place to land, but there is none. There is only the raging ocean below, now red with blood. The body of a massive sea creature rises to the surface, its belly up, tossing in the waves. My heart sinks and I continue on, looking for a place to land. There is nowhere. All the islands are gone. This is not a memory of the eagle's, but a vision of what is to come.

All of a sudden, the planet erupts with a blast of heat, an explosion which lifts me up and up, away from the planet that suddenly is no more.

Now I will never land.

I wake on a cold stone floor, my jaw clenched tight and my fists clamped shut.

Go now, Rita, don't wait.
Take Rynn's sword and
change this planet's fate.
Bring the sword to Orusk.
Don't hesitate
or, for the creatures of the Galaxy,
it will be too late.

I sit up with effort, chilled to the bone. The fog has returned and I can't see the sky anymore.

The eagle is gone.

Was it all just a dream?

No, it couldn't have been. I flew. My arms are still heavy with the effort of flapping those massive wings. I still feel the wind on my chest. The eagle led me through a vision, showing me the past and the future.

"Rita!" Parrin runs towards me, appearing from the fog. "There you are. I was looking everywhere for you. People were beginning to worry."

"I'm fine," I say.

Parrin kneels down beside me, a concerned look on his face. "What happened? Are you okay?"

"Parrin?"

"Yes?"

"We need to talk."

CHAPTER 46

I MOVE CLOSER TO the small campfire. The smell of burning wood calms my nerves. I smile at Parrin, glad that he insisted on making a fire. The party is still in full swing. The sounds of singing and laughter drift to us, but we're far enough away that I can relax and not worry about being followed. I reach my palms towards the heat of the fire.

"So you're sure it was a vision from the Gift and not just a dream?" Parrin asks. The flames reflect in his eyes which are still full of concern for me.

I nod. "It was a voice, a clear voice. It wasn't the first time I heard the same message, about the sword. I feel a power when the voice speaks. It gave me strength in the interrogation room, to get free of the chair." I shiver and stop talking. Parrin doesn't know about the interrogation chair.

He takes a deep breath then looks back at the fire. It crackles as we sit silently. I wait for him to ask me more about the interrogation room and my time as Takano's prisoner, but he doesn't and I'm grateful. For a second I think I hear the eagle's cry, but it's only noise from the party on the other side of the small island.

"General Anias told me not to touch the sword," I whisper, staring at the fire. "Even Takano warned me against it."

"What do you think we should do?" Parrin asks. I look up at him in surprise.

"We?" I know what *I* need to do. I need to take the sword to Orusk. But Parrin has nothing to do with that. He could get killed along the way.

"Should we talk to General Anias?" he asks. "We could dispatch a fleet of—"

"No. They'll only stop me from going. I need to do this by myself. The General will never let me, or anyone, take the sword. And the fleet will draw attention from the Ruling Order. I think this would be best done in secret."

"Then I'll go with you."

"No." I shake my head. "I just need you to take me to where the sword is."

"It's in the catacombs."

I turn to Parrin, surprised he knows and so easily told me. He obviously doesn't realize the risk I'd be taking in trying to get that sword.

"Okay. I can find it on my own."

I'll get Parrin to draw me a map. There's no reason to drag him into all this.

"I know I don't have the Gift," Parrin says. "And that you're probably a thousand times stronger than me. But I can help you fly a ship, to the island with the catacombs."

"Beeps will help me."

Parrin seems to think about this as he watches the fire.

"I won't be tempted by the sword," he says softly.

"What?" I ask.

"I don't have the Gift, so the sword won't be dangerous in my hands. I'm terrible with a sword." He sits up straighter. "I should be the one to carry it."

I'm about to object, but then stop. He's right. The sword would be dangerous in my hands. It could even influence me, maybe make me become evil, like the vision I had in my dream with Takano, the vision of me as a Dark Master. But Parrin will never turn into a Dark Master, he isn't Gifted.

"You're right," I say. "When everyone is sleeping, we'll go."

CHAPTER 47

"**T**HANKS AGAIN FOR DOING this," I say to Star. She unlatches the heavy bay doors and they slide open.

"No problem."

"I didn't want to sleep alone," I say sheepishly.

Star gives me a salute and walks inside. I follow in after her. Our footsteps echo in the dark cargo bay. The smell of grease and metal pinch at my nose.

"I mean, I didn't want to leave Beeps in here alone all night, either."

"I understand," Star says. "I'm just glad Charlie had the access codes for this area. Security can be pretty tight on the Base."

I hear the click of switches and the overhead lights come on. Long tables run all around the perimeter of the equipment room, covered in robotic parts and broken equipment. Star walks ahead of me to where Beeps is, surrounded by other small work-robots.

Beeps doesn't acknowledge us but remains quiet and un-moving. I run over to her.

"Beeps?"

She doesn't respond.

"What's wrong with her?" I say to Star, my voice rising.

"She's been turned off."

"Do they have to shut her off to do maintenance?"

"No." Star flips on Beeps' power switch and she comes to life, turning her head left and right. She stops when she sees me.

"Rita," she beeps. "I thought you left without me, to go find Takano."

"No." I give her a hug. "I'd never do that. They were just repairing you." I look down at her tiny compartment door. It's still dented.

"I guess they didn't get around to it yet," Star says.

"I told them I wanted to see you," Beeps says. "But they powered me off." She becomes still suddenly. Then a second later she starts moving again, turning to Star. "I have new programming."

"What kind of new programming?" she asks, her brow furrowed.

"I don't know. I can't access it, but it's taking up a lot of my memory."

I lift Beeps off the table and set her on the ground.

"Let's get you out of here."

"Are we going to find Takano now?" she asks.

"No," I say, wishing Beeps would not talk about the plans we made in secret. Star gives me a curious look but doesn't ask.

"We're going to bed early," I continue. "It's been a long night."

"But you don't like to sleep, remember?" Beeps says.

"Of course I do." I try to make a convincing chuckle, but fail terribly. "Thanks for your help, Star."

"No problem," Star gives me a smile but I can see the questions and worry in her eyes. "I think I'll stay here and work on one of the small engines."

"Sure." I smile back, hoping to reassure her that I won't do anything crazy. "If you see Parrin, can you tell him I'm looking for him?"

"Sure thing." Star already has her head in an engine and a wrench in hand.

"Thanks again," I say, as Beeps and I turn to leave. "It's good to have you back," I say to Beeps as we walk down the corridors. "That's the last time I ever let anyone take you away from me."

CHAPTER 48

B ACK AT MY SLEEPING chamber I find my black clothes from Aylvon sitting on my bed. They've been washed and folded by the service crew who travel with the large battleships and are stationed at the base, between missions.

I pull the green dress over my head and toss it aside, watching the entrance curtain in case I see the shadow of anyone approaching. I pick up the black shirt and slip my arms into the soft fabric.

"Beeps, keep watch at the door for me so no one comes in," I say.

Beeps rolls over to the door obediently and lowers her head to look under the curtain.

"Thanks."

My belt is also on the bed, with the sword sheath attached.

"We're going back for Takano," I say, putting on the pants. "I won't leave him behind."

Beeps makes an excited little sound.

"But first, we have to get his sword and take it to Orusk."

"Parrin is coming," Beeps says.

I do up the button on my pants just as Parrin barges in.

"Rita?" He throws the curtain aside and I tuck my shirt into my pants. "Sorry!" His cheeks flush. "There are no doors in this place or I would have knocked, and the curtain...well anyway, Star said you wanted to see me?" Parrin's flush deepens as he waits for me to put on my belt.

"You wouldn't happen to know anything about Beeps getting new programming, would you?" I ask.

"Um...no. I don't know." Parrin adjusts his jacket and runs a hand over his short cut hair. "Aren't you going to sleep a bit tonight? Before we go down into the catacombs?"

I shake my head no. Was he hoping to hang out with me while we wait for the right time to go get the sword? I can't go until everyone is asleep.

"Actually, I might sleep a bit," I lie.

We stand in silence for a moment.

"Okay, well..." Parrin rubs the back of his neck, looking at the floor. "I'll let you sleep then." He walks to the doorway. "Unless you'd like me to stay?"

"No," I say quickly. "I'm just going to rest for a little bit. Will you let me know when the General is asleep?"

"Yes," he nods. "I'll check on everyone once the party stops and come let you know when they're all asleep."

"Thanks."

He nods then leaves through the curtain. I sigh in relief.

"Are you going to sleep?" Beeps asks.

I smile down at her. She's starting to understand when I'm not telling the truth, and when she shouldn't either. I sit down on the bed and tell her about my visions and how Takano came to visit me in a dream the previous night. I tell her about the vision of me as a Dark Master but leave out the part about Takano and me kissing. Then I tell her about the eagle and the vision I had through the eagle's eyes. The planets being destroyed. The animals dying.

Beeps listens until I'm finished.

"So, Takano's not allowed to sleep or dream?" she asks.

Her question surprises me. After all that I've told her, her main concern is Takano's sleep?

"I guess not," I say.

"But he was with you all night on Aylvon. Did he lay awake all night?"

"Oh..." My shoulders slump. He probably did stay awake all night, even though I we were laying down together.

"What's wrong?" Beeps asks.

I pull my knees up and hug them to my chest. "If I accidentally fall asleep, will you wake me in half an hour?" I say quietly. "I'm just going to rest for a bit. I don't think I'll dream much in just half an hour, anyway. I just need to rest a little."

"Okay."

I lie down on my side and turn my back to Beeps, curling up into a ball. My belt digs into my side but I don't care. I finally let the tears fall. I close my eyes and focus in on my Gift, even though I know I won't be able to send Takano a message to where he is, I try anyway.

I'm not going to leave you behind, I call out to him.

* * *

I dream of a dark place, filled with black ashes on the ground, floating in the air. My boots are covered in soot. The planet I'm on is burning, everywhere I look there is fire. The sun is hidden by dust and even the sky is red like fire.

I have the feeling that someone is watching me and I turn to look behind me.

A hooded figure stands there, silhouetted by the red sky. *I'll show you the way to go. Just follow his suffering and pain.*

It's Dukath.

He looks different in this dream, tall and majestic, but I've seen the real Dukath and he's a lot less impressive.

He has an invisible hold on me and I can't speak or reply, only listen. He raises his arm slowly, out to the side. I look to where he's pointing and see Takano, tied to a post. He's slumped down, knees bent. He's full of bruises and bleeding through his clothes, his head bowed.

"No!" I yell, regaining my voice. But I can't move. I can't run to him.

Come save him. Dukath whispers to my thoughts. *I know he's what you I want. I'll let him go, if you bring yourself to me.*

I swallow hard. "I will come," I say. "Just stop hurting him. I'm not afraid to face you."

*No, Rita. Don't...*It's Takano this time. He raises his head and looks at me.

Takano! My heart hammers in my chest and I break free of Dukath's hold. But I can't bring myself to run to Takano. His suffering is too hard to look at.

I made a promise. I'll come for you, I tell him.

I tell myself it's only a dream. Takano is fine. But then I see the smirk on Dukath's face.

Takano might not be beat and tied to a post in the waking world, but he isn't safe either.

Don't come, Rita, Takano pleads. *He's lying to you.*

"Quiet!" Dukath's voice thunders. He thrusts out his arm and Takano cries out in pain.

"Stop!" I yell.

Suddenly the ash beneath Takano bursts into flames and he is consumed by fire.

"No!"

***

"Rita? Rita?" Beeps' cries enter my thoughts and I wake. "It's been half an hour. You told me to wake you."

I get up quickly. "We can't wait any longer Beeps. We have to go, now!"

CHAPTER 49

"W HAT THE...?" I TRIP over someone in the corridor. It's Parrin, sitting on the floor just outside the entrance to my room.

"Ouch!" he says.

"What are you doing here?"

"I was..." Parrin gets up and brushes himself off. "The General just finished his tea not too long ago and went to bed, but I don't know if he's asleep yet."

"If he had his tea then he's likely sound asleep already."

"Parrin was guarding your door," Beeps says. "While you were sleeping."

"Come on," I give Parrin a hand up. "Let's go. And no more talking. We need to be a little more quiet."

We hurry down the hall in silence, except that Beeps' gears whir as her wheels spin in one place, trying to get traction on the marble floor.

I slow down to wait for her to catch up.

No one is around and my heart races as we move amidst the shadows, trying not to get caught.

Takano told me not to come after him, but Dukath is keeping him prisoner and hurting him. Which mission is more important, saving Takano first or taking the sword to Orusk?

"Rita!" Parrin whispers loudly, startling me. He waves his hand at me to join him. I'd started going down a different hallway. How did we get separated? I need to stay focused.

I run over to him and he crouches behind a potted plant, pulling me down beside him.

The scent of earth and plant life hit me with a longing for home. The reality of how far from home I am right now, farther than I ever imagined I'd go in my lifetime, hits me suddenly.

A guard in Opposition uniform walks in through the front passageway from an outside balcony. His steps are silenced by the roar of the ocean below. He doesn't look our way as he passes by, a large gun resting in his arms.

The stone wall behind me is cold, making Parrin's warm shoulder feel inviting against mine. I feel him move as he breathes. I want to pull away, but there's no room.

Parrin watches the corridor where the guard went. I can't see the guard anymore but Parrin doesn't move and Beeps doesn't either, so I wait. I close my eyes and think of the forest back home.

How did I get here? How do I feel about Parrin? He makes me feel safe and cared for, but also uncomfortable sometimes. His nervousness around me makes *me* feel nervous.

"Okay, he's gone. Let's go," Parrin whispers, getting up.

I nod, quickly getting up, too.

Soon we're running again, Beeps at our heels. I'm glad Parrin knows the way. The plan is to get the sword. Then what? Take it to Orusk first and then hurry to help Takano?

When we reach the landing platform, Beeps and I keep watch while Parrin searches for Star's fighter plane.

"Rita!" Parrin calls, a moment later.

I turn to see him waving. He's standing beside a plane barely visible in the fog and shadows.

Beeps and I run over. We board the plane without a word. The roaring ocean below muffles our sounds. Parrin opens the hatch for me and helps Beeps get in. He sets her behind our seats, where the weapons usually go. I check to make sure she's secure.

"How far is it to the catacombs?" I ask Parrin, buckling up. It feels good to talk freely now that the hatch is closed. There's no way they won't notice a plane leaving. But then again, they're monitoring the sky for incoming planes, not the island for low flying ones, hopefully. That might buy us some time.

"It's not far." Parrin runs a hand over his hair. "I'm pretty sure Star's plane has a cloaking shield. She always talks about it."

"Oh, that would be really useful." I look over at Parrin who looks disheveled.

"Aren't you going to buckle in?" I ask.

"Oh, right." Parrin looks around for the fastening belt.

"It's right here," I reach over and pull it out for him.

"Oh," Parrin chuckles nervously. "I'm not much of a pilot I guess…"

I sigh and undo my seatbelt so we can exchange places. "Let me fly."

"I mean," he continues, "I can fly! It's just that the fog might make it hard for me to navigate. It's like flying blind," he says.

"Don't worry about it," I say, climbing over him so we can switch seats. I put on my helmet and start the engine. "You okay, Beeps?" I call over my shoulder. She beeps back with a positive reply.

The controls of the fighter plane are more sensitive than other planes I've flown before. Each small movement makes a dramatic dip of the aircraft, enough to make my stomach uneasy. I look out into the fog and see nothing. I watch the monitors instead, trying to figure out the out- line of objects on the tiny screens. I can tell which one is the water below and which is likely a small piece of island up ahead. I tilt the plane to the right, to align it with the grid on the viewer so we are flying level. A few more islands appear on the screen.

"Which island?" I ask.

"Uh..." Parrin messes around with the controls on the copilot's side and my grip tightens on the rudder. My stomach is already in knots and Parrin's uncertainty doesn't help. "I have the co-ordinates."

"Memorized?"

"Yes, it's that one, there," he points to the view screen.

"Which one?" There's a break in the fog and I see an island with ruins below.

"That's it!" Parrin says, pointing outside. "Oh, and I found some great ear pieces for communicating." He reaches into his pocket and his elbow bumps my arm. The pane tilts, reacting to every small movement.

"How about you show me after we land?" I say into the helmet headset.

Parrin nods and finally sits still as I search for a place to land.

"Can I communicate with the earpieces, too?" Beeps asks behind us.

"Of course," I say. "Right, Parrin? She can tune into our comm frequencies, can't she?"

"Yeah, no problem."

I lower the plane onto a rocky surface and the bottom crunches to a halt. I cringe. I've got to get better at landings. I hope Star forgives me for scratching up her plane, next time I see her. If we ever see each other again. I push the thought away. I can't think negatively right now. I need to focus. We have to get Takano's sword, before Dukath gets to it.

"You ready?" I turn to Parrin.

"As ready as I will ever be to raid the catacombs of an ancient Temple, where the Galaxy's most dangerous weapon is locked up."

I roll my eyes, but smile. At least Parrin isn't a negative person. That should help a lot. I turn off the engine and Parrin opens the hatch. We look down. The stones are cracked below us. They look like they're going to crumble into the ocean at any moment. Not the best place to land, but the entire Island is falling apart.

I shiver. "Beeps, you'll just have to stay in here and wait for us."

She beeps some complaint in response.

"We won't be long," I say, then climb out.

The stone is sturdy enough to hold the plane, but when we reach the stairs that lead down to the main Temple area, the rocks begin to crumble and slide beneath our feet. Wet fog clings to the ground, making the steps slippery and dangerous.

Parrin falls behind, stumbling on every loose stone that comes into contact with his foot. I slow down and wait for him. He trips again and I grab his arm at the last second, before he falls over the side of the cliff into the waters below.

"Thanks," he says.

"Come on." I pull him forward.

We finally reach the Temple entrance. Here, the ground is solid and I stop to look up at the broken ceiling, open to the sky above. A few lonely stars twinkle through the light from the eternal sunset. They seem impossibly far away, yet Takano is even farther away than those few stars.

"Which way now?" I ask Parrin.

He points to the other side of the sanctuary and I start to run. The General will find us at any moment. Then he'll stop me and I'll never get the sword to Orusk.

Parrin's boots crunch the loose gravel on the stone floor and I tense. What if there are guards? What if someone will hear us? I stop and Parrin bumps into me.

"Sorry," he says, breathing heavily.

"Where is it?" I ask. There isn't even a door on this side of the sanctuary.

"Here." Parrin points down to the ground.

I look down into a dark hole in the floor. If I'd run any farther I would have fallen in.

Cool, musty air escapes up through the hole, smelling of mildew and dust. A rope ladder hangs down into the darkness below. I step back.

"You can't be serious," I say to Parrin.

He shrugs. "As far as I know, it's down there. I haven't seen any guards around here, though. You would think they'd want to keep it guarded."

"Maybe the place is guarded by some kind of magic, or by the Gifted Masters of old, somehow," I say. But Parrin is right, it is kind of suspicious that there are no guards around. "We should probably hurry."

Parrin nods but doesn't make a move to go down. We look at each other.

"Should I go first?" he asks.

"Sure," I say.

He pulls out a blaster and I wave my hand at him.

"Put that away," I hiss. "If you shoot that thing here, the whole place will crumble into the ocean!" I crouch down and look into the hole. It's too dark to see anything and yet the fog inside the cavern seems to glow a light green. "Do you have a light?"

"No," Parrin frowns.

Voices float up from the catacombs below, children's voices; some crying, some talking. It's so faint I wonder if I'm just imagining it.

"Can you hear that?" I glance at Parrin.

"Hear what?"

"The voices."

He shakes his head then crouches down beside me to listen. I hear them more clearly this time, but Parrin doesn't react.

"I don't hear anything." He says. "Why? Do you hear something?"

I don't answer. Even if there are voices, what can they do to me? They're only whispers of those who are no longer alive.

I start climbing down the rope ladder.

I can do this. I have to. For the planets and animals. And for Takano.

I continue to climb down, imagining a long drop to the bottom. But I reach the end of the ladder faster than I expect to.

"It's not too far down," I call up to Parrin, who is still waiting at the top.

"Are you sure it's safe?"

I roll my eyes, knowing Parrin can't see me. "I'll go look for the sword by myself, if you want to guard the entrance."

"No, wait for me. I'm coming!" Parrin kicks dust down onto my head as he scurries down the ladder. I step back, and cover my mouth and nose.

The voices start up again, floating around me like the odd, green fog. I know they don't belong to real people. They're not guards or Ruling Order soldiers. *They can't hurt me*, I tell myself. They're just the spirits of ages past.

Distant screams echo down the dark chambers. I clear my throat to make a different noise, any noise, so I don't have to hear the screams.

"Hurry, Parrin," I say. "We have to get back to Beeps. She's all alone."

Parrin jumps from the ladder, landing with a thud.

"You okay?" he asks.

I can't see his face, only a silhouette of him from the light above. My eyes are adjusting to the dim light and I look down the long passageway in front of us. There are pillars on either side, made of thousands of flat stones stacked onto one another. A soft green light, like moon shine, illuminates the cavern all the way down to the other side, making it possible to see.

"Do you see that?" I ask.

"The light?" Parrin asks.

"Yeah." I wipe the sweat from my forehead. "I'm glad you see it too."

"It's the dust in the air."

He's right. It isn't fog, but a dust floating around. And it's glowing. I cover my mouth with my hand. "Maybe we shouldn't breathe it in."

Parrin nods and covers his mouth as well. "I guess we start searching now?"

I groan. It's probably in a creepy coffin or something.

We walk in silence, our steps echoing in the long corridor. I see caskets on either side of us, lining the passageway. They are closed, thankfully, covered with heavy looking stone lids.

There is no one down here guarding Takano's sword, other than the spirits of the dead.

A chill runs through me.

"Are you sure this is where it is?" I ask Parrin.

"Yes," he whispers back.

Why would they bring it here? And yet, I feel the power of the Gift all around, pushing in on me, stifling me. It's the energy of both the good and the bad side, together in one place, conflicting, but in balance.

"Look," Parrin says, pointing to a casket with a red glow around the lid's edges.

"That's it!" I lean down to push the lid aside but it's too heavy. Parrin rushes over to help me. Stone scrapes against stone, kicking up more of the sparkling dust. I hold my breath.

A loud sound echoes through the cavern, so loud it rattles my teeth and I scream. The light from the hole we came down in, goes dark.

"I think we activated a trap," Parrin says.

My heart pounds. Takano's sword is glowing red. Is it a reaction from the dust around us? Maybe the sword could help us.

I reach for it but Parrin grabs my wrist before I can touch it.

"Let me," he says. He leans in and grasps the handle of the sword. The red light stops glowing at his touch, leaving us in the dim green darkness again. I watch Parrin hold the sword, studying it curiously.

"Doesn't seem very—"

"Give it to me!" I say, my voice sounding harsher than I intended.

"What?" Parrin lowers the sword and looks at me. "It's not safe with you, remember?"

I no longer care about the dust getting into my lungs, and take my hand away from my mouth to grab for the sword, but Parrin evades me at the last second.

"No! We decided I would carry it."

"I changed my mind," I growl at him.

"I can't let you have it."

"Give it to me!" I yell.

The shout echoes through the cavernous hall and doesn't even sound like me. I push my Gift energy at Parrin and he goes flying down the corridor, landing on his back and sliding across the loose stones. He drops the sword and I lunge for it.

He scrambles to his feet and snatches the sword seconds before I do. I freeze him in place and he begins to choke.

"Rita..." Parrin says, barely able to speak. "I can't breathe."

I release him and he collapses to the floor, sending up a cloud of electric dust.

"Parrin?" I kneel down beside him. "I'm so sorry...are you okay?"

"I'm okay." Parrin's voice cracks.

He rubs at his neck.

"I don't know what came over me. I'm so sorry."

"It's fine." His right arm is behind his back, hiding the sword from my view.

"Keep it out of sight," I say, stepping away from him. "We've got it now and we need to get back to Beeps."

Parrin nods and gets up off the ground. We head back to the opening, but it's now closed by a trap door. I climb up the wobbly rope steps and push on the door. It's latched shut.

"Should I blast it open?" Parrin says, reaching for his blaster.

"I've got this," I say, closing my eyes to concentrate.

The glowing dust seems to energize me, gathering around me as I tap into my Gift. I set my fingers on the door above me and envision its shape and size in my mind. It's made of wood and is perfectly round. I see the outside latch in my mind's eye. I coax it open with my thoughts. It moves ever so slowly. I concentrate, imagining every movement that needs to happen to unlatch the door. There is a distinct click and I push up. The door opens.

"Nice!" Parrin cheers from below as the light floods down on us.

"Thanks." I wipe the sweat off my brow. "Now let's get *out* of here. The General is probably on his way since we triggered that alarm."

CHAPTER 50

"Could we not just go get a more reliable ship?" I yell down to Parrin over the loud hissing sounds. He's fixing another problem on the Eagle Starship. Every second we're not in the air feels like an eternity. We made it off the small island with the catacombs, and to the Eagle. We're so close.

"The other ships are all in the same place, so they'll notice if one goes missing," Parrin calls up. "Don't worry, Charlie's ship is perfect."

"Star's not going to like this. Her and Charlie are good friends."

The hissing stops and Parrin climbs up, his face sweaty. "It's fixed."

"Alright," I sigh. "I hope this old craft can get us where we need to go."

"Are you kidding?" Parrin wipes his hands on his pants and smiles. "The Eagle Ten is a classic! It's big enough to get us far and it's better in battle than a little fighter plane. It'll take them a while to notice it's missing. Unless Charlie needs to use it right away."

We head down an unkempt hallway to the cockpit, Beeps at our heels. She's been quiet since we made it back from the catacombs.

I take the pilot seat and Parrin sits in the copilot chair. I flip on the preliminary switches and the ship boots up. There are a lot more controls in the Eagle, than Star's plane.

"Ready?" I give Parrin a reassuring smile, knowing he gets far more nervous than I do flying in a space craft.

Parrin nods and we lift off. I look at the gauges. We're not running on full impulse. The deflection shields are on and they're draining extra power.

"Parrin, we need to conserve power. Can you turn off the deflection shields?"

"Got it." Parrin reaches up and I see the sword on his belt. Suddenly I'm out of the pilot's seat and reaching for the sword. The ship tilts, throwing me off balance. I stumble before reaching the sword.

"Rita?" Parrin says. "What happened? Are you okay?"

I get up, rubbing a bruise on my arm where I hit the side of Parrin's seat.

"Can you take the controls?"

"What?" Parrin's eyes go wide. "You know how to fly this ship, don't you?"

I hurry away before he can answer. I need to get as far away from Takano's sword as possible.

I pass Beeps in the hall, almost running into her.

"Are you okay?" she beeps, changing course and rolling after me.

I stop running and crouch down, wrapping my arms around my knees.

"I don't know, Beeps."

"You need more sleep."

"No!" I snap and Beeps backs up. "I'm Sorry." My shoulders slump. "You're right, I probably do need more sleep. But there's no way I'm going to let myself sleep and see those visions again."

"Of Takano with Dukath?"

"Yes." I get up and begin to pace the small hallway. "Can't this thing go any faster?" I yell to the front of the ship.

"I'll try," Parrin yells back. I continue pacing.

Rita...

The voice in my mind is Takano's. We must be getting closer to where he is.

"Takano?" I run back to the cockpit and grab the controls away from Parrin. He let's go in surprise.

"Forget Orusk," I say. "We're going to go kill Dukath instead."

Parrin leans back. "What about the sword and the voice telling you to take it to Or—"

"Forget that!" I snap.

Parrin sets his hand over mine on the rudder. "I don't think we should."

"*Red Leader to the Eagle Starship,*" the comm system blares, startling both of us. "*Cease and desist, I repeat, desist and return to Antineon.*"

I hit the comm button. "Star? Is that you?"

"*Yes. The General insists you return immediately.*"

"Negative, Red Leader," I reply. "We aren't prepared to do that."

"*I have direct orders—*"

The communication gets interrupted by another incoming message.

"*This is your General. I don't know what you're up to but you need to head back immediately. That robot has sensitive information that we can't afford to let fall into enemy hands, which is where I'm assuming you're headed.*"

I blink, moving away from Parrin and sinking into the copilot's seat. Parrin sits up straighter, taking a firm grasp of the rudder and rerouting our course.

"Stop!" I pull his hand away and he tenses. I tap the comm button. "General, I need to take the sword to Orusk."

"*Orusk has been destroyed by the Ruling Order. I repeat, the planet no longer exists.*"

Parrin glances at me. "Should we go back?"

I blink back tears. Could I have been so wrong?

I shrug my shoulders and Parrin turns off the comm unit. "Let's go see if that planet is still out there," he says.

"Are you sure?"

He boosts the ship into warp speed and I fall back against the seat. The stars melt away around us.

"I thought we didn't have enough power for warp speed," I yell over the engine.

"We do, if we don't intend to come back," Parrin yells back.

I nod. He's right, we don't have time to get there slowly.

There's no heading back now.

I grip the arm rests on either side of my seat as we zoom through a spiraling vortex.

I resist the urge to hold my breath, the way I used to when I was little and my dad would take me in his ship. I'd forgotten about that until now.

We drop out of warp a moment later and come to a stop in an empty stretch of space.

"Parrin, why did you stop?"

His hands hover over the controls. Then he checks the coordinates.

"I'm sorry, Rita. This is it."

"What?"

"Orusk. It's..." he doesn't finish and I slouch down in my seat. I look at the display on the ship's console. There are no nearby planets. The General was right. The planet is gone. It's actually gone. Was the voice I heard just an illusion too? Did I take Takano's sword for nothing? Or worse, was it a trick by Dukath to get me to bring him the sword?

"What's that?" Parrin says, pointing to the display screen.

"I don't know, an asteroid?"

"No. I think it's an escape pod."

I sit up in my seat. "Go closer."

Parrin does and we see that it is, in fact, an old fashion escape pod.

* * *

We wait for the shuttle pod to dock into the Eagle, watching through the view window of the bay doors until the airlock is securely closed again. The shuttle pod crashes to the floor and the receiving doors close. A cold steam rises off the pod. I tap my foot, waiting for the red light by the bay doors to turn green so we can go into the cargo bay. The bay area re-pressurizes and the light turns green.

"I'll go first," Parrin says, but I'm already pushing past him.

The door slides open with a hiss and I step into the cargo bay. The walls of the escape pod crackle with the change in temperature from the cold of outer space.

Parrin stops beside me and I hear Beeps roll in after him. The lone tiny window on the pod is crystallized with frost and I can't see inside.

"Should I open it?" Parrin asks.

I nod slowly. He walks around the pod then pulls down a lever, which unlocks the hatch from the outside.

The pod opens.

CHAPTER 51

A HOODED FIGURE SITS unmoving, hunched over inside the pod. Parrin pulls out Takano's black sword and my heart jumps to my throat.

"Put that away!" The hooded man says. He extends a quivering arm and the sword goes flying out of Parrin's hand. I try to lunge for it but I'm suddenly locked in a hold.

I look at the elderly man sitting in the pod.

"I thought all the Gifted Masters were dead," I say to him.

"Perhaps." He pulls back his hood to reveal a head of white hair and an aged face. The effort seems almost too much for him.

Parrin picks up the sword and tucks it into his belt.

"Who are you?" he asks the cloaked man.

"I'm the one who called you here. I am Kra'an."

I gasp. "Master Kra'an?"

"Yes, but first, before I answer any questions, I must have some water."

* * *

"He was a troubled boy when he came to me," Master Kra'an says in a dry voice, despite the water. He leans his elbows onto the table that we're sitting around, in the ship's small common area. I blink back tears, looking at the teacher who made such a big difference in Takano's life. He wasn't killed after all. Randon is a liar. I need to tell Takano.

Beeps rolls lightly on her wheels, watching silently from the corner of the room. She is afraid of Kra'an, but I know she's listening to every word he's saying.

Parrin pours some more water into the Master's cup as we wait for him to continue.

"Bryn's emotions were not in control," Kra'an continues, looking at me. "And neither are yours."

Parrin glances over at me, then back at Kra'an.

The elderly man breathes slowly. "I am dying and should already be dead," he says with effort. "But I held on to life to bring you here. I've had a vision. You, young master, will turn to evil." He points a shaky finger at me.

I shake my head but can't seem to respond.

"The future is always in motion and never certain," Kra'an continues. "Therefore, you do not need to fear what I tell you, only make the decisions now, which will prevent this vision of mine from coming to pass. Takano Rynn's sword can destroy Dukath, yes, but it is not the only thing that can. You must not take it back to him.

"You cannot save Takano Rynn, he is too far deep within his doubt. Only he can free himself. I have seen his heart. He will not let go of that which holds him captive, that which tears him apart.

"You must not go to him, you must not seek him out. Do not confront Dukath for he knows your weaknesses, he knows how you feel about the young Lord, Takano Rynn. He will use it to draw you in. And your feelings for him will surely be your end." Kra'an pauses to take a few breaths "Dukath's power lies only in deception."

The air vents hum as we sit in silence. I'm not sure what to say. I can't promise that I won't go to Takano, but Master Kra'an's warnings are making me worry. He continues to watch me and I shift uncomfortably in my seat.

"You and Bryn," he says, "have fused your Gifts to one another. This is why Dukath now has you on the brink of your own destruction. To your own emotions, do not give in."

My chest aches but I don't respond. Master Kra'an sinks down in his seat, as though finished talking.

"Master? Please..." I plead. "Tell me why two Gift sensitive people can't become attached. What about having Gift sensitive children? Takano had parents."

"One of them was sensitive to the Gift, the other was not. You can have attachments with others, but with your own kind, it is forbidden. For the child of such a union would go mad with the Gift. A forbidden child. It is too dangerous.

"You must save the Galaxy from the Ruling Order, young Rita. But not with the sword. Your emotions are too strong now to take it up. Turn back your course. With your friends and with patience, against Dukath you will win, but first you must let go. Let go, of Takano Rynn."

Master Kra'an bows his head and breathes his last breath.

* * *

"Rita?" Parrin knocks on the washroom door lightly.

I pace the small space. I can't face Parrin yet. I can't even talk to Beeps right now.

"Are you alright?" he asks from behind the door.

I don't answer and I hear him sigh heavily.

"Rita?" he says again. For a moment there is silence.

Then he says, "I think you should go save Takano Rynn."

"What?" I stop pacing.

"I think you should follow your heart." Parrin's voice is muffled behind the door. Did he really just say I should go after Takano? Despite all Master Kra'an told us?

I pull the door open and Parrin startles, stepping back. His expression changes to a look of pity. I frown, imagining what a mess I must look like after all that crying.

"But you heard what Kra'an said," I sniffle.

"Yes, I did. And he might be right about some of it. But I also believe the future is not written. Only you can write it for yourself."

Parrin's words spark a hope in me and I feel a bit lighter.

"Listen," he says, looking down. "I don't know what happened between you and Takano Rynn, but it's clear to me that you love him."

My breath catches at Parrin's words. Do I love Takano? If I didn't, would I be this torn as to what to do next? I would simply return to Antineon. The General and the Opposition fleet could create a plan to help Takano, if I talked to them. His father would be willing to help. It doesn't have to be me.

But I won't go back. I won't leave him in Dukath's hands for even a moment longer. I can't. Parrin is right. I do love him.

My tears start flowing again and Parrin sets his hand on my shoulder. "Master Kra'an said you fused your Gifts together?"

I look down at the ground, not sure how to answer his questions. I know what he's asking, and it's not what he thinks. We trained together, our Gifts making us better in battle when we used them together. But I don't think that is what Master Kra'an was talking about. The moments Takano and I looked into each other's minds, sharing our memories and fears, our hopes and secrets; that's when we fused our Gifts. I saw Takano's struggles in grade school, he saw mine at the Temple, waiting for my parents to return. He is the leader of the Dark Army. I can't imagine he has ever been that vulnerable with anyone else, the way he was with me in those moments.

"We shared each other's thoughts," I whisper. "And..." I'm not sure how to explain it, so I stop. Then I remember our moment suspended in the air over the forest of Aylvon.

"If you let him die," Parrin says, "you'll die too, in your heart. You'll never feel right, knowing you didn't try to help him be free of Dukath. Even if Dukath is destroyed in the end. If Takano Rynn dies, I don't think you'll even care if Dukath does or not."

I throw my arms around Parrin, startling him. He returns the hug and I hear Beeps beeping. She wants to help Takano, too.

"I can talk to Takano," she beeps. "I'll tell him not to be afraid."

I let go of Parrin. "Okay, Beeps," I say. "Thank you."

I set my hand on her little head.

A system alarm blares, making me jump.

"What's that?" Beeps squeals.

"It's the intruder alarm. Someone's on board."

CHAPTER 52

"S TAR!" PARRIN AND I say at the same time. Star's ship is docked beside the small escape pod in the cargo bay receiving area. She removes her helmet and isn't smiling.

"What is that?" she asks, pointing with her thumb behind her to the shuttle pod.

"How did you find us?" I say, not wanting to get into the details of Master Kra'an's shuttle pod just yet.

"Listen." Star puts up her hand to silence me. "I'm only here to get Beeps. It's really important that—"

"No." I shake my head.

"Just hear me out."

"Beeps stays with us." My hands tremble with the urge to grab Takano's sword from Parrin's belt and lash out at Star in anger. I clench my fists and keep them tucked at my sides.

Star presses her lips together, glaring at me. I feel a twinge of guilt. Beeps is her robot, not mine. But Beeps wants to stay with me, and the thought of being separated from her makes me unreasonably angry.

Parrin steps between us, holding out his hands. "No one's going anywhere. What do you need from Beeps?" he asks Star.

"The memory drive."

"We can't remove her memory!" I say. "She'll forget everything. She'll lose all her memories. And it's not fair to her."

"Hold on," Parrin says. "Can we just remove the part of the memory you need?" He looks at Star again.

Beeps makes a noise behind us.

"She says she only has one memory drive and everything is on it," Star clarifies for us. "General Anias sent me to get Beeps and he wants the sword returned, too. They'll send a fleet after you if you don't consent."

"They don't know where we're going," I say, lifting my chin.

"They can easily track you. I found you, didn't I?"

"Parrin? Can we change the tracking signature of the Eagle to confuse their sensors?"

"No, but I think I have an idea that can basically do the same thing," Parrin says, leaving quickly, presumably to do just that.

"What?" Star watches him go, a confused look on her face. "Why are you both doing this?"

"I'm sorry, Star. I'm going after Dukath and I'm going to kill him. And I'm not leaving Beeps behind, ever again."

"You're making a mistake."

Beeps rolls back and forth near our feet but doesn't say anything.

"The Opposition can help you," Star continues. "Why won't you let us help? You can't just go by yourself to face Dukath. We need a strategy, a plan."

"No," I cross my arms. "That will just get us all killed. Don't you see? Dukath won't be defeated that way, with weapons fire and us in a battle against the Ruling Order. Their army is too big and they have a super weapon that can destroy planets, which they will do if they want to threaten us. It's not worth the risk. I'm the one who has to do it."

There is a moment of silence and even Beeps stops moving.

Star nods finally. "Alright, count me in."

CHAPTER 53

"**R**UN THIS BY ME again?" Parrin says. He rubs his forehead as though his head hurts. He and Star returned Kra'an to the escape pod and released the pod back into space. I should have helped but I was too upset. I can't bear the thought of Takano's childhood Master dying before Takano got a chance to say goodbye to him. Beeps and I went in search of food and drinks instead.

I push a bowl of dried fruit to Parrin but he waves it away. Maybe I should have helped Star with Master Kra'an and let Parrin search for the food. I certainly didn't find the right drawers.

Star grabs some of the fruit and pops it into her mouth. "That's not much of a plan," she says to me, between chews.

"I don't know what to expect when we get there," I say, picking up a cheese flavored cracker. Now that we're finally making plans, I'm feeling better about my decision to go after Takano. "Dukath will be expecting me, he won't be expecting the two of you."

"He might be expecting the whole Opposition army," Star says.

"Maybe, but I don't think he'll see the two of you as any threat to him, even if he's aware that you're with me."

We eat for a moment and think.

"Parrin, you keep the sword," I say. "Dukath will be focused on me and if he can sense the sword, he'll just assume I have it on me. I'll wear a different sword. Then you can strike when he least expects it. Takano's sword is the only thing that can kill him."

"I know a way we can sneak onto their ship," Parrin says, running his hands over the table. He's slouched in his seat, seeming somber. Does the thought of returning to a Ruling Order ship bring back bad memories for him?

"But if they've landed on a planet, it will be impossible to keep our ship's arrival hidden, even if the Eagle had a cloaking option, which it doesn't." Star takes a drink from a bottle of water.

"He'll know I'm coming either way," I reply. "But you should stay out of sight, Star. You're our back-up. And you'll be with Beeps."

She nods.

"It's hard to make concrete plans when we don't know what to expect." I sigh, sitting back.

"But we've got the element of surprise," Parrin says, resolute. "I'm the one that's going to use the sword, not you, Rita. Dukath won't expect that." His hand moves to his belt and I fight the temptation to grab the sword away from him. It was never like this on Aylvon when Takano had the sword with him, so why is it different now?

I get up. "We should get going."

* * *

Star moves her fighter plane slowly towards the Battleship ahead, using the tip of the aircraft to push an asteroid floating in space, so the plane remains hidden behind it.

I sense Takano, but I can't sense Dukath. The thought of us being anywhere near Dukath makes my skin crawl. Maybe he isn't here after all. This could be some kind of trap. But Takano is here. His presence grows stronger by the second.

I sit on my hands to keep from reaching over and grabbing the controls from Star and blasting this fighter plane forward faster. But we're pretending to be a slow-moving asteroid passing by their ship.

I pull my legs up to my chest. There isn't much room for Beeps and me at the back of Star's plane. We had to leave the bombs behind to make room for us to sit. But the Eagle is too big to bring on a stealthy mission.

"So where should I land?" Star asks. Her voice comes through the small earpiece Parrin brought for each of us. Beeps is also locked into our frequency, so we can all communicate.

"Try to land somewhere inconspicuous, if possible," I say. "They'll probably know we're here, anyway. At least Takano will. I don't know about Dukath. I can't sense him."

"Land near the sanitation chute at the back of the ship," Parrin says. "If they don't know we're here yet then we can get in through the—"

"Hold on," Star shouts as the large Battleship comes to a stop in front of us.

Our asteroid is suddenly moving forward way too fast, now that the battleship we were following has come to an abrupt stop. The asteroid crashes into the side of the Ruling Order ship with a jolt, crunching the front of Star's already battered plane. She grumbles.

"Why'd they stop?" Parrin asks.

"They must be expecting us," Star says. "Their deflector shields are down."

"Wouldn't they be up if they're expecting us?"

"Not if they want us to board."

I adjust my ear piece. "Parrin, are you ready?"

"As ready as I'll ever be, to kill an evil Dark Lord Supreme Leader."

"Alright, then let's get this over with."

CHAPTER 54

TAKANO'S PRESENCE IS SO strong that I have no idea which direction to take in the brightly lit halls of the Ruling Order battleship. It's like he's everywhere.

Parrin wipes at his forehead, remaining silent. The corridor is eerily empty. There are no guards or commanders walking the halls. The entire ship is still, like the catacombs of Antineon.

"Are you sure he's here?" Parrin says softly, looking around.

"He's definitely here," I whisper in response.

Our boots click on the smooth floors as we make our way down the hall.

"This doesn't feel right," Parrin says.

I'm about to agree when a hooded figure appears at the end of the corridor.

My heart hammers in my chest and I can't speak. Takano stops when he sees us, his black cape swirling around him. He stands tall and silent, unharmed. Not beaten and bruised like I'd seen in my dream.

I told you not to come, he says to me.

Parrin looks from Takano to me, then back again.

"I came for you," I say to Takano. I start to walk over to him but then stop. I didn't expect to find him healthy and roaming around freely.

"Parrin, take her home," Takano says in a menacing tone, not taking his eyes off of me.

"No!" I shake my head. "I'm not leaving here without you."

Takano reaches out his hand, curling his fingers and I go flying towards him. I fall onto my knees and slide across the floor, stopping at his feet.

"Rita!" Parrin yells behind me.

"Go, wander the halls," Takano says to Parrin, his voice low and commanding. "Forget why you're here and don't come back to this corridor."

Parrin walks away in a trance. Why did I leave Star behind for backup? Her mind is a lot stronger than Parrin's. I need to contact her, but my throat is locked tight and I can't speak.

Takano crouches down to my level. "I told you not to come," he says. "Now I have to kill you."

CHAPTER 55

"TAKANO, STOP!" MY BACK hits the wall and I'm held in place with my feet off the ground.

Where's the sword? Takano's eyes grow dark.

"You told me not to touch it," I say in a tight voice. "So I don't have it."

Takano whips his hand and I go flying again. This time I stop the impact using my own Gift strength, and I spin to face him.

"I know it's here," he says.

"I don't have it."

"*Where is it?*" he shouts.

"I thought you were hurt." I quickly change the topic. Hopefully he won't figure out that Parrin has the sword.

"That's what Dukath wanted you to think."

Takano pulls me forward again and this time his hands clasp around my throat, hands that once comforted and held me when I cried. He's more powerful now than ever.

Or maybe I'm weaker, but not physically. Master Kra'an was right, my emotions are going to get me killed.

Takano wasn't hurt after all, and he doesn't want to come with me. He's under Dukath's spell and there's nothing I can do about it.

His eyes are full of anger now, but they're still the same eyes that looked at me with affection on Aylvon, when we floated above the trees.

"This isn't you," I whisper. "You're not like this."

His grip on my throat is an iron clamp, yet he doesn't hurt me or cut off my air supply, when he easily could. Despite Dukath's hold on him, he still doesn't hurt me.

"Takano, let me go." I struggle to remove his hands from my throat but can't.

"It would be better for you to die, than for Dukath to have you," he says. Fear rushes through me at his words. Does he honestly believe that?

"Like your mother died?" I say, regretting the words the moment they've come out of my mouth.

Takano releases me and I reach for my belt, but then remember that I don't actually have a sword. There were no extra ones to bring and I'm only wearing the sheath. I realize that Takano doesn't have one on him either.

He circles around me.

You still have a chance to leave, Rita. You need to go, now.

I hold my hands out in front of me, ready for a fight.

I'm not leaving without you. I made a promise to myself not to leave anyone behind.

Takano frowns. *No attachments, remember?*

"It's still my choice." I say it out loud, despite the burning in my throat. "It's my *choice*..." I clench my fists. I have to say it, though the words feel stuck in my throat. "It's my choice...to love you."

Takano stops. He closes his eyes for a moment then opens them again, the anger in them now gone. "There's no such thing as love, Rita," he says, softly. "Not for a Dark Master."

"There can be."

"It's too late for me," he shouts, startling me. Then he sighs and his shoulders slump. "But it's not too late for you."

"If you're going to kill me, then do it already," I challenge.

He frowns, a look of confusion crosses his face.

"I came here to kill Dukath," I continue. "So that you could be free. But I can't convince you to come with me and I'm not leaving without you."

"You underestimate Dukath's power, if you think you can kill him."

"And you overestimate it," I say.

He bows his head slowly and raising a black gloved hand to his face. "Why don't you just let me go?" he says softly, leaning back against the wall. *I'll never be free.*

I move closer. "I won't leave you behind."

Takano shakes his head slowly, his dark hair hanging into his eyes. He tries to hold back his thoughts from me but I see glimpses of sadness and it grips my heart. He's afraid that he'll lose me. That I'll lose myself, the way he lost himself to Dukath. Suddenly he lets his guard down and his emotions seep into me. I lift his chin so I can look into his eyes.

You won't lose me to Dukath. I won't give in to him.

Takano's warm scent bring back memories of our time together on Aylvon. I let him see those memories. Our memories. Him leaving food out for me for breakfast and cleaning the mud off Beeps.

That's you.

I set my palm on his cheek and he flinches.

There is still goodness in you. It's only your doubt that holds you back.

Then I see more of his thoughts. He's scared of my touch, scared to feel the way he does about me. His eyes flash as a memory passes between us. The kiss we shared in our dream together; a memory he's kept hidden, until now. The emotions it stirs up in him, scares him.

I move in closer.

"Rita...wait," Takano whispers. "Don't..."

I pull him to me and rest my forehead against his. He grasps my arms tight, as though to shove me away, but he doesn't.

"Don't make me feel this way," he whispers, his breathing more labored now. I set my palms against his chest and feel his heart race. Then I close my eyes and focus on his mind. His whole life has been overrun with his internal battle between good and evil. And in all that time he's never allowed himself to fall in love.

He tries to pull his thoughts away from me but I'm locked in on him now. He's never been this close to anyone before.

Rita, don't. Takano's grip on my arms tightens.

I slide my cheek against his, my heart pounding as I move my lips towards his.

Rita...wait...

Our lips brush and Takano's grip loosens on my arms. He wraps his arms around me.

"I can't have attachments" he whispers. "You don't understand."

I press my lips harder against his and feel his longing for me, like a tidal wave, crushing me, making my muscles go weak. He grabs my hair, returning the kiss with urgency.

The lights overhead flicker, then pop, sparking like fireworks above us. Glass rains down and Takano breaks our kiss to cover me with his cape as glass shatters all around us. The sound of the falling glass is like a magical waterfall.

"I think I've given you enough time for your goodbyes."

Dukath's voice crawls out of the darkness from somewhere behind us.

Takano pulls away from me. I step back, too.

The lights have been blown out and now there is only dark. I can't see where Dukath is, but I hear a sword being pulled from its sheath and a dim glow fills the corridor. It's coming from the sword Dukath is holding.

His hooded figure is hunched over and his wrinkled face looks menacing above the glow of the sword. Takano's sword.

"Parrin..." I gasp. He was the last one holding that sword.

CHAPTER 56

"RITA? PARRIN?" STAR'S VOICE blares in my earpiece. "The battleship's gone dark. What's going on in there?"

I clench my jaw but don't respond, keeping my eyes on Dukath. Does he know Star and Beeps are here too? I know he can't read my thoughts. I don't know why, but he can't and I'm glad.

"I'm coming in!" Star says into the earpiece. "Should I leave Beeps here?"

Beeps! I instinctively reach up to the earpiece and Dukath's eyes turn to me. I quickly lower my hand.

"Supreme Lord," Takano says. "Parrin and the pilot are here. And so is the robot."

My heart sinks. Of course Takano knows. He was just in my head a minute ago.

"Bring them to me," Dukath scowls.

Takano's boots crunch over broken glass as he walks away. The sound pierces my heart.

*Takano...*I try to reach for him, but he's gone.

I click on my earpiece. "Abort. Leave the battleship. Go now!"

"Reinforcements are on their way," Star says into the earpiece. "I repeat, the Opposition is coming."

Her words are interrupted by another transmission.

"Rita?"

"Parrin!"

All of a sudden my earpiece rips away from my ear and flies to Dukath's hand. He throws it down and steps on it, crushing it with his boot.

A few of the lights overhead turn back on, giving the hallway an eerie, flickering glow.

"There we are," Dukath says. "That's better." He holds the sword out to me. "I believe this belongs to you now."

I step back.

"Go on." Dukath grins. "Take it. This is what you came here for, is it not? To kill me with this sword? Now is your chance."

I start to move forward, the power of the sword beckoning me. It's so close and I know I can defeat Dukath with it. Why is he offering it to me? If I have it then I will be all powerful.

No. I shake my head. It's a trick. He isn't just going to hand over the sword.

Or is he?

I try to look into his eyes but they are hidden beneath the shadows of his hood.

An angry shout fills the hall. I turn to see Star behind me. Her yell is silenced by an onset of choking as she freezes in place. I turn back to Dukath, ready to lunge for the sword, but my body locks up, too.

"Stay here, child," Dukath says. "They'll all come to us. Be patient."

I swallow hard. The sound of Beeps' wheels zipping over shattered glass makes my heart ache. Why did I bring her on this mission?

"Come here, girl. Let me have a look at you," Dukath says to me.

I walk to him, my legs moving against my will, wobbling with each step. His presence is like the stench of death, yet I keep walking until I'm standing right in front of him.

"So naïve," he says slowly. "So palpable, so full of emotion."

I shudder at his words, turning my head away.

"You're friends are coming," Dukath says. His hand is raised, controlling my movements. My head turns to face him again.

"You should have come alone. Now they will all die because of you."

"It's me you want," I say. "So let them go. You have me now."

"Not yet, I don't. But I will. I have foreseen it." He holds out the sword to me again.

"Take it." He moves it closer and my hands begin to shake.

"No."

Dukath tilts his head to the side, studying me. I want to punch him. He won't force me to take that sword.

"You're stronger than I thought you would be," he says.

I hear Beeps behind me but I can't look to see if she's okay.

"Let them go," I say. "And I'll take the sword, like you want." I hold his gaze, challenging him. I won't take the sword, but he doesn't know that. He can't read my mind for some reason.

"You think it's me who's going to harm them?" Dukath chuckles. "It's not me, but you."

"Shut *up!*" I yell.

Dukath grins, then releases me from his hold. I slump down, almost losing my balance. My boots crunch the glass on the floor. I turn to see Star glaring angrily at Dukath and Parrin beside her, looking terrified.

Before I can run to them, Beeps zooms towards Dukath, letting out a high squeal. Her gears grind as she tries to resist being dragged forward through the glass towards Dukath.

"No!" Parrin and I yell at the same time. My hand involuntarily flies up to summon the sword in Dukath's hand.

Suddenly the ship shakes and a muffled boom rattles the walls. We're under attack.

"It's the Opposition," Star says. "You won't win, Dukath."

Dukath throws back his head and laughs.

Takano enters from the other end of the hall. "Your Leadership, an Opposition army has landed."

"I know, I know," Dukath gives a dismissive wave. "Let them come."

Takano clenches his fists but doesn't reply. I don't try to make a connection with him. Dukath will get into my head if I try to connect to Takano.

I glance over at him now. His expression is stoic as before. Does he know Dukath's plans? Or is he as oblivious as I am?

There's another jolt and the ship shakes again. I lose my balance and Takano grabs my other arm to stop me from falling into the glass.

"No!" Star cries out, reaching up to her earpiece. She has a scared expression on her face, one that I have never seen before.

"General, cancel the order to shoot! Do not hit target," she yells into the earpiece. "We've removed all the sensitive data from the robot. Do not destroy it."

My head spins. Star is talking about Beeps. But we weren't able to remove her new data. She's lying to protect Beeps.

The hallway suddenly fills with commotion; the stomping of boots and cries of the Opposition fighters as they flood in. They shoot at Takano and he blocks the shots, deflecting them into the wall. They shoot in Dukath's direction, but they aren't aiming for him, they're shooting at Beeps!

"No!" I yell as more and more shots are fired.

Beeps' little metal body flies back as they keep firing. The shots spark off her small metal body as she tries to run away from them.

"Stop!" I reach out my hand and Takano's sword flies out of Dukath's hand and into mine. My fingers close around the handle. It fits perfectly into my grasp, as though the sword was made just for me.

I turn and slash down on an Opposition fighter who is shooting at Beeps. He goes down. Then I swing at another soldier who is also shooting at her.

They begin shooting at me, but I block the shots easily. The sword makes me powerful and fast, filled with the strength and skill of all the Masters that died at its sharp edge.

I feel invincible. The sword cuts through everything in my way, even the walls, as I fight with blind rage.

Beeps is gone. They've destroyed her. And now, I will destroy all of *them*.

CHAPTER 57

THE FIRING HAS STOPPED; the screams and cries are just echoes left in my ears.

My heart hammers in my chest. The ship hums and the overhead lights flicker but there is no more movement or fighting, only the soft sound of someone sobbing.

I look in the direction it's coming from. For a moment I don't recognize the man in the brown jacket, hunched over someone in a pilot's uniform. I am not myself when the sword is in my hand, I am one with the many who yielded it before me. I try to remember the fight as my rage subsides and I look around the long corridor. There are many fighters in pilot's uniforms, all lying dead around me.

I killed them all, because they killed Beeps.

A sickening feeling stirs in my belly as my mind clears and the reality of what I've done sinks in.

The man in the brown jacket, crying, is Parrin. I blink to get a better view. He's holding one of the pilots in his arms. This pilot's blonde hair is like Star's, but stained with blood. My grip on the black sword loosens.

"Star?" I swallow hard. There is no one left alive but Parrin, and Takano, who is standing in the shadows.

And, Dukath.

I can feel his presence behind me. My grip tightens around my sword again.

You're all powerful now. His voice enters my mind. He can now speak to me in my thoughts, but why? Because of the sword?

I turn to him. *Yes, I am. And now, I'm going to kill you.*

Dukath smiles.

If you kill me, then Takano dies, too. I freeze, then look at Takano. He looks away.

He doesn't have to tell me if it's true. I can sense it, from both of them. If I kill Dukath then Takano will die, too.

"Takano?" I want him to deny it, to say that Dukath is a liar and that this is all just a dream. But it isn't. So we would have never killed Dukath together, like we'd planned. Even if Takano wasn't under Dukath's influence and we defeated him somehow, they would have both died. It was a suicide mission for Takano, and he never told me.

I close my eyes, not wanting to see Parrin on his knees with Star on the floor before him.

Star's words come to mind, *I don't want anyone to miss me if I die.*

What have I done?

I fall to my knees. They were right, Kra'an and Dukath. They knew I would turn into something evil, by the power of the Gift and of this sword.

I lift the sword and turn it towards my chest.

I've killed Star. Beeps has been destroyed. I'm no longer Rita, the Temple Girl, but a slave of evil, with the power to do great harm. But I will not let that happen. I will not turn into a Dark Master, like Kra'an prophesied; like the vision I saw in Takano's dream. I still have a choice not to.

"You still won't win," I say to Dukath.

"Rita!" *Don't do this...*It's Takano.

*Yes...*Dukath's voice hisses in my mind. *Do it.*

I shut my eyes tight. Too many voices in my head. I grip the sword handle with both hands.

Master Kra'an, I call out with my Gift, in one last plea, before I end all of this. *Help me. I've lost myself. You were right. I gave in to my emotions and have become a monster.*

A voice replies, gentle but strong.

Your death will only fuel the sword, a final act to make it all-powerful in the deeds of evil, united with the other Dark Masters who died unjustly by its crystal edge. Dukath longs to wield the sword of infinite darkness, all-powerful with anger, hate and death. This act of self-hatred will not undo what you have already done.

The sword shakes in my hand. No one moves.

Anias said that the evil way is a conscious choice, one that is chosen freely and of your own will.

I lift the sword up to the back of my neck. Takano's eyes go wide and Dukath smiles. There's still one choice left for me to make.

I take hold of my long hair, grasping it tight in my fist. I am not a Temple Girl anymore. My hair is no longer holy. *I don't want to be Gifted anymore.*

I slash the sword outward with a loud cry, slicing off my hair. It instantly disintegrates in my hand, turning into tiny specks of light that glisten for a moment then fade away. Will my Gift fade in the same way, now that I've cut off my hair? I should have done it when I first got to Central. But there's no going back now. Because of me, Beeps is gone and Star is dead. Takano is still trapped by Dukath. I didn't save him. I didn't even save myself.

You must go, to a place of which you know, Master Kra'an's voice in my head continues. *Where the voices and cries of the children of good and evil abide.*

In the shadows they exist, amidst the tombs of the great,

Still kept alive, yet they no longer live.

There they rest, until the time is right.

There you too shall hide and no longer fight.

There you will harm none who abides,

if you remain always, in the shadows inside.

Take the sword, take flight.

Take the power of its fight,

The strength of the dead Masters are now united in its light,

Take it with you to the tombs of eternal night.

There it will be protected, hidden from sight

If any should enter there,

Amidst the catacombs of despair,

You, nor the sword, will they find,

Both protected by the Gift of eternal light.

I blink, returning to the present. Takano's sword is still clasped in my hand. Takano stands in the shadows, his face full of emotion now. But there will be no goodbyes.

"You will not remember how I left, nor try to follow me," I say to him and to Dukath, by the power of the sword that is now one with me.

Then, I am gone.

TO BE CONTINUED...

ACKNOWLEDGEMENTS

THIS BOOK WOULD NOT be possible without the help of my daughter, who sat through many nights of me reading to her most of the first draft of this novel, so she could point out where anything sounded confusing! Thank you Jessica for always telling me which sentence sounds better and for helping me find the missing word all those times I'd be running around the house yelling "I need a word! I need a word!" And then becoming an amazing artist and creating these new re-release covers!

A big thanks to my best friend, Amanda, for all your support and encouragement throughout this whole process!

A very special thanks to my Mom, who always believes in my big, crazy dreams.

I want to thank my Beta readers Cindy, Ian and Emily, as well as my writer friends from the River Bottom Writers, without whom I would have never stepped forward to publish my first novel. The first day I showed up at a Thursday night meeting, with my daughter who was too small back then to be left home alone, I was terrified! RBW has helped me grow a lot over the years as a writer.

I'd also like to mention the Medicine Hat Rhyme and Reason Writer's group who have always loved everything I've ever read at their author reading events. I've never me a more supportive group of people all in one place!

Linda P, the first time I met you at one of the RBW meetings you had your fun business cards for your yet- to-be-published novel that you were already promoting! That little card, and your hopeful personality were the inspiration that led me to publish *The Virgin Diaries*, and now *Rita!*

Linda J. I will never forget the words you spoke at a presentation for the RBW years ago that changed the course of my writing career forever. You said to "always be proud of your work." Those few words made me believe that as long as I believe in my work, my books are worth publishing. Mandy Eve and Linda J thank you both for your support and encouragement.

Ken, many thanks for your uncanny ability to proof read. It's scary to think of all the mistakes that would have been printed if it weren't for your keen eye!

A special thanks to Camilla and Ashley from work, for loving my first novel so enthusiastically that it made me want to hurry up and publish another one! And Claudia, thank you for being you, and thereby making me want to be me, too.

A special thanks to Audrey's Books in Edmonton, who sent me my first ever tangible paycheck for selling my novel in a real bookstore! A whopping $9.59! I have framed the check and it will always make me smile.

I have so much love for my Wattpad readers, I don't even know where to begin. Those who read daily when I was posting this story originally as a fan fiction, every day! You know who you are. Your comments made me smile and still do. I would print them out and tack them to my cork board above my computer. In those early days of this story, I had to go park outside of Starbucks to use their wifi so that I could upload and post the next chapters every night for all of you waiting to read them!

The fan fiction community is truly the craziest bunch of people I've ever known and the most supportive readers ever! I'm so blessed to have been a part of your fan reading experience.

Grandma, thank you for always watching over me from heaven and sending all the right people into my life. I love you.

Please enjoy this special excerpt from TAKANO RYNN, book two of The Rita Series.

Takano Rynn

I CLUTCH THE MEMORY chip from the small robot, tightly in my fist. It's my only connection to Rita, these memories stored in Beeps' files. I still haven't found a compatible robot from the Opposition to install the chip into and read the files.

I lie back onto the snow and look up at the stars above Aylvon. The tree tops sway in the breeze, silhouetted by the last of the sunset as the stars take over the night sky. The wet ground seeps through my cloak and I shiver. I don't know why I came back here, to this small, abandoned planet. Maybe because it reminds me of the forest near Rita's village, where I first saw her. Maybe because this is where she found me.

Where are you, Rita? Why can't I sense you?

It's no use. She is hidden from me, hidden from Dukath. Hidden from everything and everyone by some power stronger than my own.

I can't find her. Yet, I know she's not dead.

I would have not survived it, if she were.

A shuffling noise in the dark catches my attention. I ignore it, daring anything in the forest to attack me. I could use a good fight right about now.

A memory returns. Rita walking towards me as I beckoned her with my Gift. She was so surprised when she realized what had happened, that I'd used my influence to get her to do what I wanted. She was already ahead of everyone else by realizing it had happened. Most never clued in.

We trained together here, on this planet, in this very field. She looked fragile and I was afraid to hurt her. But she was strong and quick. She was the Gift Stone I'd been searching for, and so much more. She shared the part of my life I could never share with anyone, the part that empowered me and imprisoned me at the same time. She understood.

I had made peace with the reality that I'd never be seen as a friend or a lover, or anything but the monster everyone saw me as.

Except Rita.

She insisted on looking for the good inside me, even when it wasn't there. In the end, I proved her wrong.

I'm so sorry, Rita.

I close my eyes and clench my fists.

The ground beneath me no longer feels cold but instead a burning heat against my back, like a well-deserved scourging.

It's because of me that Rita fell to the evil side of the Gift. She came to save me...

Show me where you are. I won't be afraid to love you this time.

"Rita wouldn't be happy if you died of hypothermia."

I sit up fast, sending snow flying around me.

It's the stormtrooper, Parrin. He is standing a few yards away, already cowering like he's preparing to be stricken. I *should* strike him, the traitor. I don't understand what Rita ever saw in him as a friend. He's nothing more than a coward.

I jump to my feet, reaching for my sword, but it's gone. The vision of Rita holding my sword suddenly returns; the look on her face when she saw the dead bodies lying all around her—all those she'd killed by its blade.

"What are you doing here?" I lock Parrin in a Gift hold, angry at him for making me recall that memory.

He drops to his knees and his eyes go wide as he struggles in my choke hold. I ease off a little to let him breathe, so he can answer my question.

"I came because I knew if Rita ever returns, she'll come to you first," he says in a strangled voice.

I let him go and he falls forward, coughing.

"Who came with you?"

He rubs his neck with his hands and gives me an angry glare. I don't have to read his mind to know that he's more hurt than mad, which makes me even more annoyed at his pathetic weakness.

"Just me," he says, getting up. He's still wearing that Opposition Pilot's jacket, reminding me of when I first saw him without his Ruling Order uniform.

"I should have killed you when you first betrayed me and left the Ruling Order, *Parrin*." I put him in a hold again. I've been wanting to do this for a long time. Might as well do it now. But first, I'll search his mind.

He resists but I push past his resistance easily.

Fear is at the forefront. No surprise there.

I go deeper, into recent memories. He resists with more effort, which means he's hiding something. I find it quickly. It's shame. He's ashamed of not fighting for Rita and for letting her come after me. He's the one who told her to follow her heart and try to save me from Dukath, even when I told her to stay away.

My hold wavers for a moment at this new information. Then I tighten my grasp again.

"It's your fault she's gone now," I growl between clenched teeth. "I could kill you, here and now."

Parrin's eyes widen with fear. His mind floods with memories I don't want to see. Rita's face streaked with tears, eyes full of pain because she's worried about me. Then the pain replaced with hope as Parrin tells her to go after me, despite the heartbreak it causes him to say it. He loved her enough to let her love someone else. The concept is so foreign to me.

I loosen my hold. I'm not the only one who lost Rita that day she disappeared, he did too.

I watch through his eyes as Rita swings my sword at a girl they know as Star, a friend to both of them. This is the vision he sees in his nightmares.

I lower my arm and Parrin falls to the ground.

I shouldn't have searched his thoughts. Now I have to live with what I've seen. I didn't want to know about his love for Rita or his loyalty to his friends. It only makes me despise him more.

"How did you get away from Dukath's influence?" he asks me, his tone accusing.

I have no desire to talk to him, but I answer anyway. "He let me go. He wants me to find the sword."

"Rita has the sword. Are you going to take her to Dukath all over again?"

I lunge forward and throw Parrin against the nearest tree. His back hits the thick trunk and he cries out.

"You shouldn't have followed me here," I say, dragging him forward through the snow until he lands on his knees at my feet. He grasps at his throat again, as though trying to unlatch the invisible hold. I should kill him, for being a traitor, for standing at Rita's side like he had some kind of right to be there.

I raise him up high and throw him again, this time he hits a tree branch with the back of his head and falls into the snow. I don't have my sword to finish him off. The only thing in my hand is Beep's memory chip.

My chest tightens. Rita loved Beeps.

She also loved Parrin, as her friend.

He's unconscious now, the snow tinted red beside him. My shoulders slump and I sigh.

He's not the coward.

I am.

TARKHASH FOOD

I CHECK FOR A heartbeat and sigh in relief when I find one. I've never wanted someone who I despised so much, to still be alive. If he died because of me, Rita would never forgive me. She would haunt me for the rest of my existence.

For a second, the idea is tempting.

Seeing Parrin's unconscious body lying in the snow brings back memories of my grade school friend Reagan. A memory I buried in my subconscious a lifetime ago. I killed him because of my anger. He was just a kid.

I was just a kid.

After that, I was sent away to train. Far from anyone I could harm. Far from my family, my school, my world.

I clench my fist then ram it into a tree. Bark goes flying and the pain shoots through my knuckles into my arm, making my elbow ache.

I'm my own worst enemy, not Dukath. Not the Opposition. Not the whole damn Galaxy, just... me.

Parrin coughs then turns onto his back. There's blood in his mouth.

Sorry, Rita. I just can't stand your...friend.

He blinks and looks around as though confused. I grab him by the arm and stand him up onto his feet.

"Follow me." I say, using my Gift influence on him so he'll obey.

I head for my ship and Parrin stumbles after me, having no choice but to do as I command.

* * *

I need a crew and a medic. And some servants would be nice too. I'm the strongest Gifted Master in the Galaxy and yet I'm here, attending to the wounds of an Opposition soldier.

My jaw tenses as I tighten Parrin's bandages.

"Ouch!" he cries.

I frown. Why is he so fragile?

"I'm only human you know," he says, as though answering my thought.

"So am I."

My words seem to surprise him. Did he think I was alien?

I quickly finish securing the bandage, then step away. I hate helping him. Maybe because I know he's the better man, despite his weak body. Rita would have been better off with him in the end.

I walk out of the small medic area and head for the bridge, leaving Parrin behind to tend to himself. It's time to get off Aylvon and back to looking for Rita. I'll interrogate Parrin later, when he has a little more strength. He might have some information which could help me find Rita. Maybe the Opposition has a lead, and he can tell me how far they are in their own search for her.

When I get to the bridge, I see Parrin's thoughts again. They hit me unbidden, and I have to set my hand on the wall to steady myself. The image of Rita crying for me will forever haunt me now. To Parrin, it was the moment he'd failed and I'd been victorious; the moment he realized she'd always love me and never choose him. This is the one thing in my life I somehow didn't fail at—Rita loving me despite everything.

I sigh and turn back the way I came. I need to give Parrin some water before he dies of stupidity. He lost a lot of blood and he'll need to replenish it. If I want to keep him alive long enough for Rita to see that I didn't kill him, I have to be nice.

Parrin isn't in the medic room when I get there. I go to the nearest console to search for bio-signs on board. There are two, and the one that isn't me is in the mess hall. Maybe he's not so stupid after all.

When I arrive at the mess hall, I see Parrin before he sees me. He's slouched over, resting his elbows on the table and eating something, or at least trying to. The chewy biscuit seems too hard for him to manage with the bruise across his jaw. He coughs, mid chew, then grimaces in pain.

I frown and walk over.

"That's Tarkhash food," I say just as Parrin swallows another bite. He jumps at the sound of my voice, then cringes in pain again. It takes a second for him to process what I've just said. He's already chewing another bite when the words seem to register in his brain and he spits the food out across the table.

I stifle a grin.

"Are you kidding me?" he says. "Why do you have Tarkhash food on board?"

"I'll get you something else," I say, annoyed that I'm on talking terms with one of my previous subordinates. But he's just too pathetic to be left on his own.

I walk over to the food synthesizer and push the soup and bread button. A list of options comes up, but I'm not about to ask the Traitor what he wants, so I pick a tomato-based broth.

"I've never seen one of those before," Parrin says behind me. I don't bother answering him. If he'd ever been anyone of importance in the Ruling Order, he would have had his own food synthesizer in his quarters.

I walk over to him and set the steaming hot broth down on the table.

"All I ever got was stew in the soldiers' mess hall," he continues, looking down at the soup.

"You can use the synthesizer for water too," I say, wanting the conversation to end.

Parrin nods. I pick up the energy biscuit which he'd been trying to eat earlier, to take with me to the bridge.

"I thought that was Tarkhash food," Parrin says.

I take a bit of the biscuit then turn to walk away, before he can see the grin on my face.

Parrin

"**Y**OU CAN'T JUST STICK the memory chip into the ship's system," Parrin says, coming out of nowhere.

I ignore him and continue hooking up the memory chip to the ship's main computer. It may not be a robot's body, but my ship is top of the line and can translate just about any robot language. I don't know why I didn't think to try it earlier.

"Beeps was a specialized, social robot," Parrin continues, taking a seat in the copilot's chair beside me. I give him a look that silences him, but likely not for long.

The small screen in the console lights up and a list of code scrolls by. I try to make sense of all the numbers but it's impossible.

"I needs to be installed into a robot body," Parrin starts up again.

"It worked," I snap.

"Yeah, but if it's in a robot like the one it came from, then she can talk to us and—"

"I don't need her to talk." I scroll through the data some more. There must be some program in the ship's database that can decode it.

"It's encrypted."

Parrin's voice grates on my nerves.

"Obviously," I grumble. "But why is it encrypted?"

"Because there's sensitive..." He trails off and doesn't and finish his sentence.

I glance over to see what's happened, but all I can gather from the look on his face is that his brain just stopped working for no apparent reason. I look back at the code. He's right; it's encrypted.

"We can take it back to the Opposition Base and..." He trails off again.

I slam my fist down on the console, making him jump. "Should I just read your mind, so we can get through this conversation faster?"

Parrin's eyes go wide and he shakes his head no.

I settle back into my seat. I have no leads in finding Rita, other than Beeps' memory chip. Maybe I could take it back to the Ruling Order Base and have them analyze it. But then

Dukath would have it, and I'm sure now that there's information on it that the Opposition doesn't want Dukath to see.

I rub at my eyes. When did I start caring about the Opposition?

"You'll take the fighter plane to the Opposition Base," I say to Parrin. "And get them to put this chip into a new robot, then bring the robot back to me."

He gets up immediately to do as I say, then stops.

"The fighter plane I came in only had enough power for a one-way trip here," he says.

I glance up. Was this some kind of suicide mission for him?

"We'll use my ship's power to recharge it—"

"And," Parrin interrupts, "I wrecked the wings in a crash landing into the trees so..."

I close my eyes for a few seconds before replying. "Then you'll tell me the location of the Opposition Base."

"What?" Parrin looks frightened. "I can't! Please don't make me."

"You'll tell me the location of your Base," I repeat, a little slower this time, using my Gift's influence on him.

"It's on Antineon," Parrin says.

Interesting.

I turn back to the console and search the ship's computer for information on the planet. Nothing comes up. I could be inputting it wrong or Parrin's pronunciation could be off, which is more likely.

I get up to give him the pilot's seat. "Then take us there."

* * *

"I just don't think it's fair you can read my mind, but I can't read yours," Parrin says.

It's the third time he's attempted to start a conversation, a different topic each time. I cross my arms and sit back in the copilot's seat. We're at quantum speed and should reach Antineon soon.

"How are we going to fly a Ruling Order Command Shuttle into the Opposition Base without getting blown out of the sky?" Parrin asks.

"Slow us down," I say, "out of Quantum Drive."

Parrin looks down at the control console with a blank stare, and doesn't do anything.

I wait.

"Over there." I point to the controls. He still can't seem to figure it out.

I lift him out of his chair so we can trade places.

"Hey!" he cries out as I plop him down into the copilot's seat.

I get into the pilot's seat and slow the ship down before it flies straight into Antineon at full speed.

"You could have just asked me to move," Parrin mumbles, rubbing his shoulder.

He's wearing that jacket again, the one I hate, and it's covering up the bandages around his ribs, which made me forget that he's hurt.

"Prepare the cloaking shields..." I begin to say, then decide to do it myself. I get up to switch places with Parrin again, since the controls I need are on his side.

"No, wait!" Parrin holds out his hand to stop me. "I can do it."

He turns on the cloaking shields and I look out the viewport at the planet in front of us. It's entirely covered in water. Did Parrin lie to me? How could this be the Opposition's Base?

"We should send a message to the General, to let him know we're coming," Parrin says.

My throat tightens and I can't seem to speak. The General... my father. How could I have forgotten?

I clench my jaw. I haven't seen him since he sent me away, when I was a child, and I don't want to see him now.

I slow the ship to a halt and set a new course.

"Where are we going?" Parrin asks.

"Somewhere else."

"But what about Beeps' chip?"

"We will find Rita some other way." I pause putting in the co-ordinates. Did I just say we?

No. That's not going to happen. Maybe I can drop Parrin off here and keep on going without him. Or better yet, I should turn him in, to the Ruling Order, and have him pay for his treason.

"This is Base Control. Please identify yourself." A voice comes over the comm unit. Either the Opposition's sensors have become more advanced, or my cloaking shields are out-dated. Parrin reaches in front of me to press the comm button before I can stop him.

"General? This is Parrin. Don't fire, I'm with—"

I yank his hand off the comm button.

"Parrin?" My father's voice suddenly comes over the speakers. It's strange to hear him, after so long. He wasn't a General when I left, but I'd heard he'd become one, while I was away.

"Why is your ship cloaked?" he continues. "What ship are you flying?"

Parrin looks over at me. "Do you want to explain this to him?" he asks.

I glare at him and he turns back to the comm system.

"Um...requesting permission to land a Ruling Order Command Shuttle."

"Can you repeat that?"

"Requesting permission to land a Ruling Order Command Shuttle, on base."

"Are you the one piloting this Ruling Order Command Shuttle, Parrin?"

Parrin glances over at me again and I resist the urge to punch him.

"Yes, Sir."

"Are you under any duress?"

"No, Sir."

"Parrin." I can hear my father's exasperated sigh over the speakers. "How exactly did you obtain a Ruling Order Command Shuttle?"

Parrin clears his throat. "I have Beeps' memory chip. We're just..." He moves away from me as far as he can while still holding the comm button, then quickly adds, "Takano Rynn is with me!"

"Bryn?"

I frown at hearing my childhood name again, which brings back a flood of unwanted memories.

I clench my fists. That's not my name anymore. This whole thing was a very bad idea.

"You alright?" Parrin whispers to me.

I don't respond and he pushes the comm button again. "I'm not under duress General. Your son wants to find Rita as much as we do, and we think the memory chip might help us do that. But we haven't been able to decode it."

There is a moment of silence.

"Permission to land granted. But not on Base territory. We'll send a shuttle to you once you've landed on an island at the other side of the planet. I'm sending you the landing coordinates now."

"Yes, sir."

"Parrin, may I please talk to Bryn?"

Parrin turns to me, and I shake my head.

"Um...we're low on power, General," Parrin says. "Comm systems are shutting down! I can't hear you anymore, General...I can't—" Parrin lets go of the button.

I rub my face with my hands. "Turn off the cloaking shields," I sigh. "We would have lost power to the cloaking shields way before the comm unit quit from lack of power."

Parrin is the worst liar I've ever encountered. Even Rita could put forth a lie when needed.

Parrin's hand hovers over the controls.

He seems to have turned stupid again.

I reach across and turn off the cloaking shields myself.

"You're not going to kill your father, are you?" Parrin asks me.

I wave my hand across his face to put him into an instant sleep, and he finally shuts up.

BIANCA ROWENA

Bianca Rowena was born in Transylvania and moved to Canada at age five. She studied Writing/Producing/Directing at the Southern Alberta Institute of Technology, in the Cinema/Television/Stage/ Radio program. She now lives with her family in Southern Alberta.

Visit her online at www.biancarowena.com

www.ingramcontent.com/pod-product-compliance
Lightning Source LLC
Chambersburg PA
CBHW011407310726
48972CB00011B/2879

9 781999 204112